CHRISTY CARLYLE

The Duke's Den

ANYTHING
BUT A
DUKE

DON'T MISS THE FIRST
DUKE'S DEN NOVEL FROM
CHRISTY CARLYLE

Also available from Avon Impulse…

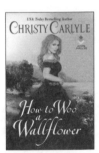

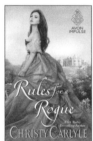

ISBN 978-0-06-285397-4

EAN

"Some would say I'm not a gentleman at all."

"Why?"

He chuckled at that, a warm, breathy sound that made her wish to hear it again. "I'm not a man you would wish to know." As soon as the words were out—words she didn't at all agree with—he took two steps back. "I bid you good night."

Distance from the heat of his body left her suddenly cold. Her wet dress let in the evening's biting chill, and she shivered so fiercely that she couldn't stop her teeth from chattering.

The stranger immediately slid off his overcoat and draped it around her shoulders. His scent was all she could smell, and the warmth from his body clinging to the fabric made her let out an involuntarily sigh of relief.

She closed her eyes a moment and her body swayed toward his. When he reached out to steady her, Diana's eyes slid open and she sensed his gaze on her. Despite the cold, heat seemed to kindle between them.

The stranger wrapped an arm around her waist and pulled her an inch closer, and she was flooded with sensation. His chest brushing against hers, the gust of his breath on her face, his crisp woodsy scent.

Without thought or calculation, she lifted off her heels and pressed her mouth to his.

By Christy Carlyle

ANYTHING BUT A DUKE

The Duke's Den

CHRISTY CARLYLE

AVONBOOKS

An Imprint of HarperCollinsPublishers

ANYTHING BUT A DUKE. Copyright © 2019 by Christy Carlyle. All rights reserved. Printed in the United States of America. No part of this book may be used or reproduced in any manner whatsoever without written permission except in the case of brief quotations embodied in critical articles and reviews. For information, address HarperCollins Publishers, 195 Broadway, New York, NY 10007.

First Avon Books mass market printing: May 2019

Print Edition ISBN: 978-0-06-285397-4
Digital Edition ISBN: 978-0-06-285400-1

Cover design by Amy Halperin
Cover illustration by Jon Paul Ferrara
Cover photographs by Media photo/Michel Legrou

Avon, Avon & logo, and Avon Books & logo are registered trademarks of HarperCollins Publishers in the United States of America and other countries.

HarperCollins is a registered trademark of HarperCollins Publishers in the United States of America and other countries.

FIRST EDITION

19 20 21 22 23 QGM 10 9 8 7 6 5 4 3 2 1

Acknowledgments

To all the friends who endure my silence while I work on a book and still remember who I am when I finally reply to their emails months later. Thank you for your words of encouragement and faithful camaraderie.

Thanks to Jill Marsal, my agent, for always knowing how to handle every question I bring to her. Jill, your advice is spot-on and invaluable.

Thanks especially to my editor, Elle Keck, for giving me so many incredible opportunities and always, without fail, helping me tell a better story. Your faith in me is humbling, and I can't thank you enough.

Chapter One

March 1845
London, Belgrave Square

$\mathcal{S}$he absolutely could not be late.

Diana Ashby approached the looking glass in her dressing room and tightened the ribbon she'd gathered around her dark, unruly hair. She'd gotten distracted in her laboratory and now the clock ticked dangerously close to the top of the hour.

An exception had been made for her and she couldn't squander it. One of her former tutors from Bexley Finishing School had arranged a private scientific lecture at his home for a few colleagues and had extended her an invitation.

Diana rushed toward the door, scooping up a notebook and pencil on the way, and reached the top of the stairs at the precise moment her mother called her name.

"Diana. Come down and greet our visitor."

She gritted her teeth and prayed this wasn't some machination to thwart her evening plans. Mama didn't approve of her pursuits or of ladies stepping out unaccompanied, but the Woodsons lived a short cab ride away, and her tutor and his wife were more than sufficient chaperones.

She descended the stairs warily, hoping whoever had come could be put off quickly. Relief washed over her when she spotted Samuel, Lord Egerton, a friend of her brother's.

Though her father had been the second son of a baronet, he'd inherited enough of a living to provide Diana and her brother with an excellent education alongside the children of England's noble families.

"I'm afraid Dominick isn't at home. Most likely getting into some mischief. I'm surprised you're not with him."

"I wish to speak to you, Diana."

Di scanned the hallway, but her mother was nowhere in sight. It was unusual to be left alone with a visitor, but Lord Egerton and his family were longtime friends.

Still, she sensed something wasn't right. A prickle of hesitation raised goose bumps on her skin.

She studied her brother's friend. Half-moon shadows darkened the undersides of his eyes and there was an odd tremor at the edge of his jaw. For a normally jovial young buck, he looked decidedly fretful as he gripped his gloves with a white-knuckled hold and twisted them nervously in his hands.

"Is something amiss with Dominick?" Her twin brother was a reckless sort. She lived in fear that one day he'd stumble into the kind of trouble one couldn't get out of with charm alone.

When Egerton shook his head, Diana breathed easier.

"Shall we talk in the parlor?" Without waiting for an answer, she led him to the room.

He shocked her by slipping the door shut behind them.

"What's troubling you?" Gentleness was hard to muster when the hands of the clock on the wall edged ever later, but she tried. They'd never been confidants, but as an acquaintance of many years, she was willing to hear whatever ailed the young man. For some reason, he'd come to her with his burdens.

"I'm not certain how to begin," he whispered, a quivery wobble in his tone. "There is an endeavor I should like to undertake and need your guidance."

"Whatever it is, I'm sure you'll do well. You always do."

He was an ambitious young man. Far more so than her brother. While Dominick had been happy to return from university with nothing but memories of frivolity and mischief, Lord Egerton had taken top marks in mathematics and philosophy and won trophies in several athletic endeavors. Di knew whatever competition he entered, Lord Egerton strove to win.

He stared at her, his mouth curved in a warm smile. The expression struck her as odd. Friendliness, she expected. But there was something more in his grin.

"You've always been kind, Diana."

The way he said her name, the care he took with each syllable, filled her with unease.

"I do try to be kind."

He stepped closer, and one hand hovered between them as if he was considering whether to reach for her. "You're also quite the prettiest girl I have ever known."

Diana took a step back. Then another. Fear of what was to come set her heart fluttering like a bird that's just noticed the bars of its cage.

"Samuel," she started, desperate to forestall what he intended to say or do. But it was too late.

In one swift move, he lowered himself onto one knee and reached for her hand.

Diana froze, her muscles tightening and her tongue thickening. His touch felt heavy and yet oddly distant, as if her skin had gone numb.

"Marry me, Miss Ashby."

Oh no. Panic sped her pulse. A single insistent hammer pounded behind her eyes. She knew what she wished to say. There was no question of her answer, but she couldn't get the words out.

"May I take your silence as an acknowledgment of what I've long known?"

"I . . ." she forced out on a gasp.

He squeezed her fingers and inched closer, as if fearful of missing a single word.

"I regret . . ." The words were almost impossible to get out. Not because they weren't true, but because panic always caused her to freeze.

But the two words sufficed.

Egerton began to crumble, the eagerness in his pale gaze turning to disappointment and then anger.

"I cannot marry you." She shook her head to make sure he could not mistake her meaning. She had no wish to cause him embarrassment or misery, but she had no desire to marry him. Or anyone. Not yet. "My inventions—"

"Good God, no." He burst up to his full height, turned his back on her, and paced the edges of the rug in the center of the room. "Tell me anything but that you're refusing me for your pastimes."

"My work is not a pastime."

"Work? You're a baronet's granddaughter. You needn't *work*, my dear girl."

"I am not *your* anything, Lord Egerton." Everything in her bristled and her blood fizzed with irritation. "I refer to my research. My designs."

"Your hobby?" he sputtered, closing his eyes, as if attempting to calm himself, before continuing. "The unladylike way you insist on spending your spare hours is something I'm willing to overlook, as long as you cease such foolishness once we wed." He came back to stand in front of her. Too close. Nearly toe to toe. "Why can't you simply paint watercolors or play the pianoforte like other ladies?"

"Because they don't interest me at all."

"You waste your time with such nonsense."

A waste of time. It's what her mother called all the hours she spent in her workshop rather than attending to the social calendar. But just because she couldn't study at university like her brother and would never be asked to speak at the Royal Society as her father had, that didn't mean her inventions weren't worthwhile.

They mattered, if only to her. One day, she hoped they'd matter to others. She just needed funding and someone to believe in her potential. If her ideas could come to fruition, her inventions could be put to good use.

"I am offering you more than anyone else will. A title, a position in society far higher than that to which you were born." Egerton spoke the words with a coldness she'd never heard from him. He leaned closer, near enough for her to smell liquor on his breath. "Your mother will not approve of your refusal."

Diana hated that he was right. She'd been given a fine education, but her family had always been on the edge of society. Marriage to a nobleman was what her mother wanted for her most of all, and she'd never imagined she could forestall wedlock forever. Just until she could make a name for herself and achieve some small measure of recognition for her inventions.

Diana could imagine marriage and motherhood. One day. But not yet.

"Do you have nothing to say for yourself? Does it not bother you to be an aberration among your sex?" He reached out to grip her wrist. "You should be honored by my interest. No other man will want a lady who cannot behave like one."

Diana yanked out of his grasp, then shoved at his chest with her forearm. Watching him stumble was terribly satisfying, but there was no use provoking him.

"There's nothing more to say, Lord Egerton. Just go."

He shot her a malicious glare. Diana glanced toward the closed drawing room door and considered shouting for a servant or her mother.

"Don't worry. I shan't waste my time with you any longer. I'd hoped you knew your duty, but you've only doomed yourself to spinsterhood."

Egerton started out of the room and she pressed the heel of her palm to her breastbone, struggling to steady her nerves.

At the threshold, he paused. "You've made a dreadful mistake today. Perhaps you don't know it yet, but you will when you're old and alone." After shooting her one last sneer, he slammed the parlor door on his way out.

Di sank onto the nearest chair, trembling, struggling to blot out his words. Part of her wanted to shout at the closed door that insults would not change her. Instead, she took a deep breath and savored the relief of having him gone.

His horrible curses echoed in her head, tangling with guilt about shirking her duty to her family. Then other thoughts swelled in, as they always did. Her mind never settled. Ideas, calculations, images of what she wished to build filled her mind.

At times like these, the whirring chaos of images and impulses was a comfort. A soothing distraction.

She could almost pretend she didn't hear Egerton's cruel words ringing in the back of her mind.

Spinster. Alone. Aberration.

The clock struck six. Diana stood and headed for the door. The young man's condemnations might be true. Perhaps she was all those things. Maybe she would end her days alone.

But there was more. Deeper, she felt an ever-present hunger. An ambition that she knew most thought improper for a lady. Yet it was a compulsion she couldn't deny. Her ideas were good and she longed to prove herself to those who would scoff at a woman inventor.

She heard movement upstairs and feared facing her mother. Later, there would be time for recriminations and explanations of why she'd turned down the first marriage offer she'd ever received.

Diana headed quickly for the door. Tonight's lecture was an opportunity to meet other scientists and speak to them of her inventions or hear of theirs. She wouldn't let Egerton's cruel words stop her. She wouldn't let anything stop her.

AIDAN IVERSON JUMPED down from the rented carriage and ducked his head as he strode into the torrent. Rain pelted his skin at a vicious slant, ice-cold drops soaking his hair and sneaking inside the collar of his coat.

His disdain for finery didn't serve him well on nights like this. Beaver hats and kid leather gloves would have proven useful against the elements, but they weren't his taste. A youth spent without luxuries meant such adornments never crossed his mind. Even now, when he owned shopping emporiums full.

Tonight he was willing to bear any discomfort.

After months of searching, he'd been given a tantalizing clue that had led him to Belgravia. With two former Bow Street Runners and one private inquiry agent on his payroll, he'd finally found an indication of where his mother had once lived. He hoped Lord Talmudge of 29 Belgrave Square might have more answers.

Mary Iverson's history was as much a mystery to Aidan as his own. He wasn't even sure she'd been called Mary, but the name lingered in his mind.

Every memory of the woman was blurred and indistinct. He recalled her as tall and thin, with hair redder than his own. But he couldn't remember the sound of her voice or if she'd said anything the day she'd abandoned him and his infant sister at a workhouse in Lambeth.

Thinking of the place brought a flood of images. Flashes of memory clouded in smoke and tears. Bits and fragments. Nothing he could hold on to.

The name Iverson was the only legacy he possessed, and he wasn't even certain if it was his mother's surname or his father's. But he'd made his name matter. After the workhouse, he'd scavenged to survive. And once he'd earned enough to gamble, he'd multiplied a pittance into a fortune.

The highest of London society knew his name, even if they didn't accept him into their circles. His wealth and instinct for profitable investments had earned him infamy.

But he needed more.

He could earn himself a million pounds and there would still be a hole where his family should have been.

Rounding the corner, he stopped and squinted through the fog-dimmed glow of a streetlamp. Several men loitered on the pavement ahead, crowded under umbrellas, forming the end of a queue waiting to enter a town house.

Drawing closer, Aidan made out a few distinct voices. One he recognized. The low rumbling tone belonged to an earl who'd sought his advice regarding an investment opportunity.

Aidan slowed and lowered his head.

He had no wish to be seen or to spark speculation among fashionable society about his meeting with Talmudge. Turning around, he searched for a side lane and found one leading to the mews behind the row of elegant, whitewashed town houses.

Footsteps echoed at his back as he entered the dim alleyway. He glanced behind but could see nothing clearly in the rain-shrouded darkness. He continued on, counting houses until he came to Talmudge's.

A fence lined the back garden. He reached to twist the latch, and the footsteps behind him hastened. Two men emerged from the shadows, one with an arm aimed toward Aidan's chest. A hard point of metal slammed against his ribs.

Footpads armed with pistols were unexpected in Belgravia, but Aidan was no stranger to a brawl. He'd fought for his supper before, even fought for his life a time or two.

"No coin to be had, gentlemen."

"We'll see," the large one barked.

The smaller man stepped closer. The glow of moonlight revealed his youthfulness. Gaunt face, huge, nervous eyes, and not a hair on his chin. "Turn 'em out."

"Your pockets," the bulky pistol wielder clarified in a smoke-roughened voice.

Aidan sensed the young man's nervousness. If he took down the large one without getting a hole through the chest, he suspected the boy would scarper.

"Afraid you didn't hear me, gents. I've no money."

His response took the behemoth by surprise, and Aidan seized the moment, lifting his arm and coming down hard on the beast's forearm, forcing the pistol away.

The man grunted, recovered quickly, and wound his own massive arm back to strike.

Aidan moved quicker. With a balled fist, he caught the edge of the brawny man's jaw. The brute faltered, stumbling back, before his pistol clattered to the pavement. Rather than retrieve the weapon, the man bent at the waist and leaned forward as if he meant to use his body as a battering ram.

A foolish move.

Aidan swiped the man's smokestack hat away, gripped his bald head, and jerked a knee up to smash his nose. A guttural yawp told him he'd found his mark, and the large man dropped onto the slick cobblestones with a thud.

Unfortunately, the younger man didn't retreat as expected.

An object came at Aidan, a flash of movement in the dark. Shooting pain lanced through his temple and he faltered, dropping to one knee. Shadows swelled in his periphery.

The youth gripped a handful of hair and wrenched Aidan's head back.

"Fool. Why'd you have to go and fight?" The lad's accent was sharper than that of his bulky compatriot, almost polished.

"I'm not fond of thieves." Aidan struggled to see and speak clearly.

"What kind of toff doesn't have a farthing to pinch? You'll forget you ever seen us if you know what's good for you."

Aidan sensed the man's movement and saw the object he'd been struck with raised up high for another blow.

"Stop!" A shout echoed off the row of town houses.

Dizziness made his vision swim, but moon glow revealed a woman. An angry woman, rushing toward his attacker, wielding a closed umbrella raised like a sword.

Hands braced on wet cobblestones, Aidan tried to force his body up. How could one blow turn his legs to jelly?

He had to stand. He had to fight. There'd been more brawls in his life than breakfasts. Now there was a woman to protect. To hell with being caught off guard by some young scalawag.

He had to protect her.

Chapter Two

*D*iana spotted the men the moment she entered the mews.

Rather than join the gentlemen queuing in the rain to enter Professor Woodson's house, she'd slipped around to the back garden. Because she was a frequent visitor of the professor and his family, the servants knew her well. She could be warm and settled before the gentlemen filed inside.

But the three men standing in the rain struck her as decidedly odd.

She considered turning back and wading through the sea of lecture goers in front. Any sensible young woman wouldn't be traipsing around alone in the dark.

Then the attack had begun, and she refused to watch a man being bludgeoned and do nothing.

"Stop!" she shouted as she marched toward the thin man.

He held an object aloft as if he intended to batter a gentleman who'd fallen to his knees in the rain-soaked alleyway.

The attacker turned to face her, and she caught a glint of white as he sneered. "What sorta tart are you then?"

"Leave 'er," a bulky man behind him said. "Don't need no harpy mucking up this job."

Rage built in her so quickly, it burned all of Diana's fear away. Something about the one man's sneer and the other's dismissive tone set her blood on fire.

Lifting the shaft of her umbrella, she aimed the pointy end at the thinner man and rushed toward him. A cry welled up from deep inside and she screamed as she closed the distance between them.

He lowered his club and shoved it into his coat. Then he glanced once at his victim and tapped the shoulder of his partner before breaking into a shambling run down the far end of the mews. The larger of the two cast her a menacing glare before following his accomplice.

The beaten man struggled to get to his feet. He was large and far too heavy for her to lift on her own, but she wrapped her hands around his arm to give him some stability as he stood. But instead of rising, he reached for her, wrapping one large, ungloved hand around the edge of her waist.

"Dizzy," he murmured.

"Then perhaps you should move more slowly."

"Can't. You need my help."

Diana assessed the man. In the moonlight, she could see a stream of blood trailing down his face. The rain had slowed to a slight drizzle, but the air had turned colder and puffs of white escaped his lips.

"I'm saving you," she told him. "Not the other way around."

She wasn't sure whether she imagined the flash of a grin.

"We should get you inside." She glanced toward the end of the lane where the men had disappeared. "I don't know if they'll return. Or if there are others."

"I don't think they will, and I'd wager there aren't others." His voice was deep and his accent not nearly as clipped as she'd expect from a man of Belgravia. Yet his fashionable clothing and polished shoes seemed those of a man of substance, just the sort who might have a home in the square.

A groan escaped as he pushed off his bent knee and got to his feet. He leaned heavily against her, gripping her hip with one hand and letting her take some of his weight.

When they stood face-to-face, the injured man towered over her. For a long moment, he stilled as if gathering his strength. It allowed her a moment to study him. He was handsome, despite the stony set of his square jaw and the grimace twisting his full lips.

He lifted his head to gaze at her in the dim light, and a strange shudder rippled down her body. As she flexed her fingers against his arm, she realized she was still holding on to him and let go.

The stranger didn't follow suit. Instead, he drew her an inch closer.

"Can you walk?" she whispered.

"The blow was to my head." His expression softened and he shot her a crooked grin. "The rest of my body is quite intact."

Suddenly his body was the only thing she noticed. He was broad shouldered, with a chest to match. Rain had soaked his shirtfront, and the starched white fabric plastered itself to his skin. The scent of sandalwood soap wafted off him.

He was still holding her, his hand an oddly comforting point of heat at her hip.

A lump formed in her throat and she swallowed it down. "I was planning to attend a lecture at Sir Beckett Woodson's home. It's just there."

"Go to your lecture." He let out a hiss when he turned his head. "I need to find a cab."

"You don't reside in the square?" Diana's curiosity was piqued. If he wasn't a resident who'd sought the back garden of his home, then what was he doing in the mews in the dark of night?

Perhaps he wasn't a gentleman at all and had some connection to the rogues who'd set upon him.

"I had business here." He gestured too vaguely for her to determine which town house he indicated. With two fingers, he touched the side of his head and winced. "It will have to wait for another day."

"Let's find you a cab." When Diana made to move away and start toward the square, he circled a hand around her arm to stop her.

"No. You've done quite enough."

For a moment she thought he was chastising her, but she sensed the intensity of his gaze, even in the darkness. His face was all sharp angles, regal brow, high cheekbones, and a notably full lower lip. But his eyes were what stood out, even in the meager light. Whatever shade they were, they were paler than her own and brightened by the moon glow.

A trickle of blood fell in a line down his cheek. Diana reached inside the tiny pocket stitched near the hem of her bodice and extracted a folded handkerchief. "You're bleeding quite severely."

"Don't ruin your—"

Before he could finish speaking, she'd already lifted the square of linen to his face.

He winced when she swiped the cloth higher and reached for her wrist. His bare hand against her skin felt shockingly warm.

"Does it hurt a great deal?"

"Not as much as the second blow would have." He released her wrist, and she allowed him to take the handkerchief into his hand. After one indelicate swipe, he stared at the stained linen and frowned. "I owe you thanks and a new handkerchief."

"I have many others." Diana glanced at the Woodson town house. "If you come with me, you can get warm and tidied up." She moved to step out of his hold.

He let her go, but made no move to follow.

"Forget about me. You've done your Good Samaritan duty for the evening." He stepped closer. "You're a rare sort of lady, whoever you are."

Diana bit the inside of her cheek and dipped her head to stare at the pavement. *Rare* wasn't the worst thing she'd been called this night. But it felt a bit too much like the other curses Egerton had thrown her way.

The stranger slid a finger along the edge of her jaw. A shocking, intimate touch, but too brief for her to take offense. She lifted her head and wished she could see him more clearly.

"I meant that as a compliment." His voice was low, almost soothing. "Any woman who rushes in to stop a man from battering me to a pulp has my infinite admiration."

"Infinite?" Being admired by men wasn't anything she'd considered until Egerton's graceless proposal. But suddenly she wished to know *this* man. His name, his story, and what had brought them to the same rain-soaked mews. "You're a different sort of gentleman, aren't you?"

Nothing about their encounter made sense. And yet standing with him, conversing with an utter stranger, felt oddly right.

"Some would say I'm not a gentleman at all."

"Why?"

He chuckled at that, a warm, breathy sound that made her wish to hear it again. "I'm not a man you would wish to know." As soon as the words were out—words she didn't at all agree with—he took two steps back. "I bid you good night."

Distance from the heat of his body left her suddenly cold. Her wet dress let in the evening's biting chill, and she shivered so fiercely that she couldn't stop her teeth from chattering.

The stranger immediately slid off his overcoat and draped it around her shoulders. His scent was all she could smell, and the warmth from his body clinging to the fabric made her let out an involuntarily sigh of relief.

She closed her eyes a moment and her body swayed toward his. When he reached out to steady her, Diana's eyes slid open and she sensed his gaze on her. Despite the cold, heat seemed to kindle between them.

The stranger wrapped an arm around her waist and pulled her an inch closer, and she was flooded with sensation. His chest brushing against hers, the gust of his breath on her face, his crisp woodsy scent.

Without thought or calculation, she lifted off her heels and pressed her mouth to his.

His lips were warm, far softer than she expected, and he responded without hesitation. When she began to pull away, he dipped his head to draw out the kiss for another moment.

He swept a finger across the edge of her cheek down to her jaw, then he released her. Diana tried for some parting words and fell silent. What did one say to a stranger one had just impulsively kissed?

He saved her the trouble. "You're soaked," he said quietly, "and I've already made you late to your engagement." Bowing, he took a step back. "I'll watch until you're safely inside."

Diana knew she should go. He was right. She wasn't sure how long they'd been standing in the mews, but she was undoubtedly late for Woodson's lecture. Shockingly, she didn't mind. This man sparked her curiosity.

He smiled at her and nudged his chin forward to urge her to go.

"Your coat?" Diana didn't wish to give it up so much as she felt the niggling prick of propriety urging her to be polite.

"Keep it. I have many others."

She smiled at that and continued on to Professor Woodson's back garden door. All the way, she sensed the stranger's gaze on her, watching protectively. One knock and a housemaid immediately opened the door to greet her. When Diana hesitated, the girl called her inside.

"In you come, miss. You're drenched."

Diana looked down the mews, hoping to see the handsome stranger one more time.

But he was gone. Not a sight of him anywhere.

A rebel impulse made her wish to go back out into the darkness, find him, and ask all the questions that filled her mind.

But she couldn't. Even she knew better than to risk that sort of impropriety.

Regret pulsed inside her and her breath hitched in her chest.

She wanted to see him again, discover his name. But it wasn't logical. She'd recklessly kissed the man.

It was far better they never meet again.

Chapter Three

Aidan dragged in a shallow breath and tried to convince himself not to rip the whole damned upstairs lounge of Lyon's Gentlemen's Club to shreds with his bare hands.

Dismantling a chair would suffice. Maybe tearing the stuffing out of a plump settee. Any destruction would do. Anything that would let him expel the rage boiling in his veins.

Gripping the balustrade of the balcony high above the gaming floor of Lyon's, he closed his eyes and fought for self-control. He focused on the sounds of the club: laughter, shouted bluster, the shuffle of cards.

Men placing wagers and exclaiming as their luck rose and fell with the roll of the dice.

The club was thriving. Since he was one-third owner, busy tables should have brought Aidan satisfaction. But the familiar buzz of activity did nothing to stem his frustration.

Everything was stained red bchind his eyes, and the loudest sound was the ceaseless thud of blood pounding in his ears.

He'd awaited an answer for months from the men organizing an industrial exhibition, only to be dismissed with a few neatly printed lines of ink. Disappointment had quickly turned to anger. Years of practice had taught him to quell the spark-to-tinder rage of the impetuous young man he'd once been, and he'd become skilled at keeping bitterness at bay.

Until tonight.

He stared down at the baize-covered tables once more, cataloging the pomaded and balding pates of dozens of men. Most were noblemen and from this view, there was little to distinguish them from one another beyond girth and hair color. All were black-suited and white-tied. A veritable army of fashionable consistency.

Aidan looked down at his own suit, a match to theirs. The finest tailored tailcoat and white-tie evening wear Bond Street had to offer. But he was different from the men below. There would always be a disparity. No matter how much money he earned. No matter how many devices he funded. No matter how many London men of business spoke his name with a mix of fear and reverence.

As co-owner of the opulent gentlemen's club, he could storm downstairs and throw every craven gambler out on his ear if the mood took him. Yet that power didn't change anything. He couldn't alter his history. Hell, he barely knew what it was.

Whatever the truth of his family, he was no nobleman. Doors would always be closed to him, and today the one he wished to enter had been slammed in his face.

He slipped a hand into his pocket and crushed the letter of refusal in his palm. Hurling it across the length of the lounge felt satisfying, but the crumpled ball landed with an unimpressive bounce.

So much for tearing the place to shreds.

"Do you prefer solitude or should I be a true friend and ask what ails you?" Rhys Forester, Marquess of Huntley's far too cheerful voice rang out from the top of the stairs.

Without waiting for an answer, Huntley headed for the cart laden with decanters and poured himself a tumbler of whiskey. He didn't retreat, but he was smart enough to say no more.

"That ball of foolscap is from Lord Lockwood."

"Lockwood." Huntley frowned and tipped his head to the gilded ceiling. "Paunchy. Walks with a cane. Speaks loudly and favors cigars that smell like the devil. Is that the one?"

"He's director of the exhibition being planned under the auspices of Prince Albert."

"I thought you were to take part in the planning." Huntley gestured vaguely. "Overseeing some of the projects or whatnot."

"I've been refused. They don't want my advice." Aidan strode to the whiskey decanter and sloshed some in a glass. He tipped it back and relished the burn. "They won't even take my money."

"Men never turn down money." Huntley rose from the settee and retrieved the crumpled letter. "You're not one to make enemies lightly. What have you done to Lock—"

"I take it you've found the answer." Aidan swigged a bit more liquid fire and refilled his glass. Lockwood had mentioned his lack of connections to members of the Royal Society, while methodically listing the titles of each man who would sit on the board of the upcoming exhibition. "Commoner blood runs rampant through my veins. Apparently, that taints everything else."

"Rubbish. My father is friends with Lockwood. They're members of the same club. Befriend the men Lockwood knows and he'll be eating out of your commoner palm."

"Which clubs?"

"White's, of course. But it's the Parthenon you'll want into. Very exclusive."

"They won't take me as a member." Aidan tightened his grip on the crystal glass in his hand until his knuckles ached.

Huntley puffed out his chest. "I'll vouch for you. Tremayne will too."

"I wouldn't ask you to." Aidan had pulled himself up from the gutter on his own. Every penny and pound he possessed, he'd earned. On his own. He'd never taken a loan. He didn't incur debts. He had business partners, but he never curried favor.

Fair transactions. An equal give and take. That's how he lived his life.

A memory filled his mind. Pale, luminous skin. Eyes as dark blue as the night sky. A fierce young woman emerging from the darkness, ready to take on his attackers. The warmth of her touch, the too brief taste of her lips.

There *was* one person he owed, and he didn't even know her name.

"I understand you're a proud man." Huntley spoke with less humor than his usual bluster. His voice dipped lower with an edge of sincerity. "But we all need help now and then."

"I'm not interested in charity."

Huntley let out a breathy chuckle. "Ah, yes, stubborn too. You're proud and bullheaded and—"

"Determined to achieve success on my own terms." Aidan tipped back another swig of whiskey and drew in a deep breath. Not enough to bring calm, but enough to allow him to speak without growling. He glanced again at the letter from Lockwood, discarded on the settee next to Huntley. "I sometimes forget how much I don't belong among men like Lockwood."

"Utter bollocks." Huntley spat the words and ran a hand through his overlong blond hair. "Acceptance in fashionable society isn't all that difficult to achieve."

Aidan scoffed and couldn't keep the bitterness from his tone. "You were born into fashionable society, *my lord*."

"Use my honorific once more and I may never speak to you again. Or give you advice."

"Are you advising me now?" There was irony in Huntley—Aidan's aristocratic friend with the worst reputation—teaching him how to gain acceptance among other noblemen. The humor of it sparked a rusty chuckle.

"There are ways in, Iverson. Money. Fashion. The queen's favor."

"I have money. Doesn't always do the trick."

"Noblemen cling to their pomposity." Huntley crossed one long leg over the other, laced his hands over his waistcoat, and let out a long sigh. "But there is one foolproof means of thrusting yourself into the bosom of good society forever."

Aidan arched a brow. "Which is?"

"Marriage, my friend." Huntley spoke with all the enthusiasm of a man mentioning his own death sentence.

"Good God, have you finally decided to give up your profligate ways?" Nick, Duke of Tremayne and Lyon's chief proprietor, bounded up the stairs and then stopped to assess them. "Our factotum told me I'd find both of you up here, but I had no idea the news would be so momentous."

"Humorous, Tremayne," Huntley said, as if he didn't find the duke's quips the least bit amusing. "I'd claim bachelorhood forever if I could. My recommendation was meant for Iverson alone."

"Iverson leg-shackled, I can more easily imagine." Tremayne approached the liquor and laid down the sheaf of papers he carried under his arm. After lifting the decanter and inspecting its meager contents, he stared at each of them accusingly.

"Look at him." Huntley flicked his fingers toward Tremayne. "Even when irked, the man's rarely without a ridiculous smile on his face."

Tremayne was, in fact, smiling. Not an outright grin, just the tip of his mouth. An expression that had become carved on his face in the past months, even in repose. Contentedness wafted off him. The change was so different from the angry, bitter man he'd once been, Iverson couldn't help but wonder at the transformative power of marital bliss.

He and Nick had met in the direst of circumstances: cold, hungry, and penniless waifs, eking out a living in the middle of a London winter. Aidan had been making his way far longer and taught Nick what he knew of cheap doss houses, day work, and which games of chance might result in dividends.

He never imagined the man would one day inherit a dukedom.

"I do recommend getting yourself a bride," Tremayne said after his first sip of whiskey. "But there must be more. Huntley wouldn't advise such a measure lightly."

"Lockwood has refused my participation in the exhibition." The words were bitter on Aidan's tongue. He had knowledge and experience to contribute. Years more than most of the pale, feckless noblemen who played at being patrons of industry could ever claim.

"The one based on the Paris Exhibition?"

"England's will be different. Better. The prince is determined to make it so."

"Industrial devices are your specialty. Why would they refuse you? How many projects have you invested in now?"

"I've lost count."

Tremayne scrubbed a hand along the edge of his jaw. "So you must win over Lockwood."

"Perhaps Lockwood has a marriageable daughter," Huntley said as he twisted his tumbler in his hand. "Two birds downed in that single bargain."

"No." Aidan briefly imagined meeting with Lockwood to ask for his daughter's hand and could only envision his own hand balled into a fist and planted neatly in the center of the man's face. "If I'm not fit for exhibition planning, then I won't be good enough for a betrothal."

"Might be worth an inquiry." Tremayne deposited his glass and inspected the club from the balcony's edge. "If not, there are plenty of noblemen downstairs with daughters on the marriage mart. Finding one who wants a rich husband shouldn't be hard."

"I wouldn't know where to begin."

Huntley arched a brow.

"I admit I have not acquired your reputation"—a muscle jumped at the edge of Aidan's jawline—"but I am aware of how to woo a lady. Just not a noble one."

Huntley let out a low chuckle. "They aren't so very different. You've befriended Lady Lovelace."

"You're also acquainted with the most beautiful duchess in England," Tremayne said without a hint of modesty.

Aidan emptied his glass and cast his aristocratic friend a glower.

How could he get Nick to understand that a duke marrying his lady steward and making her his duchess was far different from a man raised in a Lambeth workhouse daring to claim an aristocrat's daughter as his own?

"There are matchmakers who—"

"I can arrange my own courtships. Thank you very much." All this *advice* and desire to aid him in such a personal matter was beginning to make his skin itch. He wasn't used to divulging his concerns to anyone.

Aidan tugged at the tight collar of his shirt.

Huntley and Tremayne fell silent but exchanged a series of conspiratorial nods and glances.

"No," Aidan said firmly. "Whatever you're concocting, stop now."

"What's the point of owning an infamous gaming club with a marquess and a duke if we can't help find you a wife?"

The pounding in Aidan's head had become a hammer. He realized he was clenching his teeth. "No," he repeated again, loud enough for his voice to echo off the low ceiling. "If I am to marry, I will find my bride, and I will woo her with no help from either of you."

"Not even the help of an invitation?" Tremayne asked. "Mina is hosting a party next week. I'm sure at least one of the young ladies who attends will be unmarried and titled."

Aidan contemplated the whiskey decanter. "I would never refuse your wife's invitation."

Tremayne's ever-present smile widened. "Excellent."

"But no interference." Aidan lifted a finger and pointed at his friend. "If I speak to a titled lady, let it be by chance. If I choose pursuit, it shall be my choice."

"Of course." Tremayne lifted both hands in the air in mock surrender. "I'd never play matchmaker. I barely know how I ended up with a wife myself."

"If you intend to wax poetic about love, it's time I take my leave." Huntley stood and straightened his waistcoat. "Do let me know, Iverson, if I can help. I'd introduce you to my sisters, but neither is of marriage-able age and both are chiefly fond of gothic romance and giggling."

When Huntley had gone, Aidan refilled his glass until the decanter trickled out the last drops of amber liquid, and noted the papers Tremayne had deposited on the liquor cart. "Applicants?"

"Yes. More arrive every day. The reputation of the Duke's Den has grown more quickly than I expected. Who knew there were so many inventors in search of investors in the city?"

"I could have told you." Aidan had never designed a bridge or a steamship or a new type of thresher, but he knew what it was to be hungry to succeed. He under-stood the ache to be given a chance and the desire for others to recognize your worth.

"We can begin reviewing them together tomorrow." Tremayne gathered the pages. "Tonight I'll go home and ask my wife to add you to her list of invitations."

"A noble bride will solve everything, will it?" The prospect of marriage had never terrified Aidan as it did men like Huntley. Wedlock was a supremely logical transaction. He'd provide wealth. A wife would provide a welcoming home and, one day, heirs.

Tremayne turned contemplative, his brow furrowed, mouth drawn in a firm line. "Whatever lady you win, I suspect her blue blood won't be the greatest boon."

"But that's the only part I truly need."

"Is it?" Tremayne wasn't a man to speak openly of finer feelings, but the way he swallowed hard and looked Aidan square in the eye made him fear his friend was about to start. "Love can be stealthy, Iverson. Changes a man before he's aware he's stumbled and is in danger of falling. In the end, I suspect you'll be glad it did."

"I congratulate you on your wedded bliss." Aidan raised his half-filled glass toward his friend. "But I want none for myself. Matrimony is a practical solution. I intend to pursue it in that manner and seek a bride who understands the terms."

Tremayne's dark brows lifted. "Why do I have a feeling you'll head back to your office and draft a contract tonight?"

"I'll save it until the morning." Aidan grinned. For the first time since climbing the balcony stairs, his ire had ebbed. He had a goal. Now he simply needed to devise a strategy. "Good night, Tremayne. Thank the duchess for the invitation."

As Aidan made his way toward the stairs, the duke cleared his throat. "Good luck, Iverson."

"I don't need luck." As gambling club owners and men well versed in games of chance, both of them knew better than to rely on anything as fickle as luck. "I just need to find the right bride."

Chapter Four

March 1846
London, the Duke's Den

The mortification of losing her notes had Diana in a nerve-rattling panic.

She'd accomplished a great deal in three and twenty years and had this very day been invited to present her invention to a panel of investors at Lyon's.

The London gentlemen's club never admitted women onto the premises. She was the first of her sex ever invited to the Duke's Den in its short but infamous history, and she wanted to make an unforgettable impression.

But the speech she'd planned, all the details she needed to recall, were in her notes.

She had to find them. With one sweeping look, she scanned the reception room again.

Despite the fact that Lyon's catered to noblemen who occupied the club at all hours, lunching and chatting by day and gambling all night, they managed to have perfectly polished marbled floors.

Her boot heels had slipped thrice while she'd searched the room where she and a dozen other inventors had been asked to wait. Her folio was a simple affair, far too like everyone else's. Except that hers had a purple grosgrain ribbon stuck inside, and she couldn't see a glimpse of it anywhere.

While pacing and silently practicing her speech, she'd placed the folio on an obliging table. Someone else must have picked it up. She was less worried about her ideas being filched than about standing in front of the investors and forgetting everything she intended to say.

Forgetfulness and speechlessness were the twin banes of having a mind always racing with ideas.

Slow down, her mother often told her, and yet today she couldn't.

She raced through the reception room, searching tables and the hands of the men who'd also been invited to present to the Duke's Den.

Dozens of masculine eyes narrowed, assessing and saying without words that she was unexpected. Perhaps even unwanted. A drop of perspiration trickled down Diana's nape, and her heart thrashed in her chest as if trying to escape. But nothing would stop her.

She'd been planning this moment for months, years. In some ways, she'd been waiting for this opportunity her entire life. A few uncomfortable men wouldn't put her off.

She let her perusal linger on a few faces and saw discomfort, disapproval, even a few tiny nods of camaraderie.

Then, one by one, all the men turned away, as if they'd lost interest in the novelty of finding a lady inventor in their midst. Either that or they decided she was no threat to their own ambitions.

Diana intended to prove them all wrong.

Willing away the anxiousness that had her pulse ticking faster than the watch pinned to her bodice, she glanced down to check the time. They'd begun calling inventors a half hour past, and she wasn't sure where she stood in the queue. Desperation began to gnaw at her nerves.

"I've lost my notes," she said to the room and got no more than a few quirked brows in response. She cleared her throat and tried again. "Excuse me, gentlemen. I've lost my notes. Brown folio. Purple ribbon."

Shoulders lifted in indifferent shrugs. A few gentlemen gazed around and shook their heads to let her know they'd no more luck than she in finding her missing folio.

She returned to the spot where she'd left her brother

and found him sprawled on a plush settee with his head back and his eyes closed.

"Dominick, wake up," she whispered. "We might be called soon." She pushed the toe of her boot against his when he didn't respond. "And I might need your help."

"It's far too early for this nonsense," he mumbled, tugging his coat lapels up around his neck and running a hand through his dark, tangled hair. Finally, the lid of one blue eye slid open. "And what are you on about? You never need my help."

"It's nearly midmorning, and today I do."

He lifted both hands to cradle his head, as if all the revelry he'd enjoyed the night before was finally catching up with him. "Tell me in as few words as possible."

"I've lost my notes." She swallowed hard and told him, "I may need your assistance when I explain the machine to the duke."

"I know nothing about your device. You always wish to keep me miles away from your inventions." Dom jerked up on the settee and cast her a dubious look. "Besides, you've been preparing for months."

"Practicing what I wish to say in front of a mirror is easy. But sometimes my thoughts rush faster than my tongue. You know that sometimes I—"

"Freeze." Her brother edged forward and reached out to give her hand a reassuring pat. "But that's only when you're truly distressed. This is different, Di. You know what you're about and are prepared for whatever they ask." The hint of a smile began to curve his mouth. "You're not afraid, are you?"

It was a question he'd often repeated when they were children. Sometimes in a playful manner. Sometimes as a taunt. Her twin brother had forever drawn her into his reckless adventures by challenging her bravery. To prove her mettle, she'd always insisted on her fearlessness. But today, the way her knees quivered beneath her skirt belied the claim.

"I'd be a fool not to be nervous. I can't squander this chance."

He shot her one of his smiles that charmed men and caused feminine conquests to dissolve into fits of giggles.

Diana smiled too, but she'd never been much for encouraging her twin's antics.

Their resemblance—gangly and tall with dark brown hair and blue eyes—was striking enough to draw attention when they strolled London's streets together. But beyond looks, their differences weren't hard to find.

Diana strived to temper her impulses and make decisions based on facts and reason. Dom indulged every passion and trusted far too much to fortune. He swore that one day, at London's gaming tables, his luck would turn and their family's financial woes would finally come to an end. Diana hoped income from her inventions might do the same.

"My inventions are good. Some are excellent. And, most importantly, they're useful. If they could be funded and produced, they could turn a fine profit." She fell silent long enough to catch her breath. "But there's only this single chance." Her voice softened. "If my thoughts become tangled or something goes wrong, I'll need to know you'll take up the slack."

He closed his eyes and pinched the skin between his brows. "Tell me what I must do. Just assure me that I needn't operate that fiendish little machine of yours."

Diana smiled down at the box containing a scale model of her vacuum device that she'd asked Dom to watch over while she explored the spacious reception rooms. She'd fashioned every fragile part with care and tested it dozens of times to make sure every element worked flawlessly. "I'll run the machine. But I do wish we had my notes."

Dom settled back on the settee. His eyelids drooped, fluttered, and then closed.

"How much did you drink last evening?"

Her brother offered no answer, but the distinct scent of alcohol wafted off his breath. He hadn't returned home by the time she'd departed, so she doubted he'd had a chance to partake of the dark, smoky coffee that was his usual cure-all.

"Excuse me, miss." A bespectacled young man approached hesitantly. "Was it a folio with a dark purple ribbon you were seeking?"

"Yes." Diana stood so quickly she nearly knocked her model onto the floor. "Where is it?"

"Saw a gent heading toward the dining rooms carrying it under his arm."

"The dining rooms?"

"Across the lobby, miss." The young man pointed toward the entrance of the club.

"Thank you."

When she and her brother had entered an hour ago, she'd steered him determinedly toward the reception rooms. Ladies were not allowed in the club unaccompanied, and her brother had long been a member for Lyon's other offerings. Namely, its gaming tables. Thankfully, he'd been too exhausted by whatever debauchery he'd gotten up to the night before to show much interest in those rooms today.

She pushed at her brother's arm to rouse him. "I need you to escort me to the dining rooms."

"Not hungry." His mumble emerged indignant, even as his body sagged against the settee.

The prospect of dragging him along as she searched for her folio held no appeal, and she suspected allowing him a moment of sleep might make him a more useful escort when she faced the Duke's Den.

"I'll return shortly," she told him, giving his arm a gentle shake. "If they call me, hold them off as long as you can."

He nodded his assent but didn't bother opening his eyes.

Diana considered leaving her scale model next to him, but it was the one part of her presentation she absolutely could not risk losing. She scooped up the handmade box and made her way into the club's main lobby.

"No ladies allowed on the gaming floors, miss," a crimson-coated attendant called before she'd made it halfway toward the dining rooms.

"I'm searching for something, sir. Notes for my presentation marked by a purple ribbon. I think another gentleman may have mistaken them for his and has gone into the dining rooms."

The older man assessed her a moment, casting a frowning gaze over her ruffled rose traveling gown before lingering on the polished wood container clutched in her arms. A tiny dip of his chin told Diana he'd made up his mind.

"If you return to the reception rooms, miss, I'll search for your notes."

"I'd prefer to look myself." It wasn't that she didn't appreciate the man's courtesy, but time was of the essence.

"That's impossible, miss. Ladies are not allowed in

the dining room." The man nodded solemnly as if the ridiculous rule of not allowing females to walk about freely was a very serious matter.

Looking around at the club's male attendees and a scattering of members settled on plush chairs reading the morning papers, Diana wondered if she was the first woman to ever enter the doors of Lyon's Gentlemen's Club.

Every man who caught her gaze looked shocked, if not thoroughly appalled, to find a lady invading their male enclave.

Another man approached to ask the attendant a question, and Diana took her chance.

Clutching her box to her chest, she rushed toward the dining rooms, only to tangle with a cluster of tall, bulky men crossing in front of her. One of the three sidestepped to avoid a collision, but another passed behind her at the same moment, bumping her elbow and stealing her balance.

Diana reached out to steady herself, clutching at the sleeve of one of the three men. She heard the rip of seams as she stumbled backward. The wearer reached out an arm to catch her, but his hand knocked the edge of her box instead.

"No!" She scrabbled to hold on and lost her grip entirely.

The box slammed to the marble floor with a sickening crack. Diana dropped to her knees, hands shaking as she examined the container for damage. No apparent splinters. The locking mechanism remained sound, and she prayed her model had too. She'd padded the insides well.

As two of the men hovered and murmured apologies, the third, the one whose coat she'd ripped, hunched beside her.

"Forgive me, miss. I didn't intend—"

"I know!" Diana drew in a shaky breath to keep from barking some more. Her nerves were frayed, and she still hadn't found her notes. "I think it will be all right."

When he stood, the man cast a long shadow, blotting out the light from the colored-glass dome overhead. Diana tipped her head to get a look at him.

Heat flooded her cheeks as she stared.

The stranger.

She'd memorized the lines of his face, heard his voice in her head, and recalled his scent far too many times.

She'd never forget the man, and yet today he looked strikingly different.

That night a year ago, he'd been cast in cloud-shrouded moon glow, a palette of grays and dark shadows.

But here, in morning light, he was all color. So many colors.

Auburn hair. Piercing green eyes. Flushed lips. A waistcoat the shade of butterscotch under a suit of sapphire blue.

In her memory he was tall, but now he seemed almost hulking compared to the men around them. And
just as she'd remembered, his size was distributed
well, proportioned in equal measure—broad chest,
enormous shoulders, muscled thighs. Thighs that from
her position in front of him, kneeling on the floor, she
found herself staring at as her cheeks flared to an
inferno.

She fought the urge to still, as she sometimes did
when emotions churned too wildly, and glanced up at
him again.

"You," he said wonderingly.

He watched for what felt like too long. Long enough
for her to note that his gaze was markedly different
from those of the other men she'd encountered that
morning. He didn't look at her as if she was an oddity
to be assessed and dismissed. His gaze was seeking,
as if he was pondering a question and wondered if she
might be the answer.

During a lengthy perusal, his gaze skimmed each
feature of her face. Then he reached out a hand.

Just like the night they'd met, Diana wasn't wearing gloves. Neither was he. His palm was shockingly
cool against her overheated fingers. Far cooler than
the look in his eyes.

She gave him her weight so that she could rise with
some small measure of gracefulness despite the protest of her corset, and then she bent and carefully

gathered her model in her arms. Subtle scents wafted off him, mint and coffee and fresh, clean linen.

"We'll be meeting again soon," he told her. "In the Den. I'm Aidan Iverson."

Diana was used to her mind working quickly, sifting facts and sorting out problems every moment of the day, but suddenly details felt like mismatched puzzle pieces. Her stranger, the man she'd found injured in a Belgravia mews, was one of the men who would soon decide her fate. She knew she should speak, offering him a civil greeting. Even a warm one. His goodwill could change the entire course of her life.

Instead, she stood mute and clung foolishly to his hand.

"Good luck, Miss Ashby," he said, his voice deep and as cool as the touch of his palm. Then he turned and strode away.

Of course he knew her name. He might have had a part in selecting her to appear before the Den. She was the only woman who'd been selected this round.

Perhaps that would help her somehow.

He'd wished her luck. It's what her brother believed in. It's what their father had relied upon. But Diana didn't believe in luck, only in herself and her ideas.

Now she just needed to convince a duke, a marquess, and a man with searching green eyes whom she'd once kissed impulsively in the rain.

Good grief, perhaps that would doom her altogether.

"Miss?" The porter who'd spoken to her earlier approached. "I believe this is what you were looking for. Young gent says he picked them up by accident but has been reunited with his own papers."

"Thank you, sir." She took the folio and offered the old man a smile, then quickly made her way back to the reception rooms. Her brother was awake but bleary-eyed.

"You found your papers?"

"I did. And you found a restorative." She gestured to the cup of steaming tea sitting on the table beside him.

"Would you like some?"

"No, thank you." Diana assessed him as she settled nearby. He looked more alert, but the pallor of his skin indicated that his need for tea was far greater than her own.

She lifted her notes and slid a single sheet out for him to review. "Those are the words I wish to say. Let's hope I remember to recite them all and in the right order without getting stuck somewhere in the middle."

While Dom squinted at her handwriting, Diana flipped through the other documents she'd brought with her. Beyond notes on her device, she'd collected details about the investors. She'd studied each man as if he were a design problem to be solved, scouring newspapers, gossip rags, and public documents to discover as much as she could about their interests and investment habits. Only one, Tremayne, was actually a duke. The other, the Marquess of Huntley, would someday inherit a dukedom.

The third man was something else entirely.

She curled her fingers against her palm, recalling the slide of his skin against hers.

Though Aidan Iverson possessed no title, he'd built an enormous fortune in shipping and commerce, earning a reputation as a champion of progress. The Duke of Devices, they called him, due to his passion for investing in grand industrial projects.

A shaky sigh escaped as she reviewed her notes on the Duke's Den. The odds were most decidedly not in her favor. In the eight months since its inception, only twelve inventors had received funding. A mere dozen successes out of hundreds who'd come before them. And, of course, none of them had been lady inventors.

The door to the lower level of the club opened and a hush fell over the room. Leather creaked and chair legs shifted as everyone turned anxious gazes toward the man who'd entered.

Diana recognized him as one who'd accompanied Iverson earlier. The Marquess of Huntley possessed a handsome face of perfect symmetry topped by a head of chaotic golden waves. He'd acquired a reputation worse than her brother's. Nearly everything she knew of the man came from scandal rags, much of it unrepeatable in polite company.

The notorious marquess scanned faces until his gaze settled on Diana. His mouth twitched before sloping into a wickedly appealing grin.

"You must be Miss Ashby."

Diana nodded and took a breath so deep her stays pinched at her chest.

The marquess turned his gaze toward Dom and glanced down at a paper clutched in his hands. "Mr. Ashby and Miss Ashby. Won't you both come and join us?" He gestured to the open door he'd just stepped through.

Dom hovered a hand at her back and whispered, "You can do this, Di."

She nodded and started forward.

She'd planned for this. She wanted this. She alone truly understood the stakes. It wasn't just funding she sought, but recognition, an opportunity to alter the future course her mother had set out for her.

She absolutely could not fail.

Chapter Five

$\mathcal{A}$idan watched, fascinated, as Miss Diana Ashby attempted to manage both her brother and the complex flow of her presentation.

"Just hold it steady," she whispered to him.

He held up a painted diagram of the cleaning apparatus she'd designed, but the edge kept slipping, along with the young man's concentration.

"Got it," he whispered back, but his hands shook and perspiration clung to his brow. He attempted to smile and only managed to look miserable.

Even from across the room, Aidan noted how Mr. Ashby's skin had taken on a sickly shade. Aidan knew of him as a gambler, one who'd briefly been a member of Lyon's. Lack of funds had driven him from the higher stakes games, as Aidan recalled. He also remembered Ashby as one who spent as much time imbibing as testing his luck at the tables.

"We're almost finished," Miss Ashby promised.

Oddly, though they'd met with half a dozen inventors over the course of the morning, Aidan wasn't eager for her presentation to end.

The first lady to ever present to the Den was acquitting herself well, despite rushing through a few details and tripping over words he suspected normally caused her no grief. Her passion for her invention was what mattered most and it shone through. Unfortunately, Aidan couldn't fathom the viability of a machine that required so much assembly and potential maintenance. Not to mention that its success would rely on the very unpredictable buying power of London's household consumers.

He suspected Miss Ashby's device might be popular for a time but then fall out of faddish favor.

She tripped over a word and started her sentence again. Her brother dropped the diagram he'd been holding and scrambled to retrieve it. Miss Ashby's cheeks reddened.

Aidan felt a ridiculously chivalrous impulse to come to her aid, yet the lady's confident air suggested she'd refuse any kind of assistance. After the incident in the lobby, he doubted she'd trust him to help at all.

He understood her nervousness and unease.

The men of the Den could be an intimidating trio. They each possessed wealth few had achieved. But Aidan recalled a time when he was the one seeking opportunities and investors, desperate for someone to believe in his instincts.

Miss Ashby took a deep breath as she drew to a close. Then she pressed a hand to the side of her neck, where Aidan suspected her pulse was racing madly. The room was warm, and her cheeks had become increasingly flushed during the past quarter of an hour.

He tried desperately to listen as if she was someone he'd never met before. When the application to appear before the Den had come from a Miss Diana Ashby, he had no idea it was the same woman who haunted his dreams. The woman who'd saved him from being left in a bloody heap in a Belgravia alleyway.

In the past months, he'd willed himself not to think of her. But she held a unique distinction of being the single person to whom he owed a debt.

And meeting her again today did nothing to diminish how much she fascinated him.

The lady was a bit of a conundrum.

She dressed like a debutante, spoke like a scholar, and had a flare of hunger in her gaze that he recognized, but hadn't felt in years.

Every inventor who came before them wanted money, validation, but he saw something more in Miss Ashby's eyes. Determination. Desperation. Drive. The same impulses that had once fueled him.

His passion for success had cooled over the years. But Diana Ashby's was fresh. Her desire felt raw, almost palpable. When he'd touched her hand in the lobby, she'd been enticingly warm, as if some fire lit her from the inside.

He'd known that kind of fire once.

His had been stoked by anger. Guilt. Desperation.

Shifting in his chair, Aidan willed himself to stop ruminating and listen to Miss Ashby's words. He clasped a hand over his mouth and cast his gaze down at the floor.

A moment later, she paused as if she'd misplaced her next thought. When she fell silent, Nick spoke up.

"Is that all, Miss Ashby?" Tremayne had a voice that sounded far gruffer than Aidan knew the man to be.

"That is the sum of my presentation, Your Grace. But I'm happy to answer any questions you might have." Her tone rang with confidence, even eagerness. Clearly she was prepared for inquiry. She'd been very thorough in describing her cleaning apparatus.

"Do you have something in that box beside you?" Huntley pointed to the object Aidan had accidentally caused her to drop.

"Yes, of course. How could I forget? It's a scale model of my device with a mechanism that works on the same principle as the completed prototype."

"Well, let us see your machine in action," Huntley suggested.

Aidan cast a sidelong glance at his friend and business partner. Huntley was the least likely of the three of them to part with his money unless it was to secure the company of free-spirited women and expensive liquor. For the first time since they'd started the Den, the man sounded downright intrigued.

Miss Ashby's brother jumped to attention as if realizing his moment had finally come.

Diana nodded to her brother and worked the latch at the top of the container, letting the sides fall open to reveal the model she'd described. One of the tubes of the mechanism lay at an odd angle and she reached inside to adjust its trajectory. She let out a hiss of breath when the ringed metal cylinder crumpled in her hand.

Mr. Ashby's eyes bulged wide. He nudged his chin toward the box. "There's something amiss."

"It's broken." She let out the two words on a horrified gasp.

"How bad?" her brother inquired gently.

"Ruined."

Aidan winced. Their mishap had been brief, but her wooden container had hit the marble floor hard.

"Is there a problem, Miss Ashby?" Huntley leaned forward. "Is your machine not working?"

"My invention *does* work, my lord." She looked up, scanning their faces. Her gaze came to rest on Aidan, and she shot him a stare as pointed as an accusing finger placed right between his eyes.

"I regret to say that my apparatus was damaged during this morning's collision." Each word fell from her lush mouth with hard emphasis, as if she was repeating a curse and wished to get every syllable right.

Aidan stared into Miss Diana Ashby's pretty blue eyes and didn't doubt for a moment that if she could have called him up before a magistrate, she would have.

He couldn't blame her. Such an opportunity came once, and he had taken part in damaging her prospects.

"That's a terrible shame, Miss Ashby." Huntley pitched his voice an octave lower.

"It's my fault." Aidan waited for all eyes to turn his way. "When we encountered Miss Ashby this morning, I inadvertently caused her model to tip—"

"To crash," she corrected.

"The box fell."

"Slammed onto the polished marble of the main lobby."

"I did apologize." He squared his gaze on her narrowed one. "I regret the accident, Miss Ashby."

"Not as much as I do, Mr. Iverson."

Aidan swallowed hard as she glared at him. He wondered if she regretted all of it. Rushing in to help a stranger. Holding on to each other for far too long on that year-ago rainy night. The brush of her mouth against his.

He turned his gaze toward Huntley and then Tremayne one chair down. "This should not impact our judgment regarding Miss Ashby's device. The blame is mine."

Tremayne nodded and Huntley pursed his mouth thoughtfully.

"Perhaps we could just—" Her brother pulled various tubes and cables out of the box.

"No." Miss Ashby spoke the single word like a judge issuing her final edict. "We mustn't waste any more of your time, gentlemen." She snapped the lid shut on her contraption, then turned to face them.

Her expression made something pinch behind Aidan's middle waistcoat button. The intensity had dimmed. She offered no more bold stares. In fact, her gaze seemed to fix on the wall at their backs.

"If there is anything else you wish to know about my mechanism, I'm willing to answer any question put to me."

"Where does it all go?" Aidan asked her. The one matter she hadn't addressed was disposal of all the dirt her device would so efficiently collect.

Instantly, her gaze met his, her eyes lit with a blaze of irritation that tightened her heart-shaped face, sharpening the soft curve of her jaw.

"Can you be more specific, Mr. Iverson?"

"You've spoken quite eloquently of the benefits of your cleaning mechanism. Ideally, you envision a tube system in every household, which can be used for disposing of dust and other refuse. But where does it all go?"

"Did you not read my notes, sir?"

"Not *every* word, Miss Ashby." He glanced at Tremayne and scoffed. "We are petitioned by hundreds of applicants."

"I imagine you are. This is the opportunity of a lifetime and I am grateful."

The moment Aidan started to speak, she cut in.

"Yet how can you adequately judge the merit of our inventions if you do not read each word of our applications?"

Aidan inhaled sharply and narrowed an eye at Diana Ashby. He'd just been chastised.

He sat up in his chair and resisted the ridiculous urge to straighten his necktie.

"To answer your question, Mr. Iverson, I propose a central facility with furnaces that would incinerate the refuse."

"That's quite brilliant." Huntley edged forward on his chair again.

Aidan rolled his eyes.

"Furnaces," Huntley continued, "create more dust, which will cause Londoners to need a system like yours even more. It's almost diabolical."

Huntley was the one Diana Ashby had looked to with hopefulness. He'd expressed the most interest in her design, though Aidan feared the man's eagerness had as much to do with the lady's beauty as her invention's profitability.

Now she looked at him in shock, eyes wide, her expression pained.

"You mistake me, my lord." Lines formed on her pinched brow, and the pink ruffles lining the pleats across her shoulders drooped as she let out a sigh. Softly, she added, "I wish to help people."

The five words landed like a blow. Miss Ashby's drive to succeed, he understood. But her desire to help others, that was a need—almost a compulsion—that rode his shoulders every day.

Their reasons could not be the same. She was probably an inveterate do-gooder. He was a man with a terrible sin to make up for. But he understood her goal, nonetheless.

Nick cleared his throat. "Thank you, Miss Ashby." He looked past Huntley to catch Aidan's gaze. "Unless any of you wish to pledge funding for Miss Ashby today, we will move on and send her our final determination via letter."

Turning back to face her, Nick added, "I won't be investing today."

"The product is fascinating. A capital idea." Huntley slouched slightly in his chair and tapped his lower lip with his forefinger. "Shame we couldn't see it in working order."

"Indeed it is, my lord." Though she spoke to Huntley, she might as well have called Aidan out by name.

Instead, she simply branded him with another pointed glare.

"I regret that your model was damaged, Miss Ashby," he told her, speaking less forcefully and only to her.

"Perhaps you could return when your scale model is in working order," Huntley offered with almost breathless enthusiasm.

"That would be setting a new precedent," Nick put in. "We've never allowed inventors to return to the Den."

He was right. Aidan winced at the notion of inviting some of the past inventors whose presentations had gone pear-shaped to return. Some of the ideas had been truly dreadful once they were fully described, and the Den already had a waiting list.

"I understand the hesitation to alter your rules, gentlemen. You've heard what my invention can do, how it could change and simplify sanitation for London's households. Surely every inventor cannot present a working model." She pointed at Nick. "You recently invested in a suspension bridge, Your Grace. And you"—one long, elegant finger jutted in Aidan's direction—"are known for investing in engineering feats that can never become more than sketches on paper until they are funded."

When she'd finished, a hush fell over the room. Nick, who'd been taking notes, stilled his pen. Even Huntley managed to hold his tongue.

Her brother whispered something and she began to back away, gathering her papers from the table beside her. "Thank you for the opportunity, gentlemen."

She pivoted and started for the door in long, determined strides.

Aidan had the unaccountable desire to call her back and offer his funding for her invention. A household pneumatic cleaning system was nothing that interested him in the least. Miss Ashby was right about his predilections. He invested in large-scale industrial projects, engineering designs that were bold and pushed the limits of what had ever been achieved in transport and civil engineering.

He still found himself standing up from his chair, but it was too late.

She and her brother stepped across the threshold and the doors slid shut behind them.

The entire room seemed dimmer.

"Mr. Kenworthy is next," Nick read from the document balanced on his knees. "Do you want to go and call him?"

Huntley, restless by nature, enjoyed the task of escorting each inventor into the Den. He stretched his arms above his head as he rose from his seat and headed for the threshold.

Aidan stared at the closed door and realized he was holding his breath. Hoping foolishly that a certain tall, dark-haired lady would step back through.

The thought of never seeing Diana Ashby again disturbed him almost as much as the notion that he would.

He stood up and followed Huntley out the door.

A familiar tickle fluttered in his stomach, like the tug of a knotted rope around his waist. Instinct and impulse drew him toward the entrance of the club.

"Miss Ashby." He called down to where she stood waiting as her brother climbed into a hansom cab.

When she turned, the afternoon sun gilded her face, her hair. Some small, soft voice inside told him to turn back. But the way she looked at him, her expression open and eager, made it impossible not to draw closer.

"Have you changed your mind?" She looked so hopeful.

He suddenly hated himself for giving in to foolish impulse.

"Possibly." He didn't want to fund her invention for any reason other than its viability. Because he believed it could succeed. He never wished to give any inventor false hope. "I'll speak to the others."

"Why?" Her frown was like a cloud obscuring the sun. "Surely you can invest on your own. You were the only investor in Mr. McAdam's road paving substance just last month, and before you became co-owner of Lyon's Gentlemen's Club, you built a reputation on the success of projects in which you were the sole investor."

Aidan grinned. "You gathered information about me before coming to the Den."

"About all of you, Mr. Iverson."

"I admire your preparation."

"I am always prepared, Mr. Iverson. I don't like surprises."

"Not every event can be anticipated." Aidan glanced down at the box in her hands.

"No. Not every one."

She was speaking of that night. Aidan took a step closer, and she didn't retreat. "You do remember, then?"

"I remember," she whispered.

They were so close he felt the heat of her breath against his face. She glanced inside the carriage at her brother, and when she turned back, the warmth between them had chilled.

"I believe I tore your coat."

It wasn't an apology. Aidan sensed she wouldn't give him anything. Why would she?

"My coat is easily mended. I hope the same is true for your scale model."

Miss Ashby turned her back on him and handed the box up to her brother. Aidan could read irritation in every line of her body—the hard clench of her jaw and square set of her shoulders.

"You should fund my device, Mr. Iverson." She faced him again and took one step closer. "My idea is sound and my device works beautifully. If I could fund several prototypes, the public might see their usefulness. I know I could return any investment offered." She leaned in to emphasize her point, drawing so near that for the briefest moment her bodice brushed the fabric of his waistcoat.

Aidan resisted the mad urge to reach out and touch her as he'd done that night in Belgravia. But he didn't have the excuse of a bruised head and dizziness now.

"You'll regret not taking this opportunity, Mr. Iverson."

In that moment, with her rosewater scent all around him and her chin quivering beneath the plushest lips he'd ever seen, he had several regrets, but none of them had to do with investments.

He reminded himself that he was on the hunt for a wife and needed a lady of good breeding, noble blood, and domestic inclinations. A bride completely unlike the woman standing so close that he could see the splash of freckles across the bridge of her nose.

Would he regret refusing her? Possibly, but the opportunity he wanted had nothing to do with Miss Ashby's device and everything to do with the woman herself.

Chapter Six

$\mathcal{B}$eing a twin was an odd business.

Diana had never been able to hide emotions from her brother. Even when she tried, the connection between them allowed Dominick to sense her feelings.

Thankfully, whatever his instincts about her mood, he did a brilliant job of not mentioning the debacle at Lyon's on their carriage ride home. Of course, he ruined it all five minutes later as they approached the front door.

"I'm sorry, Di," he said with a sad smile.

"There will be more opportunities. And next time things will go differently." She wasn't ready to give up, and the last thing she wanted were words of pity or platitudes.

"I'm proud of you." He scrubbed a hand over his stubbled jaw. "I may not tell you enough. Actually, I may never tell you at all." He frowned thoughtfully. "You are a brilliant inventor."

Diana squinted into the sunlight casting a halo above her brother's head. "I suspected you imbibed too much last night, but now I'm wondering if at some point you stumbled and knocked your head."

He smiled in reply and she tried too, though her face felt tight and everything in her rebelled. Disappointment was still too fresh.

Besides, she and Dom had never been the sort of siblings to offer compliments. They bickered and brawled and challenged each other. That was how it had always been. But she soaked up his words and let them sink in. There was comfort in knowing that he believed in her. She didn't wish to think of those moments before the Duke's Den when it had all fallen apart.

That mortification was too much to swallow all at once. She'd ponder the disaster of it all later, when she was alone.

"I know it didn't come together as you wished, but going was terribly brave. You were the first."

A sigh escaped from a place so deep in the center of her chest that the exhale burned. "Perhaps I'll be the last."

"Then they're fools." Dom stepped closer, forcing her to look him in the eye. "Don't even think of giving up on your inventions. Father never stopped believing in his."

Diana bit back the reply that rushed up. "He was tenacious."

Dom had always idolized their late father, looking up to him despite his many failures. What she didn't mention was what her brother chose to ignore. Their father's tenacity had bankrupted their family.

At times, Diana feared she was like her father. Bullheaded, impractical, too devoted to her own ambitions to consider the needs of others. Few of his inventions had been useful and half hadn't functioned at all.

No, she wasn't like him. Tenacity they might share, but not the rest. Her inventions were practical. All of her ideas could help others. If she could find success with just a single one, the influx of funds would help her family too.

"Ready to face Mama?"

"I didn't tell her where I was going this morning, so at least I won't have to bear her disappointment."

Dom winked. "What Mama doesn't know is for the best."

Di followed her brother through the front door. No servants greeted them. They'd let one of their maids go the previous month to economize, and the cook and housekeeper were no doubt busy below stairs.

Their mother's voice, along with several others,

echoed from the front drawing room. Diana exchanged a raised-brow glance with her brother.

"I'm not going in there. I'll face her later," he said with a foot on the first step that led to the upstairs bedrooms. "First, I need to sleep."

Diana waited for him to ascend the stairs and straightened her spine before entering the drawing room. Her jaw dropped at the scene before her.

Three of her friends, young women she hadn't seen in nearly a year, sat clustered on the settee. Lady Sophronia Bales squealed when she spotted Diana in the doorway. Miss Grace Grinstead and Lady Elizabeth Thorndyke smiled warmly at her.

Her mother offered an inscrutable expression and raised her arms in welcome. "Diana, dear. You're finally home." She came forward, gripped Diana's shoulders, and planted a quick kiss on each cheek. "The note you left was rather cryptic," she whispered.

"Not cryptic, Mama. Just incomplete."

"I insist you tell me all about your morning promenade later. First, come and say hello to your friends."

Each lady stood and they exchanged hugs and cheek kisses before Diana took a seat on an overstuffed chair nearby.

"My goodness, it's good to see all of you." She let her gaze rest on each friend's face, remembering the adventures they'd gotten up to together at Bexley Finishing School. "What brings you for a visit?"

The Season, she guessed, would draw all of them to London. Of the group she'd studied with at Bexley, only a handful had yet to secure a betrothal. Those whose families could bear the expense had a fresh Season year after year, ever determined to make a fortuitous match.

"We hadn't heard from you, Di," Lady Sophie said in her high-pitched voice. "We were worried you hadn't received our invitation." She beamed at her companions on either side of her on the settee. "So we decided to come and invite you in person."

Diana frowned. "To what exactly?" A quiver of nervousness chased across her skin.

When she was working on an invention, her habit was to turn down invites to dinners and soirees, not that she received many. Just the notion of a ball made her queasy. Dancing had been an accomplishment at which she'd never excelled.

"Your classmates are planning a reunion, Diana," her mother put in before any of her friends could answer. "Apparently your invitation went astray."

"Do say you'll come." Lady Elizabeth was the most earnest of the lot. Emotional and prone to fancy, she was also one of Diana's kindest friends.

"We've brought a new invitation." Grace dipped a hand into her reticule and pulled out a cream-colored rectangle with Diana's name printed on the front in bold, swirling letters. "All the details are inside."

"My parents have agreed to host the event." Lady Elizabeth leaned forward and smiled. "Would it be very rude of me to insist you come? It will be a wonderful way to start the Season and Mama has promised to devote herself to matchmaking for all of us."

Diana fretted endlessly over her family's financial struggles, but she'd never been disappointed that she'd been spared the rituals of a Season, or matchmaking.

"Sophie and I are doing much of the planning," Elizabeth continued. "We thought we'd start with a luncheon, some games in the garden, and then a dance in the evening."

"In other words, a ball." Diana tried to hide a shudder at the prospect.

"Say you'll come. A Bexley reunion wouldn't be complete without you."

Di sensed her mother's gaze on her, searching and intense. Rather than face the question in her eyes, she stared at the empty patch of wall over the fireplace. A landscape painting had hung in the spot for years, but the previous week their mother had sold it to an art dealer in order to fill their coffers and pay the rent.

They'd already lost so much. Not merely furnishings and housemaids but dignity. The Ashbys had once been a proud lot. Her grandfather had been a respected leader in society, a philosopher who'd written volumes on man's essential nature. Her grandmother had busied herself raising six children, including four daughters, all of whom went on to marry higher than they'd been born.

It was a hope Diana's mother had long nursed for her too.

She understood her mother's wishes. If she or Dom married well, their mother could reside with one of them. Their house might be sold or let. How could she blame her mother for wishing to see her children settled and to find a bit of security in her dotage?

"Your invitation," Grace said with a smile, offering up a small buff-colored envelope sealed with a daub of wax.

Diana glanced at her mother and reluctantly took the envelope. Inside, she found an invitation to the reunion, which was to be held in a few weeks.

Diana pressed the envelope to her lap as a wave of nostalgia made her throat burn. She'd kept herself so busy that she'd neglected the few friendships she valued. Being matched with an eligible suitor didn't interest her in the least, but she was touched by her friends' kindness and encouragement.

"Will you attend, Diana?" Grace, who'd shared her dormitory at finishing school, met her gaze squarely. She was a young woman who could hide her own feelings well, but always seemed to suss out others' quickly.

"I'll come to the reunion." As soon as she'd agreed, Diana felt a strange mixture of dread and eagerness.

"Hurrah!" Sophie bounced in place on the settee, clapping her gloved hands and squealing with excitement.

"Will you stay for luncheon, ladies?" her mother asked cheerfully.

Diana's brow winged up. They hadn't hosted visitors at their home in ages, and she wondered if their cook could rustle up something better than a few cups of tea on such short notice.

"We should go," Elizabeth said. She offered Diana a nod and a soft smile, as if she was pleased with the outcome of their visit. "But while we're all in town, we should see each other more."

"I'd like that." Diana kept her own company too much. Time spent working on her inventions allayed most of her loneliness, but not all.

After lingering good-byes and promises to meet again for a stroll through the park or a visit to a museum, Diana waved until their carriage had rolled out of sight, and returned to the drawing room.

Before saying a word, her mother rang for tea and seated herself on her favorite chair as if nothing out of the ordinary had occurred.

"Are you going to tell me where you were this morning?" she finally asked.

When Diana didn't immediately offer an answer, her mother patted the arm of the settee. "Have a seat, my dear. We must talk."

Dreaded words. A little shiver danced down Diana's spine.

When she sat, her lower back twinged, a reminder of her collision with a tall, muscled man. She'd been so certain Iverson or Huntley might invest in her idea, and yet all of them had disappointed her.

"I'm not angry with you, Diana." Eloise Ashby could lie to a parson, charm a naysayer, and spoke freely but rarely said exactly what was on her mind.

Yet Diana could sense this was different. Her mother wore no false smile, and she'd settled back against the cushions of her chair as if the morning had already worn her out.

Weakness was nothing Diana was familiar with in her mother. She was never ill, never anything but cheerful about facing a new day.

Her mother's gaze settled on the empty patch of plaster above the fireplace.

"Your father gave that painting to me after an argument." A small smile teased at the edges of her mouth and she glanced at a portrait of him on the far wall. "I accepted the watercolor because it was a gift. But I require no dreadful landscape to remind me of him."

To Diana, her father's legacy was the poverty and indebtedness her family had struggled to overcome since his passing.

"I see your father in you and your brother every day."

"There is an unmistakable resemblance." An agreeable tone was all Diana could manage. Today, when she needed a bit of her mother's sunny disposition most, she felt numb. Disappointment had dimmed everything else.

"You took your invention away with you this morning. I saw you departing with your box."

Diana cast her mother a rueful look. Her father might have possessed a prodigiously creative mind, but her mother's powers of observation were impressive too. She and Dom were fools to think anything slipped her notice.

"I went to speak to potential investors, Mama."

"And what did they say?" Her mother learned forward in her chair.

"Nothing for certain." Diana's throat burned. "They will give me their final decision via letter. By the end of the week."

"Why could they make no determination today?"

"There were three of them. Perhaps they need time to consider."

"Which invention did you take? Not one of your outlandish ones, I hope."

"Invention is supposed to be outlandish, Mama. Beyond what anyone else has ever conceived."

Despite how passionately she made the argument, Diana feared her mother was right. Some of her early inventions had been rather . . . unusual. But she'd learned through trial and error. Now she strove for practicality. *That* was the one quality her father never understood.

"I've designed a cleaning apparatus."

"Pardon?" After a brief glance around the dusty drawing room that their single housemaid hadn't yet gotten to, her mother gave Diana an affronted look.

"I have a prototype in my workshop if you'd like to see."

"I do love the creative spark you inherited from your father." Her mother reached out and laid a hand gently on Diana's.

"I wish to succeed where he failed." Diana worked to keep her voice calm. Such conversations were familiar. Her mother made no secret of the distaste she harbored for her daughter's "pastime."

More often than not, she urged Diana to marry well, to do what she'd been born for, but Diana couldn't bear more talk of husband hunting.

"I want to find funding for this invention." Shoulders back, hands clasped tightly in her lap, she added, "I know that once people use it, they'll understand its value. Mama, I can triumph as no lady inventor ever has."

"Always full of fine ideas and so much zeal." Her mother's face softened and her mouth curved in a gentle smile. She reached out and cupped Diana's chin in her palm. "I hope you will continue to have both after you're wed."

Diana pulled away and rose from the settee. She approached the window, wishing she was sketching in the park across the square or visiting with a friend at the coffeehouse nearby. She longed to escape to her workshop. Why revisit an argument she and her mother had repeated a hundred times?

There was no way to win. Diana couldn't satisfy her mother without forfeiting everything. Yet her mother didn't seem to understand the essential point.

"If I could turn a profit with one of my inventions, our troubles would come to an end. The money I could bring in—"

"I will not have my daughter earning wages like an office clerk."

Diana wheeled around to face her mother. "Then who will, Mama? Dom? You?"

Returning to the settee, Diana perched on the edge and folded her hands in her lap. "Just one opportunity. That's all I need. The system I've designed isn't frivolous. It's something everyone could use, whether household servants in Belgravia or a bachelor who works in the City and can't afford a maid of his own."

After a moment, her mother let out a raspy breath. Her shoulders sagged and Diana clamored for any explanation that might make her understand.

"But the investors did not see merit in your device." Her mother's words landed as sharply as she intended.

"I don't know that for certain." Diana tugged nervously at the edge of her sleeve and felt the delicate lace trim give way. "They have not made a final decision."

"But they could have agreed today, could they not?"

Diana looked up. Her mother's gaze was too intense, too knowing.

"You've pursued your pastime long enough," her mother said tightly. She nudged her chin toward the invitation discarded on a table nearby. "Go to the reunion and the Merton's ball. Allow Lady Elizabeth's mother to take you under her wing."

Diana reached for the invitation and her hands shook as she fumbled to return the cream square to its elegantly printed linen envelope.

"Don't waste any more time, Diana."

So many hours. Days. Years of attempting to engineer a success. Out of the corner of her eye, she could see sunlight glinting on the gilded edge of her father's portrait.

She didn't wish to be like him. Wasting her days. Disappointing her family and herself.

The furniture creaked as her mother rose and came to stand behind her, wafting her familiar perfume, tapping gently at the floor with her cane. She only used it at home, where no one else might see.

"Give me the month, Mama."

"And then?"

"If I haven't found an investor for my device—" The words stuck on her tongue like the gum arabic she used as adhesive in her workshop. "I will attend the ball and let my friends play matchmaker."

Just speaking the words made her dizzy. Blood rushed in her ears. The urge to take it back was so strong, she clenched her teeth to keep from speaking.

"Thank you, my dear." Her mother let out a long sigh of relief and laid a hand on her shoulder. "You're a clever young lady. I knew your good sense would win out." She barely paused for breath before adding, "We should contact a modiste."

"Mama. There's no money for new dresses."

Her mother squeezed her shoulder gently. "I've put some pounds aside. We must be prepared."

"I intend to find the money to fund my device, Mama. Please know that I'm hoping I *won't* be going to the ball."

After a moment her mother nodded, a taut smile stretching her lips. "We shall see."

Diana placed a kiss on her mother's cheek and strode to the room the family used as an office and library. She cut a square from a piece of foolscap, dipped a nib pen in the ink pot, and scratched out a note, not bothering with the precise penmanship she'd been taught at finishing school.

This move was a bold one. A risk, to be sure, but what did she have to lose?

When she'd finished and blown the ink dry, she folded her letter and slid it into an envelope, then added an address.

> *Aidan Iverson*
> *c/o The Duke's Den*
> *St. James Street, London*

She stared down at the words and dragged in a shaky breath.

Her knowledge of games of chance was limited to rounds of whist with her brother. Dom was the inveterate gambler in the family.

Diana prayed, in this gamble, her luck would be far better than his.

Chapter Seven

The woman was late.

Hours after his clash with Diana Ashby at the Duke's Den, Aidan stood shrouded in darkness and watched for any movement beyond the windowpanes of the Earl of Wyndham's St. James town house. Clouds hung low in the sky, blotting out the light of the moon and coating every surface in a steady drizzle.

But it wasn't the cold or rain that caused a muscle to tick at the edge of his jaw. It was the waiting. Wasting minutes. He hated nothing so much as squandering time.

After flicking rain from his coat collar and lifting the fabric to shield his neck and face, he returned his gaze to the back garden of Wyndham House.

He couldn't shake the sense of déjà vu and turned his head to glance down the row of houses, half-expecting two thugs to materialize out of the fog.

His private inquiry agent had arranged the clandestine meeting with the earl's housekeeper, but Aidan insisted on questioning the woman himself. Whatever information she possessed, it was his alone. No one else's.

This time he'd come prepared. He gave his coat pocket a pat and felt the reassuring outline of a revolver. No thieving ruffians would spoil his plans this evening.

After the attack, he'd returned to Belgravia a week later and confronted Lord Talmudge, only to discover that the Mariah "Mary" Iverson who'd worked for him had been an aged widow who'd served briefly as governess. Far too old to have been the woman who'd given birth to two children during the period when Aidan and his sister were born.

So he'd hired more investigators and their work had led him here. Waiting, once again, in the dark outside an aristocrat's back garden.

He clenched his hands into fists for warmth and considered battering the kitchen door. It was far more notice than he wished to attract and yet he had no desire to waste the evening in a pointless vigil either.

In business, he traded in commodities—iron and steel, textiles and grain. But he'd learned long ago that time was the most precious commodity.

Of late, it felt as if his time was running out. Or at least that his past was catching up. Guilt gnawed with teeth that were sharper each day.

Perhaps it was the prospect of wedlock that spurred the need. The thought of children and the legacy he'd leave behind ironically made him look backward. If he didn't face his past now, he sensed it would forever haunt his future.

Light shifted behind curtains in the kitchen windows, and the squeak of a door hinge indicated someone had emerged from the house. Aidan could make out nothing through the drizzle until the glow of a single lantern lit the darkness, a circle of light that bobbed and swayed as the old woman approached.

"Mrs. Tuttle?"

"That I am, sir." She came close and held up her lamp as she gaped at him. "You must be Iverson."

Even in the dim light, she seemed determined to see him. To study him.

A flare of hope burned behind his ribs. He held his breath.

"You reckon you're Mary's son, sir?"

"Investigator Reeves said you knew her. And her children." Aidan scanned the woman's face as eagerly as she examined his, but it was futile. Even if they'd met long ago, he'd been but a boy.

"Knew Mary well, I did. Met the boy twice. Held the youngest child when she was just a babe."

"Where did you meet them?" Aidan leaned closer and the woman stepped back in alarm. "Any details you have, Mrs. Tuttle, I'm willing to pay." Sliding a hand inside his overcoat, he withdrew a pile of banknotes far enough for her to see the white of the paper.

"Detective Reeves said you're a rich man." The old woman fluttered a hand at the high neck of her black servant's uniform. "But there's more to consider than coin."

"How much do you want?" Aidan understood negotiation, but there was no time for flimflam now. He'd pay the old woman a fortune if it meant he could learn the truth and find some measure of peace.

"She left the earl's employ in 1817. Took a room in Lambeth."

"Lambeth?" The same riverside district where he'd spent his childhood. "And she said her surname was Iverson? You're certain?"

Aidan had no clear memories of his parents. His first and ugliest memories were of his days in a workhouse. Of that time, there were only a few good reminiscences. Sharp, precious recollections of his younger sister.

"I'll never forget Mary Iverson, sir. She was like kin to me."

"Then you must tell me all you knew of her. Reeves said you had documents. Letters. A journal." Aidan's fingers itched. He was half ready to reach out and dig through the woman's pockets. He'd been searching so long for any clue, any trace of his parents.

"I've nothing for you tonight, sir." The old woman

sniffed and cast a glance back toward the Wyndham town house. "Wanted to have a look at you. Discover whether I could trust you. Whether you looked aught like Mary's boy."

Aidan flinched. He hated the rush of longing that came, the need to have the emptiness inside him filled. How long had he sought belonging?

But he sensed impatience wouldn't do with Mrs. Tuttle. In his businesslike voice, he asked, "And what is the verdict?" He allowed no eagerness to seep into his tone. "Do I look like her?"

Mrs. Tuttle shuffled closer and raised her lantern again. Her perusal came like the rough press of fingertips. Aidan half expected her to reach out and grab his jaw to hold him steady.

"You do, sir."

Breath whooshed out of him. Relief expanded his chest, filling his lungs with a chilling gulp of damp air.

"Then you must give me something. If you've no information, why agree to this meeting? You understand what I wish to know."

The housekeeper began nodding her head but said nothing.

Aidan pulled out a five-pound note and held it in front of her. "There's much more where this came from. But you'll need to provide me with something tangible in return. Are there letters?"

"Perhaps, a few."

He began to shiver. Not from the cold, but from desperation. Answers had eluded him for too long.

"You shouldn't return here, Mr. Iverson. There will be too many questions if you do. May I call on you?"

"Soon, Mrs. Tuttle." Before all good sense fled and he stormed Wyndham House and turned the place over brick by brick. He lifted a calling card from his waistcoat pocket.

She hesitated for what felt like an hour, her gaze darting from the card to his eyes, his nose, his chin. The paper of his card began to grow soggy between his fingers.

"Aye, you're her boy," she finally said. "I'm sure of it the more I look."

"Then assist me."

With trembling fingers, she reached for the card and the money, but she didn't immediately pull away. Her hand came down on his and she held him for a moment before letting go.

"Mary did love her children."

Then why did she send us to hell?

"Next week, Mrs. Tuttle?"

The woman shook her head vehemently. "I must request permission for a half holiday and wait for the mistress to grant the time."

"As soon as you can." Aidan tipped a meaningful gaze down to where she clutched his card and five-pound note. "Good evening to you."

He watched her return to the house, her lamp flame guttering in the evening breeze. Then, just at the threshold, she turned back.

"Mr. Iverson? You might check the lodging house in Lambeth. Close on the river. Off the Belvedere Road. Number fourteen, if memory recalls."

"When would she have been there?"

In the lantern glow, he saw the woman's mouth tilt.

"How old are *you*, young man? She brought you into this world in that lodging house and I held her hand the whole long night. Three decades past?"

"Eight and twenty years." Long enough for the lodging house to have changed owners or to have been demolished completely. Likely too long for whoever had known his mother to remember her or anything about her fate.

"I shall visit you soon, Mr. Iverson."

"Bring everything you have, Mrs. Tuttle. And hurry. I'm not a patient man."

Chapter Eight

*A*idan arrived at the office early the next day. He'd hoped to find word from Mrs. Tuttle that she'd received her half holiday and would soon be on her way to him with his mother's journals and letters.

But there'd been no messages. Only a diary full of appointments, a day filled with talk of new business projects, and the impending weight of marriage.

Now, as the clock on the wall ticked toward six in the early evening, he found himself shifting in his chair, desperate to find a comfortable position from which to engage in the most uncomfortable of activities.

Asking others for help fit him like an ill-tailored suit, pinching here, squeezing there. But the past months had proven that this decision was necessary. His own attempts at meeting and wooing a noblewoman ranged from ineffectual to downright comical.

He'd decided to defer to an expert.

"Pleasure to meet you, Mr. Iverson." Professional matchmaker Mrs. Bertha Trellaway offered a loose handshake before seating herself in front of his desk.

She was older than he expected. Prim, petite, and nervous, judging by the way her fingers danced back and forth across the edge of the leather folio in her lap.

He'd worked off his own share of nervous energy by pacing his office before her arrival, but he was better at masking unease. It was a gambler's skill he'd honed over many years of practice.

"I appreciate that you arrived so promptly, Mrs. Trellaway." He smiled, but the lady didn't seem to take any notice.

She was a curious sort. He waited as she took in his office, scanning the items on his desk, the bookcase in the corner, a row of ledgers on a high shelf at his back. There wasn't a great deal to see. He kept the space free of anything that might distract him from work.

He didn't mind her perusal. It gave him an opportunity to assess her in return.

Aidan quite liked that she was a woman of advanced years. Age could prove an advantage. Years implied experience, and, in this matter, he needed all the help he could get. With no formal education, he often felt himself a step behind, especially when it came to etiquette and the dictates of polite society.

Three months after telling his friends he required no help to catch the notice of some eligible noblewoman at a round of social functions, he'd decided to take Huntley's advice.

Heaven help him.

Huntley had given him Mrs. Trellaway's name and insisted she'd engineered matches between the most eligible ladies and gentlemen of the *ton*.

"I have a few questions, if I may," she finally began. With a single tug, the matchmaker released a fan of papers from her folder.

The muscle under Aidan's eye began to twitch.

"What is it that you wish to know?" Aidan tugged at the knot of his tie and felt the thrum of his pulse beating against his fingertips.

He had secrets to keep and a past mostly punctuated by mysteries.

"Tell me about your people, Mr. Iverson."

"My people?" He attempted to swallow the stone that had lodged itself at the back of his throat. "I'd prefer we not tread there."

"I see." The lady's eyes bulged behind her spectacles and she shuffled the papers balanced on her knees. "Well, let's save that for later. I understand you seek a highborn noblewoman for a bride. A lady of excellent breeding and accomplishments. Dowry unnecessary?"

"Completely." The only lure he had to offer was wealth, and he wished to maintain that advantage.

Some aristocrats would sneer at how he'd earned his money, but others were feeling the wane of the railroad boom. Those men who'd invested unwisely, whose familial estates were bleeding tenants and losing money season after season, would be willing to bind their daughters to any man able to refill their coffers.

"Any preferences, sir?"

"Haste and discretion." Scrubbing a hand across his jaw, Aidan admitted, "My own efforts have not borne success."

The memory of his ham-fisted matchmaking attempts made his stomach twist. So many parties. Ear-splitting visits to the bloody opera. Smiling until his cheeks ached. He'd been a fool to think finding a bride would be easy. Ladies found him charming enough and his money drew them, if nothing else. But he was an exacting man. He wanted what he'd been born without. A name that made others take notice. Connections that would cause a nobleman to raise a glass in recognition rather than tip a haughty nose in disdain.

He wanted a legacy.

"Discretion is my byword, Mr. Iverson." Across from him, the matchmaker narrowed her gaze and hovered a pencil over her papers, as if waiting to note crucial details. "But what are your preferences in regard to a prospective bride? Do you favor fair-haired ladies or—"

Dark hair. Curves. Except for her chin, which narrowed to a little notched square.

A vision of Miss Diana Ashby filled his mind as if she'd just come strutting through his office door with all the confidence she'd exuded in the Duke's Den. He'd tried not to notice her beauty, tried not to let his gaze wander below the neckline of her frilly gown, and utterly failed. Several times.

But Miss Ashby had come to them for funding. Nothing more.

Business was business. And pleasure was a separate endeavor altogether. One that, regrettably, he rarely found time for. But when he did, he maintained an impenetrable wall between the two. Structure, management, and control made his businesses run smoothly. He had no reason to run his private life any other way.

And when he married? The wall between his public and private life would matter more than ever. He wished his home to be a haven from the cutthroat world of commerce.

"Fair-haired will do," he heard himself say. He'd always preferred ladies with gold tresses. So he had no bloody idea why his mind continued to catalog Miss Diana Ashby's charms. *Blue eyes. A divot in the center of her chin.*

"What of accomplishments?" Mrs. Trellaway's silver brows slid up her forehead. "Music?"

"Not necessary." Aidan winced at the memory of musicales he'd attended and how often he'd attempted to inconspicuously press a hand over his ear at the opera.

"Painting?"

"Might be useful." His Mayfair town house had been decorated in pale cream and dove gray before he took up residence. He quite liked the notion of someone bringing a bit of color to the walls.

"Any particular tongue you wish the young lady to be proficient in?"

"I do prefer an educated bride." He suspected most noblewomen possessed some education. A clever lady sounded appealing. "Languages, history, literature—whatever takes her fancy."

"Noted. Now, answer me this, Mr. Iverson. What one essential quality do you require in a young lady you'd consider marrying?"

Bluntly, he wanted a woman with unassailable connections. He didn't truly care whether his lady bride spoke ten languages as long as she could trace her family back for ten generations.

"Entry into polite society is what I'm after, Mrs. Trellaway. I require a wellborn bride."

The older woman narrowed dark eyes behind her gold-rimmed spectacles. "How high do you aim, sir?"

"A duke's daughter will do."

"There aren't many of those, Mr. Iverson."

"I only require one, Mrs. Trellaway." For a moment, Aidan thought she might refuse him or bolt from his office. The matchmaker shifted as if to rise. But instead of departing, she slipped a rectangle of newsprint from her folio and slid it onto his desk.

A woman's crosshatched image stared back at him. Pinched brow, cold eyes, a thin, unsmiling mouth.

"Lady Elnora is the Duke of Redmond's only unmarried daughter. She speaks French and German, paints, plays the pianoforte—"

"She's not what I had in mind."

"Interested in a pretty face, I take it." Mrs. Trellaway's smile told Aidan his preference was not unexpected.

She shifted more documents and then selected two to lay out before him. One was a small watercolor, its bright hues a marked contrast to the daguerreotype beside it. The photograph bore the image of a curvaceous woman of middle age with dark eyes and fair hair. The other lady was waifish and so pale that her eyes, hair, and brows all seemed the same snowy shade.

"Lady Bridget is the daughter of the Duke of Ainswyck," she said of the shapely woman. "And Lady Sarah is the only child of the Marquess of Cleland, who will soon inherit his father's dukedom."

"Tell me about Lady Bridget."

The older woman grinned proudly. "Thought you'd like the looks of her. Word is she's a bit of a challenge."

"I'm not daunted by a challenge."

"She's a broken-hearted lass. Apparently, some Frenchman was set to marry her and broke the engagement."

"When?"

Mrs. Trellaway shrugged. "Quite recently. Dukes' daughters don't remain on the marriage mart long."

"Then time is of the essence. How do we arrange an introduction?"

"In most circumstances, it's advantageous if we use your own connections to initiate an introduction." She glanced down again at her notes. "You count the Duke of Tremayne and the Marquess of Huntley as friends?"

"I do." The two men were the only true friends he had. Keeping secrets meant keeping personal ties to a minimum.

The matchmaker stared at him, gaze narrowed. Aidan realized Mrs. Trellaway was assessing him and he wasn't coming up to snuff.

"Any other titled acquaintances, Mr. Iverson?"

"Are a duke and a marquess not sufficient?"

She reached up to adjust the brooch at the neck of her gown and swallowed hard. "May I speak frankly?"

"I prefer that you do."

"Any sort of acquaintance with a nobleman will, in the normal course, lead to familiarity with other noblemen. Invitations come your way, I'm sure."

"They do indeed." Huntley was forever entertaining, and Nick and his wife, Mina, had begun to host dinners in their new Belgrave Square home in an attempt to establish their place in London society.

"There's something that matters more in aristocratic circles than a man's wealth or title or bloodline." Her brow folded in a worried frown, as if she was about to convey news he would not wish to hear. "Reputation, Mr. Iverson, is the most precious commodity."

"I've engaged in no scandals, Mrs. Trellaway." He'd spent years avoiding bad business deals and building trust with other men of commerce in London.

"You have not, but I'm afraid the Duke of Tremayne is considered a newcomer to the *ton* and the marquess is . . . perhaps too well-known."

"I do have other aristocratic acquaintances. Members of Lyon's and a few gentlemen at the Royal Society." He knew them well enough to exchange a civil greeting, but no better, and he suspected Mrs. Trellaway sensed he was grasping for unlikely possibilities.

"We may need to call on them, Mr. Iverson, but let me first determine when Lady Bridget will be in town. Her family resides mostly on an estate in Ireland and only comes to London for the Season."

"Whatever it takes."

"I shall make inquiries and report back to you by the end of the week."

"Very good." He could almost taste the end of small talk with marriage-eager debutantes, only to discover that their fathers were as noble as he was. When the matchmaker scooted forward in her chair, Aidan scooted back in his chair, eager to see her out.

She gathered her notes carefully and then let out an unexpected *ah*. "There is one last bit of information I require, Mr. Iverson."

"Which is?"

"Your people. The Duke of Ainswyck is as scrupulous about lineage as you are, sir."

"I came to you because I have no noble pedigree to boast."

The lady matchmaker bristled and sat up straighter in her chair. "Most of my clients *do* boast such a pedigree, sir." She flicked the papers at the edge of her folio and stared at the top of his desk as if pondering what to say. "Ainswyck's estate is nearly bankrupted. That much is true. But I fear even that inducement would not allow him to bind his daughter to a man whose history remains shrouded in mystery."

Aidan scrubbed at his jaw and squeezed his hand around the knot of tension at the back of his neck. "Tell him they were respectable. Tell him they're dead. Remind the duke of all that I can offer Lady

Bridget." Aidan turned his gaze from the woman and worked to stem a flare of irritation. Anger lay just below the surface, reminding him too much of the impulsive young man he no longer wished to be.

"I'm not at all certain I can convince the duke, Mr. Iverson." Her tone was cool, her voice dubious.

"Cost is irrelevant. Offer Ainswyck whatever he wants as an engagement gift." Aidan squared his gaze on the woman. "Only to be delivered when the banns are read." He wasn't fool enough to make a bad deal, even with a matter of such consequence.

"Your wealth is not in doubt, Mr. Iverson. But your parentage will be if I can give no answer to the Duke of Ainswyck when he asks. And I promise you he will."

"Stall him. Or make something up." Aidan stood and pushed back his chair. It was either that or tip his entire desk over in one shove.

He turned to gaze out the window, focusing on the pale ribbon of gold still lighting the dusky sky. But out of the corner of his eye, he could sense Mrs. Trellaway's unease.

"I do not think I can assist you." The matchmaker scooted forward on her seat. "If you can provide no information that I may take to the duke, then I fear any match with Lady Bridget, or any duke's daughter, will be impossible."

When she stood, a crinkling noise sounded in the office before she stepped forward and placed the check he'd given her on his desk.

"I'm sorry, Mr. Iverson."

Aidan didn't look at her or offer any parting words. For the moment, gentlemanly civility escaped him.

When the matchmaker departed, Aidan settled back on the edge of his desk. Shivers racked his body, though warmth still emanated from the grate in the corner of his office.

Like poking at an open wound, he couldn't stop from reaching inside a carved box he kept on his desktop and pulling out the faded scrap of paper inside. *Sarah*. The name was simply formed, a child's hand. And the drawing was more primitive still, a few lines meant to represent a smiling face. One tiny stick arm raised in the semblance of a wave.

He had no photograph of his sister. Just this ragged single memento and a hoard of regrets heavy enough to crush the air from his lungs.

Pushing off his desk to stand, his hand snagged on a piece of the morning post his clerk had left for him to review.

His pulse started a wild tattoo when he saw the feminine hand and the sender's name.

The Honorable Miss Diana Ashby.

He ran his finger over letters as elegantly shaped as

the lady herself. Then he tore the envelope open and unfolded her note.

Mr. Iverson,

I know you regret our collision at the Lyon's Den and the resulting damage to my model. Rather than bill you for the cost of materials, I will allow you to rectify the matter by visiting my workshop so that I may show you a working model of my design.

Sincerely,
D. Ashby
33 Cadogan Square

Chapter Nine

$\mathcal{I}$s it supposed to look . . . like that?" Grace Grinstead pointed at the various pieces of Diana's scale model that were laid out on a table in her workshop.

"No, it most decidedly is not." Diana handed her friend a smock to cover the delicate lace and fine satin of the striped day dress she wore. "Put one of these on. This space can get rather messy."

"Get? I'm afraid messy has been achieved." Grace smiled, slid her arms into the plain cotton garment, and secured it with a loose knot around her waist. "I recall that you were prone to messiness at Bexley too."

"I was not." Diana pointed at the poor broken parts of her pneumatic device. "For goodness' sakes, my greatest invention is a machine intended to make cleaning easier."

"Shall we start with this conservatory?" Grace lifted a rag from the workbench with two fingers, inspected a few of its stains, and then cast the oily fabric away. "I know you don't employ many staff, but surely one of the maids could tidy for you."

Diana sat on one of the wooden stools she'd placed out for each of them and smiled at her former boarding school roommate. "What's become of you, Grace? I remember how you used to love to ride horseback in the rain and dig your hands in the dirt during lessons in the garden. Being filthy never bothered you before."

Her friend let out a dismissive huff. "We haven't been at Bexley in years, Diana." She reached out to pick up one of the broken pieces of the model and spun it nervously in her fingers. "I've changed since then. My goals. My activities. My family has high expectations."

"Marriage?"

"Yes, of course." That she had even asked seemed to surprise Grace. "But not just any match. They wish for a fortuitous one. Mama admonishes us never to speak of finances, but the truth is ours are grim."

"I understand." Diana never spoke of her family's struggles with money either, but she suspected Grace's father, Viscount Holcomb, would be horrified to know it had been a topic of conversation.

"Do you?" Grace took in the cluttered corner of the back-garden conservatory that Diana had transformed into her workshop and smiled. "It seems that you're well occupied in pursuits beyond husband hunting."

"For now, yes." Diana took two pieces of broken metal cylinder into her hands. "My mother is losing patience."

"My father is the same." Grace moved closer and settled onto the stool beside Diana. "But I'm impatient too. Do you not wish to leave home? To have a household of your own to manage?"

"I can't say that I do." Diana craved independence, but would marriage bring that? "I appreciate having a space of my own."

Her mother did allow her more autonomy than she sometimes appreciated. Not all unmarried young ladies would get away with commandeering the family conservatory.

"What about the rest?" Grace ran her finger around a whorl in the polished wooden tabletop. "There's more than independence from one's family to make a young woman wish to marry."

"There must be." Diana glanced to her left and indicated a list that had been distributed to all the young ladies of Bexley, including the name of each student in their graduating class. She'd placed a checkmark next to the name of each friend whose marriage had been announced since they'd departed school four years ago.

"Goodness, are there truly so few of us who've not yet found a match?" Grace sounded bereft. "Now I feel like even more of a spinster."

She and Diana exchanged a glance and chuckled.

"What I meant was love."

"Ah." Diana sighed and reached for a small hammer to alter the shape of her cylinder.

"Don't tell me you don't believe in love." Grace leaned so far into the table, she shifted a few pieces of Diana's model.

"Poets tell of love. Novelists write characters who fall far too readily. But I don't have time for reading poetry or novels." Diana smiled, but didn't meet her friend's gaze. "I prefer to make decisions based on what's rational. On what I can see and touch and calculate."

"Come, Di. Are you telling me there's never been a single man who's made your pulse race? No one who made you wish to ignore all the rules of propriety we were taught at Bexley?"

Diana's fingers tensed so fiercely on the cylinder in her hand that she felt the thin metal begin to give way. Her cheeks warmed, and she willed her thoughts to go anyplace but to that night.

Aidan Iverson made her pulse race, and she'd ignored every bit of etiquette she'd been taught.

"There is someone," Grace whispered.

"No, there's not," Diana said, as much to herself as

to her friend. "I am a woman of science. Love is about feelings and fanciful notions that have no place in my life."

Grace lifted one blond brow when Diana finished. "No place at all?"

"Not right now." Diana stood and collected a bottle of adhesive and two brushes from her workbench. "Would you help me glue these chipped pieces back together? They haven't splintered and we can fit them neatly back into place."

They worked in silence for several minutes. Diana was grateful for the reprieve, but she sensed Grace's gaze on her now and then, watching and assessing.

"Love will find you one day," Grace said quietly. "When you least expect it. Your feelings may not make sense or be as rational as one of your scientific formulas, but they will be undeniable."

Grace spoke with such solid certainty that Diana stopped and looked at her.

"Is there someone who's turned your head, Grace? Someone that you wish to marry?"

Her friend's eyes widened, but she collected herself quickly, schooled her expression, and laughed lightly. "Of course. I just haven't met him yet. I only know he must be rich and willing to accept a meager dowry from my father."

"You just spoke to me of love and yet now you leave it off your list."

"Oh, love would be nice, but I suppose it's not essential. Not if every other requirement is met." Grace winked and then stared down at the table. She glued the last piece in place and glanced up proudly. "There. Now what else can I help you with?"

"Nothing, unless you can convince one of the men of the Duke's Den to fund my machine."

"I've heard of it. Quite a strange arrangement. Titled men flouting convention and inviting others to petition for funds." Grace lowered her voice and added, "My father thinks it's all quite scandalous."

"Then he'd be horrified to know that I spoke to them."

"Did you?" Grace tucked a ringlet of blond hair behind her ear and stared at Diana with concern in her gray eyes.

"Unfortunately, my presentation didn't go well." *Disastrous* was the most accurate description, but it sounded dreadfully hopeless. "I'm not giving up."

"You rarely do." Grace's smile indicated the words were meant as more compliment than critique. "What do you plan to do?"

"Divide and conquer." Diana stood and retrieved the notes she'd assembled on the men of the Duke's Den. She laid the sheets down in front of Grace. "I only need to convince one of them."

"I know him," Grace said immediately, pointing to the name of Lord Huntley. "He's an utter rogue."

"So I've gathered. As you see, most of the details I have about him are from the scandal rags." Diana tipped her head. "Do you know him personally? Perhaps you know something that would help me convince him to invest."

"I know his sisters mostly. Our families met once in Bath."

"Anything he seemed particularly interested in?"

"Flirtation, as I recall." Grace winked, then dipped her head to continue perusing Diana's notes. "Tremayne is quite broodingly handsome, is he not? He and his wife attended one of Mama's balls last year. They're terribly smitten and didn't attempt to hide it."

"I'm not particularly interested in what he looks li—"

"Goodness."

Diana leaned closer to see what had caught her friend's eye. "Ah, yes. Mr. Iverson. He is very . . ." *Handsome* didn't seem sufficient. There was symmetry in his features and masculine appeal in every slope and line. But it was the way he carried himself. The confidence he exuded that somehow didn't ever ebb into arrogance or pompous pride. She'd known from the first moment she met the man that he was kind. Yet she knew now that he could also be hard, decisive. She didn't imagine him giving in to sentiment often.

"Compelling," Diana finally said. "He's very compelling."

"He's very rich." Grace turned the page around so that Diana could see and placed her finger over a number. "Is that truly his annual income?"

"Only an estimate. I calculated based on records I found related to dividends he'd received from his investments." Diana shrugged. "Could be more or slightly less."

"And yet with all this money, he won't invest in your device?"

"He did initially refuse." Diana bit her lip, thinking of the letter she'd impulsively sent. "But I still have hope."

Grace continued sifting through the pages and rested her chin on her hand. "What if no one invests? What will you do?"

"I'll join you in the marriage hunt. Which will make my mother very happy."

"And you very miserable?"

"Perhaps." Diana couldn't imagine that possibility yet. She told herself that it would not come. She'd find funding and then she wouldn't need to marry. At least not immediately. If she waited, perhaps she'd have time to read poetry and begin to believe in something as fanciful as love.

"Why does this all matter to you so much?" Grace asked with a wave of her hand around the cluttered workshop. "These inventions. This drive to fund one of them. Are they truly your dreams, or your father's?"

"They're mine, Grace. These designs, everything you see here, is mine." Diana clenched her jaw and glanced behind her at the row of brushes, rulers, hammers, and chisels. They'd been her father's tools. In some ways, they were her legacy. But what Diana built, she built to prove her own merit, not to carry on for her father.

At Bexley she'd been teased for collecting bits of metal and wooden crates in order to build models of her ideas. After she had returned home, her mother discouraged her from scientific study. She'd never forbidden Diana from spending time in her workshop, but her mother made it clear that she believed all the hours spent there were wasted time.

If Diana could never succeed with one of her designs, then her mother would be right.

"This matters to me because it's who I am. Even if I weren't in this workshop every day, the ideas, the drive to create, would be whirling in my head. It never quiets. But I need it to be more than fanciful notions." Her mother claimed that Father's inventions had ruined their family. "I need my inventions to be real and make someone's life better."

Diana realized she was rambling, talking too fast, speaking so that she didn't feel.

Grace reached out and laid a hand over hers. "I'm sorry. Forgive me."

Diana nodded, but she could no longer find any

words. Her mother spoke about their father often, but never of his death. Even she and Dom, as close as they were, had never been able to revisit that pain.

"I wonder why. The question haunts me," Diana finally managed. "Why that particular day at that particular hour? And why did none of us know he had become so hopeless?"

Others referred to Frederick Ashby's death as tragedy, but no one dared mention that he had taken his own life.

Diana didn't pursue her inventions simply to follow in her father's footsteps. Her ideas were her own. But his life, and his death, were always in her mind.

"I won't lose hope. I can't give up no matter how difficult this path might be."

Grace squeezed her hand. "I understand a little better now." She settled back on her stool and turned contemplative. There was a look that came over her, one Diana remembered from finishing school. She was plotting, and few plotted as well as Grace Grinstead.

"What are you thinking about?"

"How I might help you. My father isn't much of a venturer when it comes to investment. He doesn't have the funds to risk. But he knows men who do. Club friends. Railroad barons mostly. One man who helped fund Brunel's steamship. He may know someone. I shall ask."

"Thank you, Grace." Diana spent so many hours alone, so much time in her own head, that it felt odd to have an ally. Odd and yet wonderful. Her heart felt fuller, and the day seemed brighter, but worry still crept in. "How can I repay you for this?"

"You must wait until I do something worth repaying," Grace reminded her. She reached out a hand and sifted the pages of Diana's notes about the gentlemen of the Duke's Den. "Though I must say that my mother would be forever grateful if you could introduce me to a man as wealthy as Aidan Iverson."

The words came punctuated with a trill of laughter. There was as much tease as seriousness in the request, Diana knew. But even that light jest caused something to knot in Diana's stomach. A burn of irritation and possessiveness when she had no right to either.

"I'd be happy to introduce you to him," she told her friend, "if I ever see the man again."

Chapter Ten

A week after Diana Ashby's presentation at the Duke's Den, Aidan paced the pavement in front of her Cadogan Square home, debating the folly of going inside.

He hated the mere fact that he *was* debating.

Decisiveness. Taking action. That's what he was known for. He'd never been a man to dither.

Dragging in a deep breath, he narrowed his gaze and stared at the rose red entrance of the Ashbys' whitewashed town house. The hue reminded him of Diana Ashby's mouth, a darker shade than the pink frock she'd worn to the Den, a shadow of the flush that had rushed up the curve of her cheeks.

The lady behind that door sparked a mix of attraction and interest that hadn't waned since the night she'd rushed toward him across slick cobblestones, determined to save him from men who were twice her size.

He'd known then that she was trouble. Brave, impulsive, and troublesome because he'd been utterly unable to forget her.

"Why the hell am I here?" he grumbled under his breath.

Her summons was like many he received from inventors eager for someone to make their ideas take flight. Despite her insistence, he didn't owe Miss Ashby this visit. Clumsiness did not equate to indebtedness.

But there was the other debt. How did one repay a young woman for recklessly saving one's life?

And there was more.

The desire to see her again had gone past intrigue and become something of a craving since the previous week when she'd torn his coat and stared at him with a disturbing mix of curiosity and interest at the club.

He *should* go inside and do exactly as she requested. Give her a chance to display her invention, apologize again for their unfortunate collision, thank her once more for saving his life, and go on his merry way.

Behaving like a proper gentleman hadn't been bred into his bones, but he knew enough of propriety to spend twenty minutes with an unwed gentlewoman and not cause a scandal.

He approached the door, knocked once, and glanced

at his pocket watch to remind himself to keep this short.

"Good afternoon, sir." A bespectacled older gentleman greeted him and took his measure in one discerning glance.

"Is Miss Ashby at home?"

The question seemed to surprise the servant. His mouth dropped open before he answered. "Why, yes, sir. And who may I say has come to call?"

"Iverson." He offered the man a calling card. "She invited me."

The old man quirked a brow and tipped his head as if he doubted every word. But he took Aidan's card, coat, and hat, and led him to a drawing room. For a London town house in a good neighborhood, the space was snug but warm and inviting. A wash of morning sunlight streamed through the curtains, enhancing the yellow shade of the walls. It was a room he could easily imagine Miss Ashby inhabiting.

"If you'll wait here, sir."

Aidan explored the space while he waited, noting every sign that told the tale of the Ashby family. Watercolor miniatures of Diana and her brother. Porcelain figurines of two identical children, a boy and a girl. A pile of books that included everything from Dickens to Copernicus. A few unpolished but framed technical drawings made him wonder if Miss Ashby's interest in engineering had been encouraged from her youth.

"Those were my father's."

Aidan inhaled sharply and caught her rosewater scent on the air. He told himself not to act like a fool before turning to face her.

"He inspired you to become an inventor?" The words came out too rough, because the sight of her was as unsettling as he anticipated.

A rush of pleasure came first and then the same jolt of attraction as when he'd looked into her eyes at Lyon's.

"I suppose he did, in some ways." Her voice was breathy too and he found himself hoping he had even a fraction of the effect on her that she did on him. "Though our designs are quite different." She approached and lifted the framed image of a technical drawing that he'd been examining.

Her nearness sped his pulse. But of course they'd stood this close before. Closer, on the night she'd let him hold on to her in the moonlight.

Having her close seemed more awkward and intimate today. He was in her home, and she looked far different than she had when he'd last seen her.

At Lyon's, she'd worn a fashionable, ruffled traveling gown, her glossy brown hair trapped in pins. Today she was downright unkempt. Her chocolate waves had been captured in a messy braid that lay over one shoulder and her plain peach gown fell naturally over her curves.

"There was no consistency to my father's fancies. He could imagine a whole city engineered to his specifications or design something like this." She held up her father's drawing. "It's a ventilating top hat."

"A ventilating . . . ?"

Miss Ashby leaned closer, her bodice brushing the arm of his coat. She lifted a finger to trace the mechanism of the design. "When a man becomes very warm—"

A sound emerged from the back of his throat. A strangled chuckle, as much because of the absurdity of the design as the fact that she was deliciously close, which had the very unsettling effect of making him overheat.

She glanced at him as if to determine whether he intended to interrupt her any further and then carried on. "By cranking this lever, the top would open to allow in some cool air."

"Why?"

She looked at him, a confused expression carving two tiny lines between her brows. "Why what?"

"If a man wishes to be cool, he can simply remove his hat." He pointed to the crank and lever design. "That seems like far too much work."

Miss Ashby returned the drawing to the table where it joined several others, then offered him a smile that made the breath tangle in his throat. "You're right, of course. Few of my father's designs ever became more than sketches."

"I can see why."

"But I assure you, Mr. Iverson, mine are already much more than fanciful nonsense." There was a delicious gleam of challenge in her gaze.

"Show me."

Without another word, she led him deep into the interior of the house, looking back now and then to make sure he still followed. Finally, she turned and headed toward what appeared to be a back garden. But as they drew closer, he realized much of the space had been taken up by a glass-covered conservatory.

The Ashby conservatory was filled with mechanical parts and tools. So many technical sketches were applied to the glass windows that they served as wallpaper, blocking much of the sunlight.

"I hoped you'd come, so I have everything laid out in anticipation. I do need a moment to prepare the device. Are you in a terrible rush?"

"No." In truth, he had two investors to meet within the hour, an appointment with his banker, and a lecture to attend in the evening. He'd intended to come and go quickly, to stay as long as politeness required and be on his way. Yet for the first time in a long while, he found himself wishing to linger.

She disappeared into a partitioned area of the conservatory and he appraised the workshop she'd created. Order reigned in the space, with nails and screws sorted by size and stored in jars on a shelf, spools of wire captured on hooks along the wall, and a neat assembly of books, seemingly organized by topic.

And then there were her creations. Strange metal contraptions with arms and levers and springs where Aidan had never imagined a spring would be needed.

One device was particularly intriguing. It was designed in a feminine shape, curved like a metal hourglass, and sat on a high stand that made it the height of a moderately tall woman. Aidan reached out to run his finger along one of the odd metal arms that marched down the length of the shapely device.

Miss Ashby cleared her throat as she stepped into the room.

Aidan snatched back his hand.

"See anything of interest?" She swept her gaze around the collection of devices and then focused on the one that had caught his notice. One dark brow edged up as she watched him.

He couldn't back down from the challenge.

"Tell me about this one," he said, indicating the shapely device.

A hint of a smile caused a dimple to flicker in her cheek. "It's a corset unlacer."

Aidan's throat went dust dry, but his mind flooded with images. Thoughts of Diana Ashby wearing nothing but a corset. And images of how he, not this many-armed contraption, might free her of such a garment. Her back to him, his fingers sliding across her skin.

When he got lost in his thoughts and said nothing more, Miss Ashby crossed the room and approached her device. She adjusted the mechanical projections so that they were all arranged in a straight row.

He watched as she ran her hands along the mechanism and wasn't sure he liked the effect the lady had on him. It wasn't just her pretty face, her lush lips, the spark of challenge in her eyes. She made him want to know everything about her.

Observing her while standing so close, he could almost hear the whirring of her mind. She radiated a determination that was as enticing as her confidence.

"You own a shopping emporium, don't you?" The glance she cast over her shoulder told him she wasn't waiting for an answer so much as stating a fact. She'd admitted to studying all the investors of the Den. He couldn't help but wonder what else she'd learned about him.

"Several."

"I've worked on a prototype that would lace a corset too." She ran a finger along the row of retracted arms. "The bottom of a lady's laces would go here and these looseners would gradually ease the laces free." She pointed to a slat at the bottom of the device's stand that he hadn't initially noticed. "By pumping the pedal, the mechanism gradually loosens the corset so that a lady might free herself."

"Do ladies generally need freeing from their corsets?"

"Trust me, Mr. Iverson, you wouldn't wish to sleep in one."

Aidan's mind tangled on the notion of sleeping and Miss Ashby, and suddenly his thoughts had nothing to do with corsets. Not much to do with sleeping either. *Rein it in, man.* His visit today was a business matter. Nothing else. She'd invited him to consider her invention, not to get lost in thoughts that would scandalize her. She turned to face him, crossed her arms, and notched her chin up with a defiant tilt. "Not all ladies have maids to assist them. And there are times when a woman wishes to become unfettered quickly."

He could only manage a nod.

"Do you think you might be able to sell them in your shop? I could take one in for a demonstration."

"Is your pneumatic device ready? I'd be interested in seeing a demonstration of the repaired model of your machine."

"Yes, Mr. Iverson." Miss Ashby pursed her mouth, as if disappointed that he hadn't jumped at the chance to feature her corset device in his shop. "It's just through here."

She pointed toward the cordoned off area she'd exited and they both stepped forward at the same time, their bodies colliding much as they had at Lyon's. She reached out and gripped his arm for balance. Aidan laid his hand over hers.

For a moment neither of them moved. Aidan was intensely aware of the warmth of her skin, the rush of her breath, and the way his own pulse sped.

His gaze traced the shape of her lips, and an inappropriate question bloomed in his mind. Had she kissed anyone since the night they'd met?

Suddenly he wanted to know. Needed to know. But of course he had no right to know.

She removed her hand from his arm, and the slide of her skin against his did nothing to stem his wayward thoughts.

"Just this way," she said quietly, and moved past him.

Inside the partitioned room, Aidan discovered that she had far more than a scale model. She had a full-sized device assembled on a long table.

"There's a pumping mechanism that has to be primed to create pneumatic pressure." She began adjusting the metal tubes of her machine and pointed to the end of the table. "Would you do the honors, Mr. Iverson?" She swiped a hand through the air. "You may wish to remove your coat. This can be dirty work."

Aidan held her gaze as he slid his suit coat from his shoulders, laid it aside, and rolled up his shirtsleeves. "I'm at your service, Miss Ashby."

She inhaled sharply and he watched her throat work as she swallowed hard. "Take that lever on top and pump. Vigorously."

He did as she bid him and felt resistance as the mechanism primed.

Miss Ashby shocked him by taking a jar from the table and emptying what appeared to be dirt onto the tiled floor between them. His shock seemed to please her. She grinned and reached for the cylinder of her device, extending the tube and bending the interlocked metal tube so that it reached the ground.

A strand of hair slipped free of her braid and dangled across her forehead. She blew it aside rather than take her hands off the device.

"Flip that switch," she commanded.

Aidan did and watched as the tube she held began to pull up dust from the floor. The speed and effectiveness were impressive, and by the time he heard the pressure wane, the black and white tiles of the conservatory were spotless.

Miss Ashby grinned in triumph, and her smile caused warmth to swell in his chest.

"Well done," he told her, because her sense of victory was contagious. He found himself reveling in her success, and her smile.

Unfortunately, he still wasn't sure he could sell enough of her cleaning machines to make a profit. Some might be taken in by the novelty of the design, but he couldn't imagine most London housekeepers forgoing a simple brush and pan to pay for a device that required priming and pumping and disposal of whatever was collected.

"Are you impressed?" she asked as she turned off the pressure valve on the device and placed the long metal cylinder back on the table.

With her? Mightily. "The mechanism works just as you described."

She dusted off her hands and came to stand in front of him. Close enough for him to see the darker lapis flecks in the bright blue of her eyes. Hopefulness radiated off her like an enticing warmth.

"Then you'll fund my device, Mr. Iverson?" She leaned closer, vibrating with anticipation. "I promise you it will sell. People will take to this convenience and I foresee its usefulness in many situations—"

"Wait." He caught her midsentence and then lost his train of thought when she stopped and watched him breathlessly, lips parted, eyes wide. "I didn't say I would fund your invention, Miss Ashby."

"But you must." The rawness in her tone echoed inside him.

He understood desperation.

She tipped her gaze down and drew in a deep breath as if working to temper her emotions. When she looked up again, he noticed her gaze land on a calendar she'd affixed to the conservatory wall. The final day of the month had been circled viciously with rounds and rounds of grease pen marks that nearly obscured the square.

"What happens at the end of the month?" he asked her quietly.

"I need to secure funding by then." For the first time since he'd met her, a bit of doubt crept into her voice.

"Or else?"

"I have agreed to give up my work." She offered him a terrible caricature of a smile. "One can't dream forever, Mr. Iverson. There comes a time to be practical."

Aidan looked around her workshop, at the dozens of sketches lining the walls, the metallic contraptions crowding the space, all the implements and bits and pieces she'd gathered around her. He'd known Diana Ashby for a handful of days, but he knew instinctively that she'd prefer any other fate to giving up on her inventions.

"Perhaps I could speak to some fellow investors on your behalf."

He hated the wariness in her gaze. She didn't trust him even to do that much to assist her.

"I am impressed with your design, but—"

"Not big enough for you, is it?" There was an angry bite to her words that she made no effort to hide.

"Size isn't the issue."

"No?" She approached a table that held an assembly of ledgers and papers, rifled through a few pages, and held one up for him to see. "You've never funded any invention that wasn't on the grandest scale. Mr. Brunel's steamship. A suspension bridge. The Thames Tunnel."

"Factories. Railroad lines. You forgot those." It was on the tip of his tongue to tell her he could be benevolent too. That he'd funded hospitals and orphanages without attaching his name to them or expecting any glory to come his way.

"What of the everyday Londoner?"

"I think you'll find that everyday Londoners use bridges too, Miss Ashby."

"What of London's ladies? They're expected to adorn their homes, to create a haven for their husbands. Why not make that task easier for them?

"Tell me. Don't mince words. Why won't you fund my invention? Is it my sex?" Miss Ashby planted her hands on her hips and fixed him with an electric blue stare. "Can you not forget for a moment that I am a woman?"

"No," he bit out.

He was completely aware that Diana Ashby was a woman. Perhaps the most appealing one he'd ever met in his life. "As you've pointed out, Miss Ashby, I've never funded a device such as yours. I invest where I believe I can earn a profit."

God, he was a wretch. There was more, of course.

He couldn't imagine entering into a business arrangement with Diana, spending time together, and not wanting her. The attraction he felt for the woman grew with every moment he spent in her company.

He'd never struggled to draw a line between business and desire. Until now.

But he could find her another investor. He knew dozens of men, some of whom might be interested in a device such as hers.

"Let me speak to some others who might see the merit in your invention."

She closed her eyes, and he fully expected her to thank him for his willingness to go the extra mile on her behalf. But the moment her lashes fluttered up, she cast another desperate look at her calendar.

"That won't do, Mr. Iverson. I don't want another investor." She turned her head, and her gaze came at him sharp as an arrow's point and lodged in the center of his chest. "I want you."

Chapter Eleven

*D*iana couldn't let him leave without agreeing.

She sensed that Iverson's promise to speak to other investors was a means of pacifying her. But when would he do it? Next week? In a fortnight? She didn't have a moment to spare.

Urgency built inside her. A determination to make Aidan Iverson see the potential in her work. If she couldn't convince him, why would anyone else be interested?

It was this man, this moment here and now, that would determine her fate. She didn't know any of the other investors he might speak to. Unlike the men of the Den, she hadn't studied their preferences and history.

But she knew him, and she trusted him instinctively. Now it was simply a matter of finding a way to convince him.

He stood stock-still for a long moment and crossed his arms.

Diana took the opportunity to sidestep toward her workbench and glance at the notes she'd collected about him. Of all the men of the Den, details about Iverson had proved the most elusive. There was very little to plumb about his history. Not even an indication of where he'd been born and raised, though his accent indicated London.

"You donated money to a hospital." Diana hadn't noticed that bit before.

One auburn brow winged up. "What else do you have there?" He reached out. "Show me your notes."

Diana stepped away from him. "Surely you know what you've done and what I might have found."

A flash of unease crossed his face so quickly she wondered whether she'd imagined it.

"I'm not an adventurer, Miss Ashby. Not even much of a rogue." Shoulders tensing, he flicked his fingers in her direction. "The only risks I take are with my bank account."

It was true. His wealth and talent for earning were what most articles touted about him. But there had to be more.

She thought back on the one single mention she'd found in the scandal rags. At least she'd guessed the bit of gossip referred to him. The *on dit* mentioned an outrageously wealthy businessman, Mr. I., and his failed attempts at wooing an earl's daughter with a fondness for stealing off to the opera on her own.

Diana sifted quickly through her notes and found the details.

"Lady Alice Ponsonby."

Iverson's lush lower lip dropped a fraction. Both brows shot up, and the sunlight pouring in through the conservatory roof lit his irritated emerald gaze.

"What of her?"

"Did you wish to marry her?"

"Miss Ashby." The way he said her name, with a little growl at the back of his throat, made her more intrigued, not less.

"Were you enamored with her?"

"That has nothing to do with why I came to visit you today." He grabbed his suit coat off the chair and violently shoved his arms inside the garment.

"What was it about her that intrigued you?"

He offered no answer, just a tightening of his jaw and a narrowed gaze.

"Are you set on marrying a noblewoman?"

"Stop." In two long strides, he was toe to toe with her.

Mercy, he was tall. And broad. She tilted her head and arched back to look into his eyes. "Am I being impertinent?"

"You know that you are."

They stared at each other, and she felt the same odd pulse that had thrummed through her the evening they'd met. Just like that night, all else fell away, and there was just this moment. The two of them and a magnetic charge in the air. Even after her research, she knew almost as little about him now as she had then.

He was a compelling puzzle she longed to solve, though she feared another question would cause him to bolt. Nothing held him here but politeness and the strange pull between them.

But she couldn't stop herself. She couldn't temper her desire to know more, to take him apart a little and understand what made him tick.

"Why did she refuse you?" she asked on a whisper.

"She didn't." His gaze fell to her mouth, skidded over her cheeks, traced the line of her nose, took in the messy fall of hair across her forehead.

"Then you're engaged to her?" Diana blinked and held her breath.

Was that a flicker of triumph in his eyes?

"No. Of course not. Both a refusal and an engagement require a proposal. I have made none. To any woman."

Warmth flooded her cheeks, kindled in her chest, spread like heated treacle through her veins. She liked that he wasn't engaged, that he'd never proposed to the earl's daughter. Far too much. But why? This man's matrimonial machinations were none of her concern.

She'd invited him to come to the conservatory for one purpose. She needed him for one purpose. The tenacious fluttering in her stomach was utter foolishness, as was her inability to stop flicking her gaze to his lips.

She'd kissed that mouth, knew the taste of him, and she could never ever do that again.

Backing up, Diana put as much distance between them as she could. Eventually she bumped into the workbench she'd installed along the wall of the conservatory. Her arm brushed a pile of papers and they fell in an unceremonious heap onto the tiles.

He approached to assist her and she bit her tongue to keep from barking at him to retreat.

"I can manage. Thank you." She gathered her papers, including the invitation to her finishing school reunion.

Iverson stayed hunched next to her, much as he had when she'd dropped her box at Lyon's, but he didn't attempt to retrieve any of the pages.

She glanced up at him and felt a tremor dancing along her skin.

His gaze fixed on her mouth. Perhaps he was thinking of their kiss too. Had he thought of her in the months since they'd met?

It didn't matter.

This silliness, these impulses, were for Grace and every other young woman of her acquaintance who was on the hunt for a husband. Diana forced her gaze back to the pile of papers and her finger slid over the embossed invitation.

A plan began to form in her mind.

Perhaps Aidan Iverson's marital machinations were a matter of interest after all.

"You didn't answer my question. Do you seek a noble-woman to wed?"

A wash of color infused the lean cut of his cheeks and she knew she'd hit upon the truth.

"My matrimonial needs seem to interest you a great deal, Miss Ashby." He leaned forward and placed his hand on the tile next to hers. "Are you offering your-self as a prospect?"

No. The answer should have come easily, but instead Diana found herself desperate for air and willing her tongue to work.

There was a question in the way he looked at her that made her insides quiver.

"Not myself, no," she finally said, though her voice emerged husky and tremulous. "But I know many noble-women. Eligible ladies who are seeking a husband of means."

Fumbling with the invitation, she lifted the cream rectangle between them as if the insignificant board of paper pulp could stave off his heat and the way his scent made her mouth water.

Twisting his head, he read the words that she'd inadvertently displayed upside down. "You are cordially invited to a reunion of the 1842 graduates of Bexley Finishing School for Ladies of Character."

"I could introduce you to them."

All the warmth radiating off Iverson seemed to chill. He stood and straightened his cuffs. Unlike at Lyon's, he offered no hand to help her up.

Diana collected her papers to her chest and rose to stand beside him. "I know which ones are kind and timid, which are clever and full of fire."

"Like you?" The interest in his question shot a strange glow of pleasure through her. She wasn't imagining the hunger in his gaze, and she couldn't deny how much he intrigued her. But she was no noblewoman.

"Some may be like me, but—"

"I doubt that very much, Miss Ashby." He ran a hand roughly through his neatly cropped red-gold waves and let his palm settle at the back of his neck. He squeezed as if to ease tension that settled there. "And in exchange for these introductions, you would expect me to fund your machine."

There was no question in his tone. He understood, and she was grateful for that much.

"If I don't wish to marry any of your aristocratic acquaintances?" He busied himself with arranging the points of his shirt cuffs, as if her answer was of little consequence.

"Then I suppose . . ." That possibility hadn't been in her mind. She hadn't thought that far.

He pointed to her calendar on the wall. "You have a deadline, Miss Ashby. From whom? Your mother?"

She must have given something away because he nodded in understanding.

"What did you agree to do if you found no investor?"

"I've already told you. I promised my mother I would give up my research and designs." A sharp pain shot through her every time she faced the prospect of abandoning her inventions.

"For what? To be idle?"

"A kind of idleness, yes." Diana huffed out a long sigh. "To fetch a husband. To take my place on the marriage mart."

Iverson's gaze sharpened. His shoulders squared and he crossed his arms in front of him. He looked commanding. Confident. As if he knew that in this gamble she'd attempted, he held all the cards.

"I must be sure I'll get a return on this investment, Miss Ashby."

"But you're a man who likes to take risks. You're known for it."

"Calculated risks. I never risk blindly, and often I require a guarantee."

"A guarantee? Then there's no risk at all." She braced a hand on her hip and tried to think how best to make her half-formed plan irresistible. "What kind of guarantee do you require, Mr. Iverson?"

He started to speak, then snapped his mouth closed again. After scrubbing at the light dusting of stubble along his jaw, he began pacing, walking deeper into parts of the conservatory she rarely used and then returning.

Finally, Iverson slowed his perambulations, coming to stand close to where she'd rested her hip against her workbench.

"You," he said, infusing the word with unequivocal power.

"Me?" She wasn't at all sure what he was insisting upon.

"If none of your noble ladies suit and we have not found a buyer or have no promise of profits for your device by the month's end . . ." He hesitated, drew in a lungful of air, and asked, "Will you agree to be my bride, Miss Ashby?"

The look he gave her wasn't triumphant. Not a hint of arrogance lit his green eyes. What she saw in his gaze was something else. Need. Uncertainty.

Marry him? A man she'd met twice and whose history was as murky as London fog?

"The Ashbys claim only a baronetcy that passed to my uncle. I'm not at all a good prospect if you wish for a noble bride."

He frowned, contemplating her argument. But she knew before he spoke again that he wouldn't give way. "If we find a buyer for your device and I have some indication of a return on my investment, I shall release you from the guarantee. You do believe in your device, don't you?"

"Of course I do."

He said no more. Words weren't needed. She knew the options before her.

"Will you provide assistance once my devices are ready to sell?"

"Help finding buyers?" He offered one firm nod. "Of course. I will assist however I'm able. As an investor, your success will be mine."

Diana weighed it all in a moment. "I agree, Mr. Iverson."

He offered her his ungloved hand and she laid her palm against his. His skin was deliciously warm.

"When do we begin?" he asked quietly.

Diana's head began to throb. She had no experience playing matchmaker but she knew at least one of her school friends well enough to know where she might be on a Tuesday morning.

"Can you meet me in Regent's Park tomorrow at ten?"

"I can."

"That's when we will begin."

"Very good, Miss Ashby." He held her hand a moment longer, keeping his gaze fixed on hers. Finally, he pulled away.

Diana curled her hand into a fist to hold on to his heat.

The hint of a smile tilted the edge of his mouth. "You don't negotiate much, do you?"

There was no mockery in his tone, just amusement. Still, Diana couldn't help but bristle.

"No, but I was successful with this one."

"There's one essential element we've yet to address." He ducked his head and looked up at her through thick auburn lashes. "We've yet to discuss an amount."

Diana let out a gust of breath and a blush warmed her cheeks.

"My investment in your invention, Miss Ashby? At the Den, we generally begin at one hundred pounds."

"Then I'd prefer two hundred." She was trembling inside and prayed whatever her expression, it gave none of her uncertainty away.

Rather than challenge her or negotiate any further, Iverson simply smiled. His grin took her breath away. It softened his square jaw and drew creases at the corners of his green eyes.

"We have a deal." He glanced down at her hand but didn't reach for her again. "I'll bring a check tomorrow. Until then, Miss Ashby."

Chapter Twelve

*T*ell me again. More slowly this time. What precisely have you agreed to, Di?" Dom's question echoed in the confines of the brougham, but Diana refused to let her brother's early morning churlishness quash her joy.

Leaning toward the carriage window, she closed her eyes and soaked in a bit of the sun's warmth.

Dominick slouched in the center of his bench, yanked his collar up, and did his best to avoid the light streaming in from either side.

"Mr. Iverson is going to fund my pneumatic device." She'd been up most of the night, sick with excitement and trepidation. Everything she'd dreamed of achieving was in front of her. She could taste victory and knew precisely how success would feel.

She breathed in the prospect like fresh morning air.

"I don't understand, and it's not because I'm awake on three hours of sleep." Dominick pressed a thumb to his brow and winced. "Why is he now doing what he refused to do a week ago?"

"People change their minds." Diana turned her gaze out the carriage window and prayed her brother couldn't see through her as he often did.

She'd rushed through her explanation for their morning outing. Convincing him to accompany her as chaperone had been quite the challenge. Early hours didn't suit her brother.

"There's a great deal you're not telling me," he said accusingly. "I can see all of it churning in your head."

"Good. Then you don't need me to explain."

"*Diana.* Why are we headed to Rotten Row when you've never given a toss about promenading with London's debutantes?"

"We're going to Regent's Park, not Hyde Park." Apparently he'd been too busy complaining about the early hour to listen when she'd given directions to the cabbie.

"Where's the fun in that? I won't know a single soul in Regent's Park."

"You'll know me and Lady Sophie." Diana cleared her throat and added quickly, "And Mr. Iverson."

Dom squinted at her for a long silent moment before leaning forward on his bench. "Tell me what's going on."

"I think Sophie and Mr. Iverson might suit."

Her brother tipped his head one way, then the other,

a bit like their cat when a dapple of sunlight flickered across the carpet.

"Suit? Each other?" He drew out each word slowly, as if he doubted the meaning of every syllable.

Diana nodded and pulled out the notes she'd begun making as soon as she'd gotten out of bed. What she knew about Mr. Iverson one side, what she knew about Sophie on the other, and any areas that might intersect. They were woefully few.

Dom's large gloved hand gripped the edge of her foolscap and he yanked it out of her grasp.

"Hey!"

"You're playing matchmaker with the man who's funding your device?"

"I am engineering an introduction." Diana snatched her notes back. "Sophie wishes to marry. Mr. Iverson is seeking a bride. Introducing them is logical."

Her brother crossed his arms and glared at her. "People aren't like your inventions, Di. You can't fix them together with a bit of wire and glue."

"I don't plan to fix anyone." She bit down hard to keep from telling him everything. He didn't need to know yet. Perhaps not ever.

Luckily, the carriage stopped before he could ask anything more.

"Here we are," she said brightly.

Her brother glowered almost as fiercely as she grinned.

"This is ridiculous," Dom mumbled before exiting the carriage and offering a hand to help her down. "Matchmaking is a terrible business. If it goes pear-shaped, they'll blame you. And any man who sets his heart on Sophie Bales is bound to be disappointed."

"I disagree. Sophie is a charming young lady. Let's hope it goes well, shall we?"

She'd long wondered about Dom's feelings about Sophie. They'd developed an instant antagonism the first time they'd met and bickered during every encounter thereafter. But it was odd that he'd never reacted as vehemently to any of her other friends.

They entered the park on the south end and Dom immediately gestured vaguely toward a young lady dressed in yellow at the far side of the promenade.

Diana lifted a hand to shade her eyes, squinting to be sure it was Sophie.

"You're right," she told him. "It's definitely her."

"The hair is unmistakable. A strange color. Not a simple cornflower blond, more like a polished guinea coin."

Diana stared at her brother until he met her gaze. He only spared her a glance before weaving his way toward a line of oaks with benches underneath.

"I'll be over there, trying not to singe under that fiery orb in the sky."

"We call that the sun, Dominick."

"Call it what you like. It's relentless and I'm more suited to London's gloom. I need darkness to thrive."

What he needed was a desire to do anything other than gamble and carouse and drink himself into a nightly stupor. But he'd admonished her against trying to fix others, and he was the most resistant to aid of anyone she'd ever known.

After he settled onto a bench, Diana started off toward Sophie, looking down once more at her notes. What did Mr. Iverson like besides making money and investing in order to make more? She'd listed engineering, science, and the opera, since he'd encountered an earl's daughter there often enough to make the gossip rags take notice.

The man was quite brawny. She wondered if he spent time at sport. Visits to Gentleman Jackson's salon perhaps?

Images flashed in her mind. Visions of Aidan Iverson sparring in a boxing ring, his muscles flexing as he moved. She imagined the feel of him, the hard plane of his chest, the sculpted muscles of his arms. If she touched him after such exertion, he'd be warm, probably breathless.

Footsteps crunched on the pebbled path, and she looked up just in time to avoid bumping into the man whose half-naked physique still lingered in her mind's eye.

She reached out to keep from tumbling and her palm landed on his waistcoat, plastered against fabric heated from his body and snugged within an inch of its life against his broad chest.

"Mr. Iverson."

"Have you been researching me again, Miss Ashby?" He stared down at the sheet of foolscap crumpled between her fingers and trapped against his stomach.

His given name was printed on one creased edge of the paper.

Diana stepped back, flattened the page against her skirt, and handed him the notes.

He kept his gaze fixed on hers as he took the paper, then glanced down quickly before looking up again. "You're wrong about one thing. I hate the opera."

Diana narrowed an eye at him. When he attempted to hand the notes back to her, she indicated the other list. "You may wish to review a few details about Lady Sophie."

Diana started toward Sophie and he followed, his head bowed to read her notes.

"Hmm, she's fond of botany, I see."

"Do you like botany?" This might be easier than she'd imagined.

"No, not at all."

Diana glanced at him, pointlessly noting how a strand of reddish-gold hair had fallen over his brow. "Do you see anything else there that might assist you?"

"Assist me?"

"To woo Lady Sophie." Sophie wasn't too far ahead of them and Diana lowered her voice lest her friend overhear.

"I have my own methods for wooing, Miss Ashby."

"Do you?" His claim stoked her curiosity.

"Of course I do."

"How well do they work?"

He didn't answer, just cast her one intense glance that she felt like the sweep of his fingers against her face that night in Belgravia.

She fought the urge to ask him to detail his methods, but she lost the battle. "Which did you try on Lady Alice Ponsonby?"

"You mention her so often, Miss Ashby. Perhaps you'd like me to introduce you?"

Diana let out a surprised chuckle. "That won't be necessary. I merely mean to point out that the methods used on her didn't work, Mr. Iverson. You'll need others to woo Sophie."

He made a little grumbling sound. His jaw was set and a muscle ticked near the sharp, clean-shaven edge.

"I merely wish to see our arrangement to a successful end," Diana told him. "Perhaps you could pretend to like botany."

"Why on earth would I?"

"To be more appealing to Lady Sophie, of course." Diana had lowered her voice to a whisper. Sophie sat on a bench and seemed thoroughly engaged with her sketchbook, but she preferred her friend didn't hear them scheming behind her back.

Mr. Iverson shocked her by stepping off the path and into the shade of a leafy maple tree. He reached out, hooked a hand around her arm, and gave a gentle tug until she stepped closer.

"I think there may be some part of our agreement you don't understand, Miss Ashby."

He released her, but Diana felt a band of heat where he'd touched her and couldn't stop herself from rubbing her fingers over the spot.

"Our terms are clear to me, Mr. Iverson."

"Not our terms. My intentions." He pursed his mouth and glanced away before looking at her again. "I will not pretend to be anything other than what I am. I have little to offer a lady like Lady Sophie, so my intent is to be honest about what I can provide."

"Which is?"

He started to speak, then held his breath. His gaze captured hers, and for a long, pulse-racing moment they stared. Diana got lost in imagining him as a husband. He didn't seem like the domestic sort. There was an energy about him, as if he loathed standing still. Yet here he was, still and watching her. Waiting. Though she was the one who'd asked the question.

"Wealth," he finally said. "That's all I have."

"Is that true?" She didn't know him well, but she knew it wasn't.

"What else do you see, Miss Ashby?"

"Resolve. Intelligence." Diana bit her lip a moment before adding, "Kindness." The overcoat he'd given her that night in Belgravia still hung in the back of her wardrobe.

"You're the kind one. You rushed into danger and likely saved my life."

Somehow he knew where her thoughts had gone.

"Perhaps I'm reckless."

He tipped his head. "It's quite an appealing combination."

The longer he looked at her with admiration in his gaze, the harder it was to recall why they were here.

"She's just there." Diana pointed toward Sophie, needing to remind him and herself about the business at hand.

But he didn't go off in the direction of the young woman he was here to meet. He took one step closer to Diana.

"Do you truly think a man woos a woman by affectation and pretending to share her interests?"

They were standing too close. As close as they had that stormy night. She remembered all of it, every minute, far too vividly.

"I possess no expertise in wooing," he admitted quietly, "but I won't play act. Lady Sophie needs a rich husband?"

Diana nodded sharply.

She'd been taught that speaking of other's circumstances wasn't seemly. But it was no secret that Sophie's father was much like her own. A man with a creative mind and no interest whatsoever in managing his finances. If anything, Sophie's circumstances were worse, since her father was an earl with an estate to manage and a mother known for her spendthrift ways.

"Then a rich husband is what I'll offer her." Iverson reached up to tighten the knot of his neck cloth and swept a hand through his tumbled auburn waves. "Presentable?"

"Yes, you'll do," Diana said, when in fact he looked ridiculously appealing. Sunlight loved him, finding all the gold in his hair, all the flecks of amber in his green eyes.

One of his brows winged up, and she realized he was staring at her cheek. "You have a . . ." He gestured toward his own ear. "Your hair has come undone."

Before she could reach up, he swept two fingers gently across her cheek and tucked a long strand behind her ear. Heat kindled in every patch of skin he touched and when he hesitated, letting his fingers linger at the sensitive spot behind her ear, a shiver swept down her body.

"There," he whispered. He lifted his hand and stepped away, but her skin still tingled everywhere his fingers had been.

When he turned back, she realized he was waiting for her. She was, after all, the one who'd agreed to make this introduction.

She stepped out from under the tree and approached her friend, calling out softly so as not to give her a fright.

"Sophie, I thought I might find you here."

Sophie turned and let out a squeal of excitement. "Diana!" Her enthusiasm had always been contagious. "What's lured you out of your laboratory?" Tossing her sketchbook aside, she stood and took Diana's hands, giving her a quick kiss on each cheek. "Say you have the day free and can join us for dinner this evening. We can take in the shops and stroll Hyde Park and have more fun than you can imagine."

Diana's throat went oddly dry and she longed for a sip of tea. Instead, she took a deep breath and said, "I came to find you and to introduce you to Mr. Iverson."

In her enthusiastic greeting, Lady Sophie had somehow failed to notice the large, broad, auburn-haired man a few steps behind Diana. But she noticed now and her gaze warmed appreciatively. Sophie always had an eye for a pretty face.

"How do you do?" Sophie smiled and offered her hand.

Dutifully, Diana performed the niceties. "Lady Sophronia Bales, may I present Mr. Aidan Iverson."

Iverson took her friend's hand and offered a curt

bow. "My pleasure, Lady Sophronia, I assure you. Miss Ashby speaks highly of you and has mentioned your fondness for botany." He stepped toward the bench and looked down at Sophie's sketchbook. "You're quite proficient at drawing too, I see."

"Do you think so, sir?" Sophie batted her eyelashes a bit too obviously.

Diana struggled not to roll her eyes. "Mr. Iverson is an investor who—"

"Oh, I know who Mr. Iverson is," Sophie put in. "You once met my father, the Earl of Caldwell, but you may not remember him. He spoke of your cleverness. You advised him on an investment."

"Ah, yes, I recall quite clearly, my lady. He wished to invest in the railroads."

Sophie's titter of laughter didn't quite match the flash of sadness in her eyes. "If only he had taken your advice."

"There's still time. A few opportunities remain to invest in solid railroad enterprises."

"Are there?" Sophie stepped closer and laid a hand on Iverson's arm in her eagerness. "Would you speak to him?"

Diana found herself watching the two of them as one watches strangers on an omnibus, fascinated with a conversation that she felt she had no right to observe. She looked at the trees, at the grass, shaded her eyes and glanced up into the cloudless sky. Anywhere but at her friend and the man whose body she'd just been imagining so vividly.

She stepped away and caught only a few words of their conversation. But as they walked, they strode back toward the spot where she'd retreated.

"If you wish it," Iverson said in the warmest tone she'd ever heard him use.

"Tomorrow evening?" Sophie clapped her hands together excitedly. "My mother is hosting a very small dinner party. But you must come. You too, Di. We have so much to catch up on. Both of you must join us."

"And me too?" Dominick spoke from where he leaned against the trunk of a thick oak.

Diana hadn't noticed that he'd abandoned his bench on the far side of the park, but she had a sneaking suspicion why he had. She narrowed her gaze at her brother, but he pointedly ignored her.

Sophie's smile faltered. "Are you truly available for supper, Mr. Ashby? I was given to understand your evening schedule is quite . . . rigorous."

Aidan turned to offer Diana a questioning look.

"My brother is forgetting what night it is, I believe. He agreed to attend . . . a play with our mother." Diana had to stop her brother from ruining everything. He was a confirmed bachelor. An inveterate rogue. He wasn't prepared to offer for Sophie, but he was just ornery enough to throw a wrench in her plans.

"Did I?" he asked with a quizzical frown.

"You did, Dominick," she said through gritted teeth.

"Ah yes," he said, examining his fingernails as if the exchange barely registered his interest. "*The Taming of the Shrew*, I believe. My favorite play." He looked up and his gaze shot straight for Sophie.

She let out a little huff of frustration.

Iverson took a step to position himself closer to Sophie. With his bulk, he effectively blocked her view of Dominick. "I would be pleased to join your family for dinner, Lady Sophronia. Though I can't speak for Miss Ashby."

He offered Diana an inscrutable look, and she couldn't determine whether he wished for her to beg off or attend.

Impulsively, she said, "I'd love to come."

Iverson blinked, as if her reply was unexpected, but a flicker of mischief lit his gaze.

Apparently, he wasn't entirely disappointed.

When Dominick strode toward Sophie and inquired about what she'd been sketching, Iverson approached Diana.

"I almost forgot to give you this." He lifted his hand toward hers and offered her a folded piece of paper. "My investment."

Diana clutched the check against her palm. This was real. She could build a dozen pneumatic devices and afford to purchase the best materials.

Rather than rejoin the others, Iverson lingered, watching her. For a man who'd just received an invitation to the home of a noblewoman eager to be wooed, he looked strangely ill at ease. A frown etched lines in his brow.

"We should prepare a strategy for tomorrow evening," he whispered to Diana.

"Now you wish for my help?"

"You're familiar with Lady Sophie's family. I'd like to know more."

Diana considered where they might speak. If he visited Cadogan Square again, her mother would ask too many questions. As a woman, she wasn't welcome at Lyon's Gentlemen's Club.

"I have a meeting in Knightsbridge tomorrow." He withdrew a calling card from his waistcoat pocket along with a stub of pencil. After scribbling a moment, he handed her the card. "Meet me at this address at two?"

She nodded her agreement and he turned back to Sophie, joining Dominick to assess her drawings.

Diana let out the breath she realized she'd been holding.

This matchmaking business was going well. Better than she could have imagined. Iverson already had an invitation.

So why did she feel as ill at ease as Mr. Iverson looked?

Chapter Thirteen

$\mathscr{A}$idan finished his meeting at Darlington's early, and restlessness made it impossible to await Diana's arrival in the upstairs administrative offices. He took to pacing the display floors and what he saw pleased him—colorful shelves, busy employees, and a plethora of shoppers.

The business he'd purchased the previous year was thriving.

Old man Darlington had been ambitious, attempting to combine a draper, haberdashery, and stationer into a single shop. Aidan had expanded the space physically, buying up a nearby building, and increased the variety of its offerings. The shopping emporium had soon become one of the most successful in Knightsbridge.

As he strode through the section of ladies' clothing, Diana and her corset unlacer came to mind. The tickle of a smile drew the edge of his mouth up. Then he frowned.

"That display doesn't look quite right," he told the shop's manager, who'd been an uninvited shadow while he wandered the aisles.

Mr. Wickett, tall, elderly, and efficient, dipped his head and stared over his pince-nez at Aidan. "Not quite right, Mr. Iverson?"

Aidan suspected the man's haughty tone worked well on the shop's other employees. "It's too crowded. Space the gloves out a bit. Let people see them clearly."

"Shall we ensure that every finger is visible, sir?" He held up his wrinkled hand, all fingers splayed, and arched one graying brow.

Aidan narrowed an eye at the old man, but for some reason the manager's dry sarcasm didn't bother him today. "Don't forget the thumb, Wickett."

Now that he looked, the lace was displayed haphazardly too. He pointed toward where a dozen styles were stacked in upright bolts. "Shouldn't they be arranged by color?"

Wickett stared at him a moment, let out a sigh, and then made a notation in the small notebook he always carried. "I will see it done, Mr. Iverson. Is there more we should fix?"

"I'll let you know if I see anything." The moment the words were out, what Aidan saw caused his breath to tangle in his throat.

He was expecting her, of course. But somehow the sight of Diana Ashby always managed to take him by surprise.

She stepped through the shop's front doors and stopped, eyes widening as she took in the display floors. Her lips parted, as if she was awestruck.

Aidan felt a surge of pride unlike he'd experienced for any of his investment endeavors in a long while. He almost felt guilty for disturbing her perusal when he strode forward to greet her.

"You're right on time, Miss Ashby." He had the urge to take her hand, but she had her hands folded around a folio she kept tucked against her chest.

"I expected the address to lead me to an office." She spared him only a glance before continuing to take in the items on display.

"There are several upstairs, but I thought we could discuss strategy at the tea shop across the street."

She nodded but then stepped past him. "You own all of this?"

"I do."

"Will you show me the rest?"

Aidan smiled at her eagerness. Not even Wickett's arched brows as they passed could diminish the pleasure of being able to show Miss Ashby something that he'd built. Not in the way she did, of course, starting from an idea to create a working machine. Aidan's talent was for seeing potential, improving what was faltering, or championing inventions that others saw as newfangled nonsense.

As they explored the shop, he enjoyed hearing her sounds of interest or surprise. At the section containing ladies' accoutrements, she stopped and tapped a finger against her lip. A shopgirl stood on a ladder returning a bolt of fabric to a shelf high on the wall.

"A simple pulley system would save her the trouble of climbing."

Aidan frowned as he considered her idea.

"And those workers carrying items up and down the stairs. Do they do that all day?"

"Stock is carried from the delivery dock to the departments upstairs."

She twisted her lips into a thoughtful moue. "A pulley system might be useful there too, though I've been working on a lift device that uses the same pneumatic pressure as my cleaning system."

Aidan chuckled as he watched her. He could almost hear the calculations clicking in her mind. He might see things that needed tidying, but she saw ways to improve how the world worked.

"Are you always like this?" The question emerged bluntly, honestly, before he had a chance to soften it.

She offered him a wary look. "How do you mean?"

"You see that things could be better and come up with solutions."

"I suppose I do." A bit of the wariness faded, but her tone remained cool. "The ideas come unbidden at times."

"It's admirable." He meant the compliment. "And I understand the impulse."

The curve of her cheek flushed pink, then she tipped her head dubiously. "Do you?"

"I don't have a scientific mind like yours." He hated the prospect of her discovering how woeful his formal education had been. "But I do admire innovation. Progress is always a consideration when I invest."

She assessed him and then leaned close enough for him to catch her floral scent on the air. "Corset unlacers and cleaning devices aren't progress enough for you, Mr. Iverson?"

"I believe you are in possession of two hundred of my pounds to fund your device, Miss Ashby."

"Yes. I haven't forgotten our deal." There was a strange note in her tone. A thread of uncertainty.

Aidan almost reached for her. He lifted his arm; the impulse to soothe whatever concerned her was so strong. He'd touched her too often already, and yet it wasn't enough. He wanted to every time he was near her.

She swallowed hard. He'd given too much away. Something must have been there in his gaze or in the quickening of his breath. But she didn't step back.

There was a boldness in the way she held his gaze that made his pulse quicken.

"We should discuss a plan for this evening," she said quietly.

"Yes." He knew he should be more interested in the dinner at Lady Sophie's. "Shall we head across the street?"

As they made their way toward the front door of the shop, a broad-shouldered gentleman barreled past, and Aidan reached out to keep the man from bumping into Diana. But he took care not to touch her.

She'd reminded him of the deal they'd made, and she was right to. He'd never had trouble achieving his goals. Something had changed that disturbed his peace of mind, but he needed to focus on his plan.

And he would start tonight.

DIANA TRIED TO concentrate on arranging the notes she'd brought on the table in front of her, but she kept glancing at Mr. Iverson. Something had changed since they'd exited his shopping emporium. He shifted in his chair, rearranged the cutlery on the table, and refused to meet her gaze.

She looked out the window at Darlington's. She was impressed with the scale of the business and its variety of offerings and wondered how much of that had been Iverson's doing.

"Why is it called Darlington's?"

He quirked a brow questioningly.

"Shouldn't it be called Iverson's?"

"I don't require my name on everything I own." He finally looked at her and settled back in his chair. "The shop is known as Darlington's and has built a reputation on that name. I've built enough of a reputation with my own name not to need it on a storefront."

His claim was clearly true, but it only raised more questions in her mind. "Reputation is important to you. That's why you wish to marry a noblewoman?"

"That's not why." He shuttered again, sweeping a hand through his hair before scooping up his teacup. Finally, he said, "As a commoner, some doors will always be shut to me."

"Why must you open them?" Diana understood his meaning. Her commoner family had never received invitations to the best society events, and some young ladies at Bexley had treated her differently. But as a lady inventor, she expected many doors to be shut to her, whatever her family's lineage. "Is it more money that you want?"

His eyes widened slightly as if she'd caught him off guard. Then he worked his jaw, as if considering how to reply. "There are changes I could make, influence I could offer if I made it through those doors."

"So it's not just about wealth?"

He took another sip of tea and cast her a smile over the rim. "That too."

"When will you know you have enough?" She was asking herself the question too. The drive inside her never waned. She feared stopping, resting, letting any moment go to waste. But someday she wanted to.

"There's no limit to ambition." The words came with a tinge of defiance. Then more quietly, he added, "When you've gone without a meal, you become very determined never to go hungry again."

"You've been hungry?" She knew his words weren't intended as a metaphor, but the pain in his eyes told her that he was speaking of his own history.

"Not for many years, and never again," he said too brightly.

Diana imagined him as a boy and the thought of him going without something as basic as a meal twisted a knot in her stomach.

"And what of your ambition, Miss Ashby? Where does your hunger come from?"

Diana flicked at the edge of her sheaf of notes with her finger. She much preferred when she was asking the questions. When she didn't answer, he leaned forward, an elbow on the table to get closer.

"Is it your father?"

"No." The word emerged louder, more vehement, than she'd intended. A few ladies at a nearby table watched for a moment before turning back to their tea. Diana let out a sigh and admitted, "In part because of my father. His love for invention and science colored my childhood. His books were the first I learned to read. But my ambition is for me too."

Iverson was resting both hands on the table and looked more at ease than he had since they'd sat down. His expression was open. He was listening and seemed to want to hear more.

"My head is full of ideas. I want them to be useful, at least some of them. I need to prove to myself and everyone else, I suppose, that one of my designs can succeed." Diana felt heat creep into her cheeks. She had said too much, admitted too much.

All her unnatural, unladylike ambition was on full display.

"Then we must find buyers for your cleaning device," Iverson said decisively.

Diana knew he didn't trust that her machine would succeed, but she had no doubt of his determination. She needed to be as resolute about her half of their bargain.

"Shall we discuss Sophie's parents?"

His brow dipped, as if he was disappointed by the change in subject. Then he sat back in his chair and assessed the several sheets of paper she'd laid out on the table. "You know quite a lot about Lord and Lady Caldwell, I take it."

"Only a bit, but I thought I'd assemble information about the other young ladies I plan to introduce you to." Diana lifted the notes she'd prepared on the earl and countess and slid them toward Iverson. "Unless you've decided to marry Lady Sophie."

He let out a chuckle and the green of his eyes brightened. "You must think me quite the mercenary. I spoke to the lady for a quarter of an hour in a public park. I'm not prepared to decide just yet."

"Perhaps after tonight you'll know." His wealth would appeal to the earl and countess, and she couldn't imagine why Sophie's gregarious charm wouldn't appeal to him.

"Don't rush me, Miss Ashby," he said with the hint of a smile. "I mean to choose wisely."

"And I mean to help you." Diana looked down at the meticulous notes she'd assembled, but she sensed Iverson's gaze on her.

"You already have." When she looked up, he was smiling. The expression softened the hard edge of his jaw, drew little creases near his eyes. A warmth kindled in Diana's chest that felt wonderful but worried her all the same.

She couldn't lose herself in how much she enjoyed talking to him and spending time with him. Matchmaking. That's why they were here together, sharing afternoon tea.

Diana couldn't give in to the charm of Aidan Iverson's smiles.

Chapter Fourteen

The minute Aidan stepped into the Earl and Countess of Caldwell's St. James Square drawing room, he understood why they struggled to maintain their modest country house and had drained their noble coffers dry.

If their furnishings were any indication, the couple reveled in excess. Not to mention shockingly bad taste.

He took in the monstrosity of a drawing room and wished he could shield his eyes. He was no connoisseur of fine decor, but he admired beauty and order. The Caldwell home displayed neither.

Massive pieces of modern art clogged the walls, elegant examples of Chinese and Japanese pottery sat crowded on doily-covered tables next to figurines of milkmaids and dogs. The entire fireplace surround was gilded and not an inch of mantel was visible beneath an assembly of clocks and crystal candlesticks and assorted bric-a-brac.

Despite his own penchant for collecting, Aidan felt uncomfortable among the clutter.

Among the collection of guests too. He'd been to dinners peopled by aristocrats before, but there was an air of tension in the Caldwell drawing room. He'd been greeted warmly, but sensed eyes on him, questioning whether he truly belonged.

There was no pretense about his purpose. Lady Caldwell had addressed him civilly but with a narrowed, assessing gaze. She was quite like every matchmaking mama he'd ever met, so he'd endured her inspection as well as he could, made polite conversation with Lady Sophronia, and then retreated to a corner where he could watch the young lady and consider what sort of wife she might be.

Unfortunately, his gaze kept straying to another young woman.

Miss Ashby caught him looking and strode over, weaving between guests and massive potted ferns.

"May I offer a bit of advice?" She took up the empty patch of carpet next to him and spoke quietly out of the side of her mouth, as if practicing her ventriloquist skills.

"You may offer. But just know that I don't agree to take your advice."

She glared at him. He sensed the heat of it against the side of his face and smiled, but he wouldn't look at her. The lady was a mighty distraction.

Even from across the room, he'd caught her rose scent and enjoyed watching her speak to other guests. A Lady Digby and a Lord Abernethy, a friend and cousin of the countess, had occupied her in a lively discussion about books and a new lending library in town. When she finally stepped away from them, he wasn't disappointed that she immediately turned her attention on him and approached his corner.

"Try not to look quite so miserable," she told him as she took a glass of lemonade from a passing servant's tray.

"Do I? I'm not." He wasn't. Not when she was standing so close. He gave in and glanced at her, finding her profile—long dark lashes, plump cheeks, and upturned nose—far too appealing. "I'm merely assessing."

She looked at him then. The first time their gazes had met since she'd arrived. He felt the same frisson that always flared between them.

Every time he looked at her, he felt a rogue tug at the corner of his mouth. But, of course, it wouldn't do to smile like a fool whenever she was near. He did allow himself this grin though, even if only to disprove her claim.

"How about now?" He kept his gaze on hers as he leaned in front of her to take his own glass of lemonade from a servant's tray. Her sharp inhale felt like a victory. "Do I still look miserable, Miss Ashby?"

"You look . . ." She assessed him in a slow perusal. He watched her eyes shift from his nose, his mouth, down to his chest, and then up again to meet his gaze. "Less miserable."

"To progress." He lifted his glass.

She raised hers hesitantly and clinked her glass gently against his. "What do you think?" she whispered. "Of Sophie."

"I've barely spoken to her. Too soon to know." In truth, he had formed a few opinions about the lady. She seemed pleasant and eager to be so. Almost to an irritating degree. She was lovely and jolly, but perhaps too much for a man who considered attending lectures on electrical devices an enjoyable pastime.

"What more do you wish to know?" Miss Ashby turned on him, a hand perched on her hip. "I did provide you with a helpful list."

"I never trust lists. They're too simple and rarely detailed enough. I need to know a great deal about any prospective bride."

"Did you know a good deal about the Lady Alice Ponsonby before you pursued her at the opera?" she asked archly.

"Scandal sheets don't seem your style, Miss Ashby, and yet you're quite stuck on that tale." He pressed his lips together to hold back another grin. "I assure you the story was entirely overblown. You mustn't believe everything you read."

Taking two steps, Miss Ashby turned to face him, her brow scrunched as she glowered at him. "I do not make a habit of reading drivel, Mr. Iverson, I assure you. And unlike you, my name has never appeared among such pages."

She sipped her lemonade, and Aidan noted a quiver at the edge of her mouth. She lifted a hand to pat at her coiffure, and he could think of nothing but how the glossy, artful waves would look if he could give in to his urge to remove every pin and take them down.

Steady, man.

Diana Ashby was not why he was here. He scanned the room for Lady Sophronia, but she'd slipped away. There was no one to distract him from the tall, irritated, rose-scented beauty in front of him.

He reached for another glass from the nearest servant's tray and gulped down a mouthful of lemony sweetness. "What else have you read about me?"

"There isn't much." She seemed annoyed by that fact. "Details are scarce. Almost as if you're hiding something, Mr. Iverson."

The lady was coming far too close to the mark. Aidan deposited his empty glass on an obliging table and crossed his arms.

"We all hide something." Over the years, he'd learned a dozen techniques for assessing others. Physical tics, little oddities of movement, the way the black of an eye contracts and expands. He'd needed those skills to survive on London's streets. They'd been useful when he'd entered the world of commerce too. It was good to know who could be trusted and who planned to take him for a fool.

In eight and twenty years, he'd never met a single man who wasn't hiding something.

He desperately wanted to know Miss Ashby's secrets.

"I don't hide anything," she retorted a bit too quickly.

"Truly?" He lowered his voice to a whisper. "Not a single fear or wish or memory that you keep tucked away deep inside?"

She touched her hair again, patting at one perfectly pinned coil, and said quietly, "Nothing that would interest you, Mr. Iverson."

"I doubt that very much, Miss Ashby. I'd like to know your secrets."

"Why?"

"I'm a curious man." And because she fascinated him as much now as when she'd been a stranger who had kissed him in the dark. More.

Without any parting words, she headed toward the settee where Lady Sophronia had taken up a spot after returning to the cluttered drawing room.

As if she somehow sensed his wayward thoughts, Miss Ashby offered him one questioning glance over her shoulder before Lady Caldwell called to her, urging her to answer a question from Lord Abernethy.

A sigh escaped before Aidan squared his shoulders and made his way over to the lady who'd invited him to her home. Lady Sophie veritably bounced with anticipation as he approached, and she tittered like an overexcited bird when he reached her side.

"Thank you so much for coming, Mr. Iverson." Gesturing to the expanse of blue damask settee beside her, she asked, "Would you like to have a seat?"

"Of course." But rather than claim the space beside her, Aidan dropped into a nearby chair. He didn't wish to seem too eager or too familiar. "Thank you for the invitation, my lady."

"Please do call me Sophie, and tell me about the next grand project you'll invest in, Mr. Iverson." Lady Sophie leaned so far forward that he feared she'd topple onto the carpet. No one could accuse the lady of appearing disinterested.

"Some projects are quite secret." He lifted a finger to his lips and drew the expected giggle from the noblewoman. "But I'll leave it to Miss Ashby to tell you of her device. I've agreed to offer my support."

"Oh no." Her heart-shaped face collapsed into a moue of disappointment before she glanced in Miss Ashby's direction and whispered, "We're all hoping Diana agrees to join us this Season. She has never had one, you see. We all wish for her to be settled."

Aidan tugged at his ear and worked to stifle a flash of irritation. "You don't approve of Miss Ashby's engineering pursuits, I take it."

"Di is quite clever." Lady Sophie's mouth curved in a sad smile. "And she's one of my dearest friends, so how can I not approve of whatever takes her fancy? But none of us believes she's truly happy." The noblewoman leaned an inch closer and said conspiratorially, "The responsibility she feels should not be hers to bear."

"What responsibility?"

Lady Sophie retreated, scooting back on the settee and refusing to meet his gaze.

Before he could press her more, the dinner gong sounded and everyone sprang into motion. Lady Sophie seemed particularly relieved to escape the necessity of answering his question. He expected to escort her in, but her cousin, Lord Abernethy, approached to do the honors instead.

Aidan glanced around the room and noticed Miss Ashby lingering near the threshold. As soon as she caught his eye, she gestured in a jerking motion, indicating that he should follow her.

In the hallway, all the dinner guests filed one way, but Miss Ashby had ducked off into a room two doors down from the drawing room. After making sure no one noticed his departure from the throng, Aidan stepped inside.

The billiard room smelled of cigar smoke and spilled liquor. The interior was so dark, he wondered for a moment if he'd entered the correct room.

"I overheard you speaking to Sophie."

Her voice sent an odd shiver spiking down his spine. "You mean you were eavesdropping."

"There aren't many guests. Your voices carried." She stepped closer.

As his eyes adjusted, he could just make out the shape of her face and the curves of her body in the pale cream gown she'd worn. In the darkness, he noticed everything, the shift of the fabric, the click of beads embroidered along the hem, and the heat of her nearness.

"She is concerned about your happiness," he told her.

"You should be more concerned with hers if you plan to marry her."

"Don't rush me, Miss Ashby. You agreed to introduce me to several debutantes. I intend to meet them all."

She huffed out a long-suffering sigh. "You should strive to talk less about me and ask Sophie about herself."

"Are you giving me lessons in wooing again?"

"Perhaps someone should. Speaking of one lady when you're in the company of another is considered bad form," she said, and then started past him toward the threshold.

He knew they should return to the others. He knew they would soon be missed. But he wanted the moment alone with her to stretch on just a little longer.

"I propose an exchange, Miss Ashby."

She stopped beside him. They stood shoulder to shoulder, her bare arm brushing the sleeve of his suit.

Aidan turned and dipped his head so that his mouth wasn't far from her ear. "One of your secrets for one of mine."

"I told you, Mr. Iverson," she said breathily. "I don't have secrets."

"Pity. That leaves you nothing with which to negotiate."

She tilted her head, and in the light through the half-open door, he saw a flash of interest in her blue gaze. "You first."

He opened his mouth to speak, but she lifted a finger between them.

"I'm only agreeing to this so that I can know which of my friends might suit you best."

"Of course."

"Go on, then."

"That night, a year ago. I think on it often." His own heart began hammering in his chest. Every word was true, but the admission felt too raw, too revealing. The next breath stalled in his throat as he waited for her to respond.

He heard only her breath quickening.

"That's my confession. That's my secret. Now it's your turn, Miss Ashby," he prompted.

She was silent so long, he thought she might balk. But finally, she whispered, "I think on that night too. Far too much."

Aidan reached for her, not desperately as he had that night, but slowly, letting his fingers skate across her skin before clasping her arm. He swept his thumb against her skin. She was so warm, so soft.

She tipped her head back, knowing exactly what he intended. That only made him want her more.

Aidan took her mouth in a hungry kiss and she opened to him instantly. He swept his tongue inside, tasting the tart sweetness of lemonade. Then he lifted his head to look at her.

"We should get back," she whispered.

Without waiting for his reply, she pulled out of his grasp and slipped out of the room. A moment after she'd left, he followed.

As he made his way back to the drawing room, he sucked in a deep lungful of air. Then another. Diana's scent was all he could smell, and his body responded as if she was still close enough to touch.

Control yourself, man.

He reminded himself why he was there. He wanted Diana Ashby. That was no longer possible to deny.

But he wanted more. Power. Success. Belonging.

He forced his mind to the industrial exhibition, to the prospect of gaining entry to an exclusive club like the Parthenon and then finding no door in London's social, political, or financial world closed to him.

Straightening his tie and tugging at the lapels of his coat, he drew in one last calming breath.

He needed his wits about him tonight. He had an earl's daughter to woo.

Chapter Fifteen

Diana looked down and checked the address she'd scribbled on a scrap of paper before exiting the hack. Once she'd determined it was Iverson's office building, she stopped on the pavement and worked to steady her nerves.

She hadn't seen the man since Sophie's dinner party three days ago. He might have made a decision to propose to her friend, for all she knew.

What she did know, what had played in her mind for days, was that she'd kissed him. Again. That had to stop.

Between her and Aidan Iverson, there was nothing but a business arrangement.

She'd been telling herself that for three days and still wasn't quite convinced.

He'd invited her to his office to discuss prospective buyers for her device. Just as he'd promised he'd do. The man was scrupulously maintaining his side of their bargain. And, practically speaking, she was too.

Practical matters were, after all, where she excelled.

But she couldn't resist peeking at herself in the reflection of the spotless window glass. After lifting a hand to pinch some color into her cheeks, she tucked a few wayward curls back into her simple coiffure.

She growled at her own reflection in frustration. Nervous energy boiled inside her and she wished that human beings could release steam as easily as water set on a hot burner.

Rather than go inside and face him, she paced, traversing the same stretch of pavement back and forth until the muscles of her legs warmed and her nerves settled.

She turned back toward the steps leading up to Iverson's office. Half a dozen steps. Easily scaled. Harder to overcome were the odd impulses that seemed to rear up whenever he was near.

Once inside, she knocked at a frosted-glass door, and a youthful, slick-haired man answered with a pleasant smile.

"You must be Miss Ashby. Mr. Iverson is expecting you." He led her to a small, tidy room with a massive desk and chairs tucked against wainscoting on the opposite wall. Nothing luxurious. Just sensible and practical furnishings. She liked the space immediately.

The clerk rapped once quietly on what Diana guessed was Iverson's door, but there was no response from the other side.

"Mr. Iverson will be with you soon." The young man rounded a large desk and stood anxiously behind his chair. "My name is Mr. Coggins. May I offer you a cup of tea while you wait?"

"No, thank you."

He seated himself and began working a device on his desk that cut paper. A simple bladed wooden lever sliced through a pile of foolscap he'd placed underneath when he pressed down. But the device was giving him trouble. He stood and wiggled the machine, adjusting the wooden platform where the paper was neatly arranged.

When he pressed again, the metal fittings screeched under the weight of his push.

Diana was intrigued. "May I assist you, Mr. Coggins?"

"Oh, I don't think you can, Miss Ashby. It's simply stuck. Always works eventually."

Diana stood and approached, leaning over the desk to get a closer look.

Mr. Coggins blushed furiously and his eyes widened when she joined him behind his desk.

"I think it's actually the fulcrum that's damaged." Diana pointed to the spot where the lever pivoted on a large metal screw. "A bit of oil might help, but it seems that the center pin itself may be at fault. See how it's a bit crooked?"

Coggins stared at her dumbfounded and finally said, "I shall see what I can do to repair it. Thank you, Miss Ashby."

"Well, that was quick." Mr. Iverson emerged from his office and tipped his head as he assessed the two of them with a bemused expression. "Has she already replaced you, Coggins?"

The low timbre of his voice with that teasing lilt caused exactly the reaction Diana had vowed not to allow. Her pulse jumped at the base of her throat and she willed herself to let nothing show on her face when she looked at him.

"I very much hope not, sir," Mr. Coggins said. "Though she has provided helpful advice on the paper trimmer."

Diana turned to face the man she'd come to see. She swallowed hard before managing a polite, "Good afternoon, Mr. Iverson."

Unlike her, he looked completely at ease. He'd settled against the frame of his door, his arms crossed over his chest. "Shall we begin, Miss Ashby? Or would you like to continue assessing the cutting machine before you join me in my office?"

"I think my work here is done." Diana offered Mr. Coggins a friendly nod, then approached Iverson. She kept her gaze fixed forward and moved past him across the threshold without sparing him a glance.

"Whichever chair you like," he told her.

As he closed his office door, Diana chose the leather upholstered chair in front of his desk.

She'd brought a notebook and pencil in an oversized reticule and she dug them out and waited, expecting him to take a seat in his desk chair. But as ever, Aidan Iverson didn't behave as she expected. He claimed the chair next to hers and reached for a stack of papers on his desk.

He wore no suit coat and had rolled his shirtsleeves up. Diana couldn't help but notice the way his waist-coat strained across the muscles of his back as he leaned forward. She also noted the dusting of auburn hair on his forearms and a mark just inside his left wrist that she thought might be a tattoo.

When he turned back, she was too slow in averting her eyes for him to miss her intense perusal. He didn't seem to mind at all that she caught his flash of a smile in response.

"These are brief descriptions of each buyer to whom I would like to present your device. The first owns a modest shopping emporium that caters to housemaids and domestic servants. The second is a man who's funded a few other promising inventions for domestic use. The third is an American who takes the best of what we create here in Britain back to his shopping enterprise in New York."

Diana scanned each page with interest. Mr. Coggins, no doubt, had written out a detailed summary about each man, but someone else had scribbled notes in the margin. That hand was bold and strong, with an abundance of capital letters and words underlined for emphasis. Personal details were included. "Has a daughter named Emily." "Enjoys summers in Brighton." "Frequents a bawdy theater near Vauxhall."

"You've met all of them?"

"Mmm. I know two of them quite well and can arrange a meeting with the third."

"Perhaps we should start with these two." Diana handed him the sheets describing the shop owner and the American entrepreneur.

"You think they'll be the most promising prospects?"

"The shop owner will understand the purpose of the machine if his products are aimed at domestic servants. That's half the battle. And the American sounds like a man who'd be intrigued by an innovative device."

"Agreed. Then I'll do my best to arrange a meeting with each of them."

"Thank you." When she tried to hand the documents back, he waved her off. "Keep them. Study them. I know how you enjoy research."

He looked at her a bit too long, his gaze intense and questioning.

"I have information for you too." From her reticule, she extracted a folded sheet of paper describing her dearest friend from Bexley.

This introduction would fulfill her promise to Iverson but also give Grace Grinstead what she jokingly requested, an opportunity to meet one of the wealthiest men in London.

"As you see, Miss Grinstead is quite accomplished."

"She has many interests."

"Isn't that what gentlemen want in a wife? Accomplishments?"

He looked up at her, a little furrow knitting his brow. "I'm not quite a gentleman though. Am I, Miss Ashby?"

Rather than answer and give in to the urge to question him about just what sort of a man he was, she pointed to the list in his hands.

"Not only is Grace fond of animals and quite well read in zoology, she has a natural talent for drawing and painting." He would soon see for himself that her creative sensibilities carried over into her personal appearance too. She was the most fashionable young woman Diana had ever known.

"She is the daughter of a nobleman, just like your opera lady."

"One more mention of the opera lady and I'll insist you accompany me to the longest, loudest opera in the history of London theater."

"I've never been before." Diana couldn't quite keep the wistfulness from her tone. Her mother had once been fond of the theater, and she remembered evenings in her childhood when her parents would attend the opera or a play.

"Do you wish to go?" Iverson turned a surprised glance her way.

"Perhaps, but not as punishment."

"I promise you. It *is* punishment."

Diana laughed. "Maybe you have no ear for music."

"That is where you're wrong, Miss Ashby." He cast her a mischievous look and held her gaze before flipping the page to read the last of her notes. After a moment, he added absently, "I play music rather proficiently."

She got lost in studying his profile, watching his eyes scan the words she'd written. He lifted a finger and ran it along the edge of his lower lip. His fingers were long, elegantly shaped, and she could easily imagine them skidding across piano keys or pressing the strings of a violin.

Those thoughts turned quickly to memories of his fingers on her skin, tracing the line of her cheek, dancing a delicious trail of heat up her arm.

She wanted him to touch her again.

Instead, she asked, "Can you prove that, Mr. Iverson? In science, nothing is true until it's proven with evidence."

"What shall be our exchange?"

Diana bit her lip and considered. "I can . . . juggle, depending on the objects, or flip a coin between each of my fingers."

After holding her challenging look without blinking, Iverson stood and approached a polished wooden cabinet in the corner of the room. Glass doors revealed an intriguing collection of statuary and rocks and delicate figures carved in marble. But when he opened the doors and reached in deep, he retrieved a violin from a drawer underneath.

He lifted it carefully, positioning the bottom edge against his neck, just under his chin. "Any requests?"

"You choose, but I do have a fondness for Mozart." Somehow her love for the composer persisted despite a fearsome piano tutor who'd rapped her knuckles when she made a mistake.

"Mozart, it is." He positioned his fingers along the strings, drew back the bow, and began to play. The notes were delicate and resonant, then they climbed to a lively tempo that made her want to move.

He paused too soon and glanced at her, as if waiting for her verdict. Or for her to urge him to play more.

"Well, carry on," she told him.

He smiled and continued to play the sweet, spritely parts of Mozart's Second Violin Concerto. The music made her wish to rise from her chair and take a turn around a ballroom. Ridiculous. She was a terrible dancer and she loathed balls.

Her fingers tapped along, knowing the song, recalling where it would rise and fall. Soon her foot was tapping too.

Iverson noticed and smiled, even speeding the tempo just enough for her to notice.

"Feel free to dance," he told her, lifting his mouth just slightly from the instrument.

"I'm a terrible dancer, and this is a place of business."

"But you want to."

"I do." Even as she admitted the truth with a smile, Diana shook her head. "I truly am a dreadful dancer."

"Prove it." He stopped playing and nudged his chin toward her. "I know how fond you are of scientific evidence."

Diana wanted to rise to the challenge, if only to keep that playful light in his eyes alive.

Before she could stand and make a fool of herself, pummeling knocks sounded at his office door.

Iverson lowered the violin and glared. "Come in, Coggins," he barked.

The young man pushed his head into the room warily, staring first at Iverson, examining the instrument dangling from his fingers, and then staring in shock at Diana.

"Visitor for you, Mr. Iverson. I knocked but you must not have heard."

"Coggins, I've cleared the hour to meet with Miss Ashby."

The secretary's brows winged up like two black birds startled from a wire. Again he glanced from

Diana to Iverson and back again. "She says it's urgent, sir."

Diana bent in her chair to glance past Mr. Coggins and see the woman who was so eager to see Iverson. A paramour? Another prospective bride?

Aidan gestured toward his secretary. "Name?"

"Says her name is Tuttle."

The name seemed to shock Aidan. His skin went ashen and his jaw slackened. "Ask her to wait a moment."

Coggins flicked his gaze to Diana and then retreated.

"I must speak to her immediately." He sounded regretful, but there was a nervous edge to his tone. "We'll need to reschedule our appointment for another day."

Glancing down, he seemed surprised to find the violin still in his hands. He placed the instrument on his desk and then approached, speaking quietly. "We'll finish this another time."

Diana nodded and turned toward the door. At the threshold, she stopped and turned to face him. His hand slid around her waist and settled where it had the first night they'd met. A heated weight that seemed to fit perfectly against the crook at her hip.

She looked down at where he held her and he withdrew his hand immediately.

"I'll wait for you," she told him quietly. "We can continue our conversation when you've finished."

"No." His reply emerged loud and emphatic. "Go on about your day. You needn't wait for me."

Diana shouldn't have felt hurt by his abrupt change in manner. They didn't know each other well enough for her to have the right to any information about his other business or personal matters. Though she realized now that she dearly wished to.

"Then I shall see you tomorrow, Mr. Iverson."

His brows dipped. "Tomorrow?"

"I've promised to visit the zoo with Miss Grace Grinstead, and it will be a perfect opportunity for you to meet her." Diana folded the notes he'd given her about potential investors and tucked them into her reticule. She tried to pretend his coolness didn't pain her.

Business. Practical matters. That was the reason for her connection with Aidan Iverson.

"Meet us at ten near the entrance. Don't be late." She decided insisting was better than petitioning.

When she looked up to await his answer, she saw a battle raging behind his eyes. Despite the coolness of his manner, there was something else in his gaze. Longing. Pain. A look of unease that made her throat ache to offer words of comfort.

"Tell me she doesn't like the opera, and I'll be there at nine-thirty."

Diana smiled. "Read your notes, Mr. Iverson. She likes zoology, art, and taking the waters at Bath."

"Excellent. Tomorrow, Miss Ashby." He shocked her by reaching for her hand, his ungloved skin warm against hers. He lifted her fingers to his lips as he had the night they'd met. Diana could say nothing. Her heart was in her throat, but she stepped beyond the threshold of his office and then glanced over her shoulder. One nod was all he offered. He looked like a man going to the gallows, aware of his fate, willing to face it, but dreading every moment.

In the outer office, a steel-haired woman stood and turned a dismissive glance on Diana as Coggins led her to Aidan's door.

As she stepped inside, she heard the woman say, "I've come about your mother, sir, just as you requested."

Coggins pulled the door shut, and Diana's mind flooded with questions. Who was this woman who brought news of Iverson's family? Was he estranged from them?

"Mr. Coggins, would you answer a question for me?"

The young man gave her a wary expression. "If I'm able, Miss Ashby."

"Do you know that woman?"

"Not at all. Her arrival and insistence on seeing Mr. Iverson was entirely unexpected. Forgive me for interrupting your time with him, miss." He cleared his throat. "I didn't know he was musical."

"Nor I." Diana had enjoyed herself. Perhaps too much. But she wouldn't apologize for how much she liked seeing a new side of Aidan Iverson.

The young man turned his attention back to his work, assuming he'd been dismissed. But Diana decided to try her luck again.

"I have a harder question for you, Mr. Coggins."

The clerk blanched and seemed to steel himself. "As you wish, Miss Ashby."

"What do you know of Mr. Iverson's past?"

"That one's rather easy." He looked pleased. "I know nothing at all. I'm afraid you'll have to inquire of him if you wish for those answers."

"Oh, I intend to, Mr. Coggins."

Chapter Sixteen

$\mathcal{L}$ambeth was as grim as Aidan recalled from his youth. Soot hung in the air and infused every breath with a metallic tang. There were more chimneys now, hundreds of blackened spires choking dark smoke into the air. There were no grassy squares, just brick buildings clustered together and a thick parade of people and carts shuffling between them.

After escaping the workhouse, he'd stayed in Lambeth for several years, working first as a chimney sweep and sometimes a mudlark, retrieving anything of value he could dig up from the muddy shore of the Thames. He'd spent his days covered in grime and his nights shivering against cold cobblestones when he couldn't find a cheap doss house.

The memories were so grim that he could hardly bear to recall them. When he did, he looked back as if on someone else. A pathetic waif. He sometimes wondered if that boy deserved the riches he had now.

Everett Street was one he'd traversed often, and it was eerie to know that he'd done so dozens of times with no knowledge that he'd been born within the grimy brick walls of a lodging house in the center of the street.

Aidan rolled his shoulders and squeezed at the knot of tension at the back of his neck before knocking on the front door. He told himself to temper his hopes. If the Mary Iverson who'd resided at this lodging house was his mother, she'd done so more than three decades past. There was no reason to believe she might still be alive, or anyone who would remember her and why she'd abandoned her children.

It was several minutes before an old, sickly-looking man leaning heavily on a cane opened the door. He scanned Aidan from head to toe, bending forward to inspect his clothes and boots.

"Hello, sir," the man finally said. "I take it you're not after lodgings. Who are you here to see?"

"Mr. Callihan. Would that be you, sir?"

"Aye, that I am."

"Then I'm here to speak with you. May I come in?"

The old man hesitated, his hand braced against the door frame protectively, but finally relented. "There's the front parlor if you wish to step inside."

Aidan stepped into the room the old man indicated and found it filled with personal mementos, photographs, and framed drawings.

"Ask me what you will, sir, but first tell me your name."

Aidan turned and fixed his gaze on the landlord's dark eyes. "Iverson."

The man's trembling, wrinkled hand came up. He clapped it over his mouth as his eyes bulged. "You're the boy."

"Yes." Aidan stepped forward and barely resisted gripping Callihan by his shirtfront. "Tell me what you know about my mother. About Mary Iverson."

The landlord stared at him for a moment and then bent on his cane to make his way across the room.

Aidan held his breath, struggling to maintain calm. He waited, somehow, for the man to open a small tin box and extract a piece of paper. Callihan shuffled toward him and stretched out his hand, offering the fragment of newsprint.

A death notice for one Mary Iverson. His fingers trembled so fiercely, Aidan almost dropped the fragile, faded clipping. She'd died so long ago, two years after he'd escaped the workhouse. All those years he'd imagined her, wondered who she was and where she might be. For most of those years, she'd been dead and buried.

"Tell me everything." He pointed to the threadbare chairs arranged in front of the fireplace. The old man collapsed into one with a heavy sigh, hooking his cane over the arm.

"The story is a sad one, sir."

"I know."

Aidan scanned every item in the parlor, wondering if one of the photographs had any link to his mother. In one of the rooms above his head, Mrs. Tuttle had watched over his mother while he came into the world. Perhaps she'd given birth to his sister here too.

"Tell me all of it, Mr. Callihan."

"I know less than I suspect you'll like." The old gentleman inhaled sharply. "I was hired to help with repairs here at the boardinghouse. Knew your mother was in a delicate way when she first arrived, and I took a liking to her." He frowned. "I mean nothing by that, sir. We became friends."

"Did she ever tell you where she hailed from?"

"From London, sir." Callihan shrugged. "Like most."

"Her family." Aidan clenched a fist against his knee. "Did she speak of them?"

"She spoke of her past rarely and of her predicament even less. Had many secrets to keep, Mary did."

"Who fathered her children?" There had always been the possibility that he and his sister did not share the same sire.

"I cannot say, sir."

"You must know something, Mr. Callihan." Aidan's patience was a fraying, broken thing. Edging forward on his chair, he said quietly, "Anything."

The old man lifted an arm, almost as if he wished to lay a comforting hand on Aidan's shoulder. "I would gladly tell you if I knew. Mary never revealed the father of her children to me. She lived here while you were very small and returned shortly after your sister was born."

"Returned where?"

"Back to her employer. The Earl of Wyndham."

Aidan didn't have to be a mathematician to fit the equation together in his head. The probability was that Wyndham, or someone in the earl's household, was his father.

"Never saw her for many years after she returned to Belgravia. Then one day she appeared." Callihan's eyes took on a glassy faraway look. "She was ill, in a bad way. I think trouble might have found her after she left the Wyndhams. Might even have run afoul of the law." Slowly, he turned his gaze on Aidan. "I cared for her until she passed. Saw to her burial and that notice." Flicking his wrist, he indicated the scrap of newspaper still clutched in Aidan's hand. "Keep it if you like, sir."

"My sister. Mrs. Tuttle said you mentioned my sister to her when she visited you."

The old man's gaze grew wary. He fussed with the

doily pinned to the arm of his chair. "Can't recall, Mr. Iverson. An old man's mind tends to stray. Sometimes I say things that mean nothing at all."

Aidan shot up from his chair. His days of brawling with other young men as hungry and desperate as he'd been were long past. But the same urge to strike out burned in him now, to get rid of the pain, to feel that he had some measure of power.

"I run a gambling club, Mr. Callihan. I know when a man is lying to me." In two steps, he was in front of the landlord's chair. Aidan towered over the frail man, but he felt as powerless as he ever had in his life. "Tell me the truth."

Pain and guilt were as clear in Callihan's eyes as if Aidan were looking in a mirror.

"Please." The word felt odd on his tongue. He wasn't used to pleading with anyone. For anything. He'd worked and fought and maneuvered for everything he'd acquired.

"There is one thing, Mr. Iverson."

"I'm listening."

The landlord grew silent so long, Aidan wondered if he'd reconsidered confessing more. He was just on the point of urging him when Callihan took a deep breath.

"There is a young lady." He wheezed out a long sigh. "I believe she is your sister, sir. But she doesn't wish to be known."

Blood rushed in Aidan's ears. He stalked to the mantel and gripped the edge, but it did little to stem a wave of dizziness that made the corners of his sight dim. Memories rolled in. Fragmented images of a girl with red-gold hair and a sweet smile.

Sarah was alive.

"How is she?" His voice quavered. His knees had turned to mush. "Is she well?" He turned back to face the man.

The man's gnarled hands came up and he waved them at Aidan as if to push him away. "I don't know. She wears a veil and comes infrequently. Only thrice in the last two years."

"Why does she come?"

"I can't tell you that either. I never invite her. She said she wished to help me. Gives me a few pounds every time she visits."

None of it made sense. "Why would she pay you?"

Callihan didn't answer. Instead he used his cane to push himself out of his chair and hobbled toward a small table where a cup of tea that must have long gone cold sat. He took a sip and then turned to face Aidan.

"I believe she means the funds as a gift. She said once the money was for Mary. I took that to mean a repayment for how I cared for her and saw to laying her to rest."

Aidan began pacing the confines of the tiny parlor, his boot heels echoing against the polished wood not covered by the rug. "What sort of lady is she?"

The envy he felt toward the man was a living thing, clawing at him from the inside. Callihan had known Aidan's mother and met his sister. Wealth, power, access to some damnable club seemed a pathetic substitute for those memories and connections he would never have.

Callihan made little aggrieved sounds as he considered his answer. "She's a very finely dressed lady, sir, and speaks the queen's English. A true lady."

More mystery. Every step in his search showed him that the knot of his mother's life and history was more tangled than he'd ever imagined.

But he wouldn't stop. Aidan had to find his sister. He wouldn't disturb her life. If she'd risen from the poverty they'd been raised in to become a fine lady, he'd never endanger her future.

Yet he had to see with his own eyes that she was alive and well. Perhaps he was selfish, but he needed to know.

"Anything else you can think of, Mr. Callihan? I intend to find my sister."

He nodded his balding gray head solemnly. "Thought you would, sir. Won't say I blame you either. But there's nothing more to tell. She comes in fine clothes, says hardly a word, and offers me an envelope."

"Do you have any of those envelopes?"

"I may have the last." The landlord leaned heavily on his cane as he got to his feet and shuffled toward a side table and slid out its single drawer. "Yes, here it is."

Between them, he lifted a cream-colored envelope. Aidan snatched at it eagerly, but it offered nothing. No writing, no watermark to indicate the maker, and no indication where it had come from or any clue that might help him find his sister.

"No help at all, is it?" Callihan sounded as bereft as Aidan felt. He'd never seen an old man who looked so weary.

"*You* have been helpful. Thank you." He pulled two crown coins from his pocket and offered them to the landlord.

"Very generous, young man. I remember you as a kind child."

There was no more to say. No more the man could give him, despite how much more he wanted to know. He headed for the threshold, almost as eager to be out of the lodging house as he'd been to enter it.

He had a puzzle to solve and only a few pieces.

The only real link he had now was his mother's connection to the Earl of Wyndham. Mrs. Tuttle no doubt held those answers, and he needed to find a way to get the woman to divulge more than she had. When she'd come to his office, she'd brought no journal or letters, only the detail that she'd visited the lodging house and that Callihan had a story Aidan would wish to hear.

Now what he wanted most was to find his sister.

He had fresh answers, but more questions than ever before.

Chapter Seventeen

The next morning, Aidan discovered an unexpected crush waiting to enter the Zoological Society and decided the throng was probably for the best. His planned introduction to Grace Grinstead would be less awkward if they weren't the only Londoners loitering outside the society's grounds.

This introduction had to go better than the last. He'd had Coggins send a thank-you note to Lady Caldwell, but he couldn't imagine continuing a pursuit of Lady Sophie. Another man would appreciate her jovial nature far more than he ever could.

Based on Miss Ashby's notes, Miss Grinstead seemed a more serious sort of lady. She was not as highborn as Lady Sophie, but Aidan had met her father once and knew him to be a sober, diligent sort, despite whatever financial woes his viscountcy might be facing.

He was determined to make this morning a success.

Aidan had taken special care with his suit and allowed the valet to have his merry way with a new-fangled necktie. A formal introduction to a highborn noblewoman was what he'd sought for months, which made it quite inconvenient that the prospect of seeing Diana occupied most of his thoughts as he'd dressed and shaved.

She was the reason he stood tapping his thigh eagerly, scanning the crowd of those waiting to see the animals. And when he finally caught sight of her, it was Diana who set his pulse thrumming. She wore a peacock blue gown that was so different from the other ladies' pastels that a man couldn't help but notice her.

He studied her curves with far too much interest, the determined set to her jaw, the bloom of pink in her cheeks. He told himself that half the ladies present had equally appealing features, but still he couldn't take his eyes off her.

As if she felt his notice, she turned. Even from a distance, he saw her eyes widen and her mouth soften into something that was almost a smile.

He felt an answering tug at the corners of his own mouth. But then she pivoted and spoke to a lady a few steps ahead of her. Miss Grinstead, no doubt.

Aidan assessed her quickly. Tall, blond, buxom, and dressed in an elegant peach traveling costume and ostentatious beribboned hat. Any man would be blind to not find her pretty.

Aidan kept his gaze fixed on Miss Ashby as she turned and bent her head to speak to Miss Grinstead. The two laughed, and the appealing sound carried on the breeze. Then Miss Ashby struck out a hand in a sweeping motion as if commenting on the landscape. She stopped and pointed at him a bit too theatrically, drawing her companion's notice his way.

Initially, Miss Grinstead didn't seem interested in taking the bait. She offered him a single assessing glance and then turned back to the queue.

Miss Ashby wasn't put off so easily, as he knew well. Hooking an arm through her friend's, she turned the lady bodily and they began strolling his way. After a moment, Miss Ashby picked up her pace and rushed ahead to greet him.

"Mr. Iverson, fancy finding you here," she said loudly, then lowered her voice to add, "Her parents are very strict, so it's extraordinary that they've allowed her to step out without a chaperone. I am entrusted with that duty, so we must make this brief outing count."

Aidan nodded. "Understood."

"Grace, may I present Mr. Aidan Iverson," she said as soon as her friend reached her side.

The young woman pasted a tight smile on her cupid bow mouth and offered him a nod. "Have we not met before, Mr. Iverson?"

"Not that I recall." He would have remembered her striking looks as well as her marriageable status.

"The Duke of Tremayne held a ball a few months past."

"Ah yes." Aidan remembered the evening. He'd stopped in to speak to Tremayne, unaware they were hosting a ball. "I don't think I had the pleasure of meeting you that night."

"You didn't dance." Her eyes finally settled on him fully and she subjected him to a thorough head-to-toe inspection. "I recall wishing you'd stayed. There was a distinct lack of gentlemen to dance with."

"Perhaps another opportunity will present itself." Aidan couldn't help sparing a glance at Diana. She was a vibrant, rose-scented distraction in his periphery, no matter how he tried to focus on Miss Grinstead.

"You're the man who invests in all of the industrial machines, are you not?" the young lady said, drawing his attention again. "My father, Lord Holcomb, is quite fond of investing in industry too. He's forever going on about an exhibition where the prince is planning to display England's industrial marvels to the world."

"I'm aware of the exhibition," Aidan said tightly. He searched his mind for a memory of any Lord Holcomb he might have encountered during his years in the London business world.

He turned his attention to Diana again and she tipped her head toward the zoo. "They've opened the gates. Should we join the queue and go inside?" Without waiting for an answer, she started off toward the entrance and her school friend followed.

"Are you coming too, Mr. Iverson?" Miss Grinstead asked with a glance over her shoulder.

"Yes, I've long wished to take in the displays." He caught up to the two of them and positioned himself beside Miss Grinstead, careful to keep a polite distance. He needed to focus on the reason for this introduction, not on the dark-haired lady inventor he'd been looking forward to seeing all morning.

"Do you like animals?" Miss Grinstead asked brightly.

Miss Ashby shot him a pointed look behind her friend's back.

"I appreciate animals most ardently," he replied, trying to infuse a note of sincerity into his tone. He didn't dislike animals, but he'd experienced them mostly as poor pack horses or stray dogs who were as desperate as he'd once been to find their next meal and a safe spot to sleep for the night.

"Which kind?"

Aidan tipped his head back to catch Miss Ashby's notice. He shrugged and she did the same.

"Mammals, amphibians, reptiles?" Miss Grinstead asked, as if the distinctions were at all helpful.

"Those with claws fascinate me," Miss Ashby put in. "Nature has provided taloned creatures such a clever and useful device."

Aidan arched a brow in her direction. Why did her preference not surprise him at all?

"You'll be pleased, Di," Miss Grinstead tittered at her friend. "They are adding more fearsome creatures, so I'm given to understand. If we're lucky, we may see a tiger or lion today."

Aidan wasn't keen on seeing wild and fearsome animals caged, but he followed the ladies inside the grounds and stopped with them at the first surround that contained a group of lithe, active monkeys. The long-tailed creatures jumped from tree branch to tree branch, stopping only briefly to stare down and assess their observers.

Miss Grinstead moved closer, fascinated with their every movement. Aidan allowed her to lecture him on the eating habits of primates for over a quarter of an hour. When he could take no more, he retreated and let her continue to ogle the creatures on her own.

His pulse ratcheted up a beat when Miss Ashby approached. "You're doing much better this time," she whispered.

"Do you intend to give me marks every time I speak to one of your friends?"

"One would think you'd welcome a lady's advice on how to woo another lady. Particularly one of her dearest friends."

Miss Grinstead moved on and looked back to see if they intended to follow. The next area featured a high cast-iron fence closing in a few majestic elephants. They were enormous beasts with long, fierce tusks.

"Quite extraordinary, are they not?" Miss Ashby enthused.

"Yes." Aidan couldn't help but agree. Their size made them impressive, but there was something in their mien that held his gaze. The one closest to the fence turned its head to appraise him and then unfurled its big petal-like ear as if offering a wave of greeting.

"They're not terribly exciting as animals go," Miss Grinstead commented after a period of watching the creatures perambulate around what seemed to Aidan a far too small enclosure. "Quite wrinkled and slow moving. But they're loyal and make excellent animals for carrying heavy loads. Hannibal used them as war animals during the Second Punic War, as I'm sure you know."

"They may not look like much, but there's a majesty to them," he said, not truly caring if Miss Grinstead heard.

"Not every creature can be beautiful, Mr. Iverson," Miss Ashby said quietly. "But it doesn't diminish their intelligence and value."

Aidan cast her a shocked glance. Her blush deepened to a bright red. He sensed somehow that she was referring to herself, but the notion was ludicrous. Miss Ashby was quite possibly the cleverest women he'd ever known. She had to know that she was beautiful.

"Of course, my dear. One can rarely judge an animal's cleverness based merely on morphology." Miss Grinstead patted her friend's hand and then tugged Miss Ashby toward another fenced circle of green where three lanky-limbed camels stood.

Aidan watched the two women awhile before following. From a distance, he noticed that Miss Grinstead wasn't quite as intrigued with the animals as he'd initially assumed. She was fascinated all right, but it wasn't with the caramel-coated camels pacing their fenced domain. Her gaze was focused beyond the creatures on a thin, sandy-haired young man who stood on the other side of the ringed enclosure and looked back at her with answering interest.

It soon became clear to Aidan that it wasn't a passing moment of mutual admiration. They seemed to know each other enough to communicate without words. The gentleman pulled a fob watch from his waistcoat pocket and tapped its face. Miss Grinstead returned the minutest of nods.

She turned to Aidan and Miss Ashby and asked, "How do both of you feel about reptiles?"

"We're here to see any and all creatures," Miss Ashby said with a nod, but Aidan didn't miss the little tremor of a shiver that shook her shoulders. "Lead the way, Grace," she said with a smile.

Miss Grinstead rose onto her tiptoes and looked off

into the distance. The young man who'd attracted her attention was nowhere in sight.

"I think," she said, lifting a hand to block the sun as she scanned the grounds, "that they've just opened the Reptile House to the public. Shall I go and check rather than force you to make a pointless journey?"

"A journey? The park is only a couple miles wide. Of course we'll accompany you."

Aidan dropped his gaze to the ground and contemplated his options. He could reveal what he'd seen or let Miss Grinstead carry on with her subterfuge.

After a deep breath, he decided to allow the young woman to have the moment she craved. How could he blame her for wishing to escape the confines of what Miss Ashby had described as strict parents?

"I wouldn't mind spending a bit more time with the camels," he said. He expected Miss Grinstead's pleased nod of agreement, and he wasn't surprised by Miss Ashby's irritation either.

"Why tarry, Mr. Iverson?" Miss Ashby demanded. "Surely you're not fatigued already."

"I am, actually." He ignored Miss Ashby's *tsk* and focused on Miss Grinstead. "We'll wait here, Miss Grinstead, and look forward to your return."

"Nonsense, Grace. I'm going with you." Miss Ashby cast him a disappointed look before striding off to catch her friend, who'd already started toward the far end of the park.

But Miss Grinstead stopped her and whispered in her ear. When the noble lady continued on, Miss Ashby stayed put and then strode back toward him, a frown pinching her brow.

"What did she say?" he asked.

"Only that she wished to have a moment on her own." Her blue eyes were shadowed, her mouth working as she contemplated the young lady's odd behavior. "I was tasked with being her chaperone. Shall I go after her or respect her wishes?"

Miss Ashby looked so worried that he found himself stepping closer, wanting to reach for her, though nothing he was about to say would reassure her.

"I believe Miss Grinstead has an assignation planned," he told her matter-of-factly.

"That's ridiculous. Grace is sensible. Her mother would lock her away if she so much as contemplated anything scandalous."

"Maybe that's why she finds the prospect so appealing."

"Do you think so?" She craned her neck, trying to see past the crowd that her friend had disappeared into. "We should go. We should stop her."

"Perhaps. But why not give her a few moments to speak to the young man?"

Miss Ashby turned to him and crossed her arms.

"You're considering marrying her. Don't you wish to stop the lady from pursuing her own ruination?"

Aidan sighed deeply. She was right. He was getting used to the fact that she often was. Even if he would never woo and win Miss Grinstead, neither of them should stand by and let her cause a scandal on their watch. "Do you have any notion where the Reptile House might be?"

"No, but I'm sure someone does."

They threaded their way through the zoo's visitors, sidestepping crowds gathered at each fenced exhibition area. As they continued, the clusters of people thinned and they had a clear view of the couple. They were strolling near a half-built structure in tall grass that hadn't been as neatly trimmed as the rest of the grounds.

Miss Ashby picked up her pace and Aidan lengthened his stride to keep up. She stopped in her tracks and gasped when the young man dropped to his knee.

"Oh no. Oh heavens no. We're too late." Her voice pitched high and panicked, and she shot him a miserable glance before lifting a handful of her skirt and starting off at a dash toward Miss Grinstead.

Aidan caught up with her and clasped her gently around the arm. "Slow down. Running through the Zoological Society grounds like a thief trying to escape a bobby will draw more notice than anything they're doing."

She was exhaling quickly, her breath coming in shallow gasps. She pressed a hand to her middle, where he suspected her corset wasn't doing much to help her breathe.

"Perhaps she doesn't want this," she said. "I know the dread of having a man offer for you when the proposal is not expected or desired."

"Do you?" Aidan realized he still held her arm and nothing in him wanted to let her go. "Who was he?" He wanted to know everything about the proposal she'd rejected. He wanted to know everything about her.

"It doesn't matter, and now's definitely not the time. But we must stop Grace from making a decision she might regret." She tugged at his hold and he released her. When she started off again, it was at a more sedate pace. Though he could tell from the straight set of her shoulders and the jerky movement of her feet that she was aching to break into a run.

"Grace," she called out when they were still too far to be sure the noblewoman would hear.

From every indication, she didn't. The gentleman was still on bended knee in front of her, and all of the young lady's focus was on him.

"I wonder who he is," Miss Ashby mused. "What sort of a gentleman would cause her to risk this kind of scandal?"

"One she's enamored with?"

Miss Ashby shot him a scowl. "Infatuation, perhaps. She's never allowed out on her own often enough to have made the acquaintance of any young man without her family's permission."

"Infatuation has led to many marriages." He thought immediately of Nick, Duke of Tremayne, who'd gone to Sussex to reclaim his ancestral estate after inheriting a dukedom and come back as smitten as any man he'd ever known.

"Do you plan to be infatuated with whatever lady you choose to marry?" She didn't look at him as she asked the question, though they walked side by side.

"No," he told her honestly. "I intend a practical transaction."

"You do like exchanges." She tipped her head his way and tripped over a stone on the path.

Before he could reach for her, she'd laid her hand on his arm, hanging on tightly for a too brief moment before letting go.

"Exchanges are fair," he told her as they continued walking. "But there are always factors one can't predict."

"Such as?" She stared at him as she walked.

He found it difficult to look into her eyes. The lady had a fierce determination to get answers, and he understood it. He wanted to know things too. But there were secrets he didn't wish to share, deeds he couldn't bear to revisit.

The curiosity in her gaze was dangerous, and the way her mouth trembled when they looked at each other too long was pure temptation.

He looked out across the field to where Miss Grinstead and her gentlemen friend were standing face-to-face. They'd clasped hands, as if they'd sealed an agreement.

"Mr. Iverson, what is it that you can't predict?"

All his vows to avoid Diana's gaze were useless. He'd always liked the curiosity he saw in her eyes. The truth was that he wished for her to know him. Not as an investor who'd negotiated her into playing match-maker, but as a man who longed to know her too.

"Infatuation, Miss Ashby," he said hoarsely.

She stopped and turned to look at him, not noticing that Miss Grinstead and her paramour had progressed from holding hands to embracing. He pointed toward the pair.

"Grace!" Miss Ashby called out, and the couple sprang apart.

Miss Grinstead gazed back at them in shock, followed quickly by resolute determination.

"You cannot speak a word of this to Mama, Diana," she said with surprising calm when they'd gathered on the far side of the half-constructed building. "I will choose the time and place to tell her. And Papa."

"Tell them what?" Diana kept her gaze focused on Miss Grinstead's young gentleman.

Aidan could almost hear her mind buzzing with questions.

"Mr. Hambly and I plan to marry." The blonde beamed at the young man beside her. "He asked and I have accepted." Then she shocked Aidan by turning her gaze on him. "I am sorry, Mr. Iverson, if you were hoping to make a match."

"I did entertain that hope." Aidan found her bluntness appealing, but he also admired her courage.

"First we'll need your father's approval." Mr. Hambly spoke for the first time and sounded far more dubious than his fiancée.

"And if you don't receive it?" Miss Ashby, Aidan was learning, always considered the worst possible outcome first.

"Then we shall consider other means," Miss Grinstead said with conviction.

She and Hambly stared at each other with an intensity that indicated, at least for now, the viscount's daughter was prepared to face whatever consequences might come.

"We'll find a way," he said reassuringly.

"Love should prevail no matter what. Don't you think?" Miss Grinstead asked the question of all of them.

Mr. Hambly nodded solemnly. Miss Ashby said nothing, but Aidan sensed her gaze on him, as if she was waiting for him to offer an answer.

"Yes." He couldn't look at two smitten fools and not feel some niggle of sentimentality.

When he turned, he found Miss Ashby staring at him, her lips slightly parted, her blue eyes lit with a tantalizing gleam.

"Love should prevail," he heard himself say, almost as if he was listening to another man speak.

He expected the sentiment to shock Diana. Would she ever believe he wasn't heartless when he'd claimed marriage should be as simple as any other business transaction?

It was only her response he wanted. He didn't care if anyone else heard his answer. His gaze lingered on her while he waited for her to reply.

She started to speak and then fell silent, and he cursed the fact that they weren't alone and he couldn't press for those words she held back.

Finally, she sucked in a breath and turned to her friend. "Grace, we should return to Grosvenor Square."

Miss Grinstead made no argument and parted from Mr. Hambly with a few whispered words. The two ladies began striding off toward Regent's Park. Diana had offered him no formal leave taking, and the omission left him feeling irrationally bereft.

"We have an appointment tomorrow, Miss Ashby," he called to her. "Don't forget."

He wondered if she heard him and considered calling out again, more loudly. Hambly watched him quizzically out of the corner of his eye.

His heart skipped a beat when she turned back. Across the short distance, he could see that a bit of the warm gleam had gone out of her eyes. "Of course, Mr. Iverson. Our business arrangement is what matters most. I won't forget."

Chapter Eighteen

*W*hen Diana knocked on Mr. Iverson's Mayfair town house door the next morning, the maid who greeted her seemed completely unprepared for what met her on the other side.

The girl tittered and gasped as Diana maneuvered the case containing a perfect working model of her device through the front door, but made no move to assist her. Diana focused mainly on trying not to scratch the door's pristine sapphire paint.

"You needn't do that alone." Iverson emerged from a room midway down the hall and joined them in three long strides.

Her instinct was to demur. Being rescued wasn't her way, but doing everything on her own was exhausting too. On the verge of accepting his help, Diana turned to glance at him and was struck speechless.

He looked . . . different.

Every moment she'd spent with the man, he'd been immaculately dressed. Even that night in the rain.

Today he was garbed in tall boots, worn trousers, a simple black waistcoat, and a white shirt with sleeves rolled up to his elbows. He looked like a country gentleman who'd just come in from taking a gallop across the heath. His hair was disheveled too, sun-kissed auburn waves hanging looser near his brow.

"Thank you," she said, and made no move to stop him when he gracefully hefted the oblong wooden case onto his shoulder. His waistcoat hugged the muscled contours of his chest and pulled snug at his waist. When he turned to head down the hall, she couldn't help but let her gaze dip lower to where his trousers shaped themselves across his taut backside.

"How in God's name did you transport this on your own?" He looked back, but she couldn't tell if he'd caught her staring.

"I didn't," she said a bit too huskily. "Dominick helped me."

He peered at the empty space behind her. "Where did you lose him?"

"At a coffeehouse in Piccadilly."

"He often leaves you unchaperoned, Miss Ashby."

The words sounded like a chastisement, yet there was a glint of mischief in his eyes.

"I'm quite safe here, am I not?" As soon as the question was out, an odd energy charged the air between them.

He didn't give her the reassurance she expected. Instead, he hefted the rectangular box higher onto his shoulder.

"You should have asked the maid to let me know you'd arrived. I would have helped you get the machine out of the carriage."

"I managed on my own."

He looked so impressed at her feat, she was tempted to tell him of all the other times she'd transported strange pieces of equipment or raw parts from one end of London to the other.

"Come this way," he said, then called out to the skittish young maid. "Tea in my office and please direct our visitor there when he arrives."

Iverson's study was almost as surprising as his clothing.

Diana expected the space to be austere like his office, but this room—part study and part library—was one of the most appealing she'd ever seen in her life. Beautifully bound books lined the walls and vivid blue velvet drapery covered two floor-to-ceiling windows. They'd been pulled open, allowing morning light to flood the room and cast a glow on the wood-paneled walls.

"I'll change before Mr. Repton arrives."

"Why?"

He tipped his head and narrowed his gaze, then swept a hand down to encompass his waistcoat. "I've been out riding this morning."

"In Hyde Park?"

That drew a burst of laughter that caused an answering tickle in her stomach.

"God, no. Hampstead. Plenty of open fields and no one to take much notice of a man on a horse."

"Were you raised in the countryside?" Despite his reputation as a man of commerce, she could easily imagine him in the country.

She sensed immediately that she was treading where he did not wish to go.

His expression shuttered, and he drew in a long breath before answering. "Not in the countryside, no. Here in London. South of the river."

Two steps and he'd strode past her. She expected him to leave her alone without another word. But on the threshold, he turned back.

"I won't be long. Help yourself to tea when it arrives."

Diana couldn't resist exploring after he'd departed. She started with the bookshelves, running her gaze along titles as varied as Marcus Aurelius's *Meditations* to a book about a traveler's journey to Spain. A volume of Pope's poetry sat next to a book with a beautifully ornate spine. When she pulled it out, she discovered it bore the intriguing title of *Ghastly Tales*.

"Tea for you, miss." The young maid entered the room, deposited a polished silver tea service on a table near the desk, and left Diana alone again.

She ran her fingers over the embossed design on the book. For years, she'd had a rogue desire to read something fanciful, but she never allowed herself to take the time. Her own family library was full of books on mathematics, science, and engineering. Topics that pleased her father. She'd never found a book of poetry at home, and despite her education at Bexley, her mother insisted that ladies should not read novels.

"You've found a book you like?" Iverson said from the doorway.

She still held the ornately gilded book in her hands and quickly replaced it on the shelf.

"The cover is beautiful. What are the stories like?"

"Frightening." He came into the room, wearing a perfectly tailored black suit. His hair had been wrangled back into neat waves and she imagined disheveling all of it again with her fingers. "Some might call them terrifying."

Diana's brother had often regaled her as a child with his own made-up ghost stories, and they'd frightened the wits out of her. "Do you like being frightened?"

"I prefer fictional frights to true terrors."

"Have you experienced many?" Somehow, she already knew the answer.

There were only a handful of facts she knew for sure about Aidan Iverson, but much more that she sensed bubbling under the surface. She had only one truly agonizing memory that she found difficult to share with others—the death of her father. She suspected Aidan had many more.

"The last time I experienced any sort of violence, a very helpful Samaritan appeared. I'm grateful to her."

Diana drew in a sharp breath and clenched her jaw. He knew exactly the memories his words would evoke. After months of wondering, she couldn't hold the question back any longer.

"Why were you in a Belgravia mews the night we met? Did you know the men who attacked you?"

Instead of answering, he picked up one of the upholstered straight-back chairs in the corner of the room and placed it behind his desk, next to a much larger leather wingback.

The question hung in the air like an echo, and the longer he failed to answer, the more she wished to repeat it. Over and over, if necessary, until she got an answer.

"I thought we could both sit on this side. United in our efforts to woo Mr. Repton. Is there anything you'd like to know about him to better prepare you before he arrives?"

"I memorized your notes."

"Then you know as much about him as I do."

"They were very thorough." She studied him a moment. "You notice a lot about people. Little details that others might miss."

He shrugged as if to downplay her praise. "A gambler's skill. You learn to look for details, tells that give away people's intentions." He gestured vaguely toward where he'd placed her case on a long table. "Do you need help assembling your machine?"

In her curiosity to inspect the room, she'd neglected to set up the pneumatic pump.

"I need to prime this. It won't take me long." She approached the table and extracted all the pieces, taking care not to drop or bump anything. The metal tubes were sturdy and the pump was made to take exertion, but the memory of the disaster at the Duke's Den would always stick in her head.

"Let me help you." The sincerity in his tone made her relent.

"Take that lever and pump until you feel resistance." Diana approached and reached for his hand, placing it just so on the metal bar and indicating where it hooked into the pneumatic device.

His hands were warm, and the brief contact sent a shiver up her arm. She turned her attention back to assembling the rest of the device, if only to distract herself from her reaction to him.

"I'm seeking to solve a mystery," Iverson said quietly behind her.

Diana spun to face him. He'd approached and stood not far behind, his gaze uncertain. Wary. She waited, sensing that if she could just hold back her tendency to demand answers, he might give them freely.

"I didn't know the men. They were thieves with a violent bent. I was in Belgravia that night to seek information." He tilted his head to stare at the ceiling, flicked his coat back, and braced his hands on his narrow hips. "About my family."

"Why?" So many thoughts raced through her head that she couldn't form a question other than the single word. "Are you estranged from them?"

"More than estranged. I never knew my father, and I barely recall my mother. My sister and I were left at a workhouse when I was three. The place is gone now. Burned, along with all details about my mother and father or any other family I might have."

"And your sister?" Diana moved a few steps closer, aching to reach for him.

They'd held on to each other once. Strangers on a rainy night whom fate had brought together. She had no regrets about the familiarities she'd allowed or the kiss she'd taken.

Now she wanted to offer that comfort again. A touch. An embrace. Anything to ease a bit of the misery in his gaze.

"Lost," he said on a broken whisper.

Diana closed the distance between them and wrapped

her arms around his waist. Her head fit just underneath his chin, and she pressed her cheek against his chest.

Heat crept up her face as he tensed, and she considered retreating.

But then his arms came around her, pulling her into his body. This close, she could feel the mad thrash of his heartbeat and the unsteady gust of his breath against her hair.

"I want to help," she whispered.

"You are," he finally said, his voice deep and husky and warm.

"No, Mr. Iverson." Diana tipped her head back to look at him. The afternoon light brightened his eyes to a cooler green. "With solving your mystery, I mean."

"No." He tensed again, but didn't let her go.

There was a finality in his tone, but Diana couldn't stop herself from trying.

"Taking matters apart, finding answers to questions that sometimes haven't even been asked—those are the only things I'm truly good at."

He turned his head and loosened his hold. Being near him, touching him in such a familiar manner, was entirely inappropriate. She knew all the rules of etiquette by heart. They'd been drilled into her at Bexley and she'd excelled at learning them all. But they seemed far away, and he was here before her, tall and warm and holding her protectively close.

The rightness of it wasn't something she was prepared to examine, but she very much wanted to help solve his mystery.

"There is something you can do for me." He stroked a hand down her back, almost absently, as he spoke. "Will you call me Aidan? At least when we're alone."

"I—"

He lifted a finger and let it hover over the edge of her mouth.

"You'll say it's inappropriate. But when have we ever bothered with that?"

Then he touched her. One tender stroke along the edge of her cheek, a hairsbreadth from her lips.

He'd touched her that way once before. She remembered every second. The rain, the warmth radiating off his body, the taste of his lips.

His eyes traced the movement of his finger, his gaze focused and intense.

Diana lifted onto her toes and pressed her mouth to his. Purposefully. Slowly. This wasn't the impulsiveness of an unexpected encounter in the rain. She wanted this.

AIDAN COULDN'T THINK. His brain refused to form a single rational thought. All of his strategies failed him.

What was worse, he could feel the walls he'd constructed beginning to crumble.

There was only what he wanted. What he needed. This moment. Diana, soft and warm and in his arms. She'd stepped there of her own will. In her fearsome determination, she'd chosen him, and he wanted to give her everything in return.

But some part of him resisted. Some instinct urged him to plot and plan how this should go, to hold on to some shred of control.

Yet one blink of sable lashes, one look into her eyes, and she unraveled every bit of him.

He cupped her face in his hands, marveled at her softness, and told himself not to frighten her. Not to ruin this moment as he had others.

Dipping his head, he kissed her softly. But it wasn't enough. He deepened the kiss, urging her to let him in. Then she did, moaning into his mouth as he kissed her.

He deepened the kiss. She set something loose inside him. Made him believe in possibilities that terrified him. She made him want to risk everything, anything, if he could keep on holding her. Kissing her.

"Aidan," she whispered.

The sound of his name on her lips shot a rush of pleasure straight down his body.

"Diana." She was what he needed. To all that he kept locked inside, somehow she possessed the key.

There was much he wished to tell her. Things he needed to make her understand.

Before he could gather a coherent thought, two

distinct raps sounded on his study door and she dropped her arms from around his waist.

"It's all right," he promised, and held her a moment longer.

When he released her, the loss hit him like a blow.

He let out a long exhale, struggling to rein in his urges and gather his thoughts before stepping over to open the door.

"Repton," he said jovially to the stout man across the threshold. "Right on time."

"Anything other than timeliness is inexcusable," the older man said with a hearty chuckle. He had a round belly, a bald pate, and a laugh that made his jowls wobble.

"Miss Diana Ashby," Aidan said as he gestured toward her.

Of course, one glance at her and he didn't wish to stop looking. Her cheeks were pink, her mouth flush from their kisses. There was a fire in her gaze that set off an answering inferno inside him.

"I've heard a great deal about you from Mr. Iverson." Repton strode forward and offered her his hand.

"I hope he's mostly told you about my pneumatic cleaning system, Mr. Repton."

The old man chortled. "Why, yes, of course." His eyes widened behind the polished brass rims of his spectacles as he took in the machine. "Do you mind if I . . . ?" He wriggled his fingers in the air.

"Touch it?" Two tiny lines formed between her brows. "Certainly. I plan to demonstrate its effectiveness for you today too. This is a complete working model."

"I wish to have a look first, if I may."

Diana's jaw tensed as the man stepped toward her machine.

Aidan approached to whisper to her. "It's all right. Let him look all he likes. If he's to sell these in his shops, he'll want to know them intimately."

She snapped her gaze to Aidan's, and then stared at his mouth.

The urge to send Repton packing and resume what had only just begun between them was terribly tempting. But he knew what this opportunity meant to her. If Repton bought her machine, it could bring Diana the success she longed for, both recognition for her inventions and financial reward.

"You say you can demonstrate it now?" Repton dipped his head and gazed at them over the rim of his spectacles.

Diana stepped forward and repeated the procedure she had done in her laboratory. This time the pump was primed and it was only a matter of shaking a bit of dust on the carpet and using the metal hose to pull up the particles.

Aidan held back. He was anxious to assist her if necessary, but he was acutely aware that she needed to show mastery of her machine on her own. A few paces back, he could also keep one eye on Repton, gauging his response. The man was decidedly intrigued. His brows did a merry dance on his forehead and his eyes widened and narrowed during the demonstration.

"Well done, Miss Ashby," he said when she was finished. "But may I try the machine for myself?" He extracted a plump envelope from his coat pocket, tore off the edge, and poured out what looked to be a combination of ash and dirt onto Aidan's study carpet.

Luckily, he'd chosen a deep burgundy rug to cover the floor.

"The pump mechanism may need to be reprimed," Diana told Repton when he strode up and lifted the main tube of the device in his hands.

"Why don't you do those honors, Iverson?" Repton directed over his shoulder.

Diana shot him a disgruntled frown, but he nodded. She had to understand that no buyer would sell a product he hadn't tested thoroughly. To do so might harm his own reputation.

When Aidan approached to reach for the lever and prepare the pump, Diana stepped in front of him.

"I can do this," she said softly, but with a thread of steel behind every syllable.

His hands brushed her body and he couldn't resist letting his palm linger at her back for a moment where Repton couldn't see. She was trembling and he kept his hand in place far longer than he should have, attempting to offer whatever meager comfort he could.

Once the pump was ready, Diana flipped the lever and Repton struggled to hold the tube steady as he ran it over the mess he'd made. Unlike Diana, he allowed the opening to connect with the carpet, where it stayed.

"If you just—" Diana tried.

"I can manage on my own, Miss Ashby." Repton ignored her attempts to set him right and fumbled with the hose for a while longer before he finally understood the principle. "Oh yes," he said as the device cleared every scrap of detritus he'd deposited. "This works quite well."

Diana's face lit in a grin, and Aidan couldn't help but smile too.

"Can I assume that means you'd like to enter an order for a few devices, Repton?"

"Now let's not get ahead of ourselves, Iverson." The American dusted off his hands as if he'd just personally cleaned the floor with a brush and pan. "Have you created many of these devices, miss? Or is this your only prototype?"

"Currently, this is the only working model, but with Mr. Iverson's investment—"

"I ship out to New York in two weeks. Can you have five completed by then?"

Aidan could feel Diana's fear and uncertainty from

across the room, but he could also taste her eagerness. This was what she'd been waiting for.

"Yes," he told Repton confidently. Whatever she needed—supplies, tools, even warehouse space—he could provide to make this sale successful.

Diana clenched the edge of her skirt in her hands and cast him a questioning glance. "I'm not sure that's true."

"Well, is it or isn't it? Time waits for no man." Repton shifted his gaze between them, finally setting his perusal on Diana. "Or woman, Miss Ashby. I came here under the belief that you would have enough devices to make the journey worth my while."

"No promises of the sort were made, Repton," Aidan reminded his longtime business associate. "But we will ensure that you don't go back to America without five of Miss Ashby's machines. At least."

The old man did his usual squint, as if he was giving the matter deep thought. But Aidan knew he would capitulate. At least to this part. Wrangling over cost would be a separate matter. Aidan had stated a price in initial correspondence with the American, but he knew that negotiation over money was the aspect Wilbur Repton liked best.

"I shall check in a week on progress. If all is on track, we can discuss a final sum at that time."

"Very good." Aidan stepped forward to seal the verbal agreement with a handshake, as was Repton's way.

The old man wrenched his arm vigorously and offered one of his signature belly-deep chuckles. "It's very new. And a lady inventor. Might make for an interesting selling point."

"Indeed." Aidan patted the man on the back as he saw him toward the threshold. "We'll have progress to report in one week."

When he turned back to Diana, he half expected her to rush into his arms. If she didn't, he was considering rushing into hers.

"You've done it," he told her. Excitement bubbled inside him. Not the usual exaltation over an investment well-chosen or a project seen through to a successful end. It was the pleasure of knowing what joy this moment must give her.

Yet she didn't look at all joyful.

She'd settled her backside against the front of his desk and crossed her arms. "You remember I'm here now, do you?"

"Forgetting you would be quite impossible, Diana." He could easily get used to the sound of her name on his tongue. He liked dispensing with the formality between them.

"But you both did at the end. You deciding that we can do the impossible, and Repton spoke of me as if I wasn't still in the room."

They had been asses now that he thought back on the exchange. He'd gotten carried away with deal making and forgotten that it was as much her negotiation as his. "You're right. He's used to me. We've been business associates for years."

She lifted a hand and began nibbling on the edge of her finger. "We'll need materials. I'll need time in my workshop. Maybe even additional manpower."

"Can I assist you? I could help obtain whatever construction materials you need, and I have two useful hands."

Diana glanced down at his hands, and he wondered if she was imagining what he was—touching her, tracing the line of her jaw with his finger, shaping her waist, her hips, and all the curves he'd not yet explored.

She dropped her gaze to the carpet and swallowed hard. "I thought I was to assist you in finding a wife. That will take time too."

Aidan wasn't sure if she meant the words to hurt, but they stung like the jab of a knife. Most of all, he hated that she was right.

She began gathering the parts of her device and returning them to the case, shoving and dropping each piece into place. When she was done, she slammed the lid shut and attempted to heave the container onto her shoulder.

"Let me."

"I can manage."

But she couldn't, and she didn't argue or push him away when he approached and lifted the case into his arms. He let her lead and followed her to the front door. All that he wished to say remained tangled in the center of his chest.

"Have Thomas fetch a hansom for Miss Ashby," he told the maid. Then they stood in awkward silence in the hallway.

"Diana—" he finally started, unsure of where to begin, knowing only that he had to try.

"That was quick," she said when the clop of horses' hooves sounded on the bricks outside his town house. "It works best if we put the device in first before I climb in." She veritably sprinted for the carriage and waited while he maneuvered the box inside.

Once he was finished, he braced a hand on the carriage wall. Their bodies were inches apart.

"Diana, what happened in the study—"

"I have one more lady for you to meet," she said in a cool, clipped tone. "Her father is a duke's heir and will one day inherit. She's very beautiful."

"*You* are beautiful and clever and determined, and apparently inclined to pretend you didn't want that kiss as much as I did."

"I did." Diana dipped her head and stared at the cobblestones. He half expected her to take the admission back. When she looked at him, however, her gaze was resolute. "But we had an agreement, Mr. Iverson. You've kept your part of our bargain and I must keep mine."

"Agreements can be nullified. Altered." He didn't want to talk about bloody business. He was well aware of what he'd agreed to, but here in this moment with her, he didn't want money and matchmaking between them. He only wanted her.

"Tomorrow evening at seven. Can you take me in your carriage?"

Aidan swallowed hard at the images her question evoked. "Take you where?"

"The home of Lady Elizabeth Thorndyke and her father, the Marquess of Merton. They are hosting a spectacle of sorts and I've secured an invitation. I'm allowed to bring one guest."

Aidan frowned. "What sort of spectacle?"

She smiled back, and it was warm and open enough to give him hope. "Based on your taste in reading material, I think you'll approve. Lady Elizabeth is quite fond of ghost stories and specters and has decided to host a séance."

Aidan had heard of the faddish entertainment and its popularity with some in London society, but he'd never considered attending one himself. But an evening spent in Diana's company? "Very well. I'll come for you at half past six."

Chapter Nineteen

Oh."

That was the single word Aidan got out. Not even a word, really. Just a sound. A gasp of air.

Diana descended the stairs of her family's Cadogan Square home in a purple dress that hugged her curves as closely as he wished to. She'd arranged her hair in a pile of lovely curls that framed her face. But it was the look in her eyes that set his pulse racing.

She looked pleased to see him, her blue gaze lit with warmth.

He'd feared after the way they'd parted the day before that she'd wish to forget their kiss. But her eyes—lingering on him, open and eager—said otherwise.

He told himself to stop gaping, that they needed to depart for the Marquess of Merton's town house soon or risk being late. But there was no place else he wished to be.

"It may seem as if I've overdressed for this event."

"No, it does not."

She smiled. "Bess is rather exacting about fashion."

"Bess?"

"Lady Elizabeth."

Ah yes. The agreement that once made so much sense and now held as much appeal as a lifetime of nights spent at the opera.

Except, of course, there was the guarantee. He should never have asked her to offer herself up as a bride if he could make no match with the other ladies. Now, it was becoming increasingly clear that was the option he'd always preferred.

Diana Ashby drew him. She always had. Her confidence. Her fearlessness. From the moment they'd met. She'd drawn him with a pull as powerful as one of the magnets in her workshop. And now he knew with certainty that no duke's daughter or any other woman would ever intrigue him as she did.

Of course, he still harbored ambitions too. Almost every day the newspapers featured details about the exhibition being planned, and he was no closer to gaining entry to the Parthenon club or Lord Lockwood's good graces.

But none of that changed how much he wanted to kiss Diana again.

The question was whether she wanted the same.

"I've prepared a few notes." She lifted a slip of

paper from a reticule dangling from her wrist and offered it to him.

"Of course you have." He overreached when he extended his hand. Desperate to touch her, he let his fingers linger against hers a moment before retrieving the folded square of paper.

She didn't retreat, and he savored the little catch in her breath.

He looked down at the careful lines of ink and could barely muster an ounce of interest in the list of Lady Elizabeth Thorndyke's hobbies.

"What's this one?" he asked, pointing to a word he'd never seen before.

Diana leaned closer and he caught her rich rose perfume and something deeper, earthier, her own unique scent.

"Lepidopterology is the study of moths and butterflies," she told him very seriously, her brow furrowed as if his lack of knowledge on the topic appalled her.

Aidan pressed his lips together to stifle a smile.

"She's fond of other bugs too, but her mother has dissuaded her from collecting any more of them."

"Is there nothing people won't study?"

"I don't think there is." She walked behind him to collect a wrap that had been laid out on a table near the front door. "Everything is worth study, Mr. Iverson. All mysteries are worth solving."

"Didn't we agree you'd call me Aidan?"

"You asked." She dipped her head, almost shyly, then looked up with a devastating smile. "I didn't agree."

"Details of a negotiation are important."

"They are." Looking up toward the top of the stairs, she added more quietly, "My mother is ailing upstairs, but she has a very keen sense of hearing."

"I hope it's nothing serious."

"Thank you for being concerned. It's just a cold. My mother is very strong. She would refuse a doctor, even if she needed one."

Aidan suspected she was speaking of herself as much as her mother.

"She approves of me escorting you this evening?"

Diana swallowed and notched her chin up an inch. "I didn't ask her. I'm practically a spinster, and I loathe asking Dominick to chaperone."

Spinster, she was not. But Aidan decided not to argue her out of the claim. At least not now.

"Shall we depart?" He offered her his arm, and she stared a moment as if wary of touching him.

After much hesitation, she laid her hand against his sleeve and let him lead her to the carriage. He'd brought his own and liked settling inside with Diana on the opposite bench. A strange rush of possessiveness washed over him. He'd never imagined the simple act of sharing a carriage ride with a woman would bring him pleasure.

They rode in silence and he studied her profile as she gazed out the window. He wanted to trace his fingers along the lush curve of her lips, the tip of her nose, even her furrowed brow.

What worried her this evening? Was it the same stew of dread and anticipation he'd been struggling with all day?

The deal they'd made had once made sense to him. As logical and practical as any exchange he'd ever agreed to, but now all that made sense was this. Him. Her. Together and feeling the undeniable pull between them.

She'd worn gloves, and the fabric was stretched taut as she gripped her reticule like a drowning man grips a tow rope.

"I take it you reviewed my notes?" she asked quietly. "About Bess. She's very clever and has more interests than any of us."

"When will you provide me a list of your interests?"

She finally looked at him, her expression unreadable. "You know mine. I like taking things apart and creating something new from the pieces."

"And solving mysteries?"

"Are you asking me to help you with yours?"

"You know I can't do that. I won't embroil you in my history when I don't even know it myself."

The corner of her mouth tipped up. "I'm the one who chased off two thugs with the tip of my umbrella. You needn't protect me, Aidan."

The lady could convince him of nearly anything just by the way she said his name, the way she slowed over the two syllables when she was usually given to rushing through every sentence. It was madness to consider letting her assist him unravel the knot of his past. But tonight he was feeling reckless.

He reached inside his coat pocket and pulled out the envelope Callihan had given him. He'd examined it dozens of times since that day. The paper had been carefully cut, folded, and glued. Someone had taken time and care to create a container for the five pounds of charity Callihan received.

"I was given this by a man who claims he got it from my sister."

She took the envelope from him with infinite care, the way he handled one of his delicate ancient artifacts. "There's nothing to distinguish it, is there?"

"No writing. No watermark." Aidan looked onto the darkened streets passing by, considering how much to tell her. "He doesn't know her name or where she resides. I have an investigator who haunts the neighborhood now, in case she reappears."

"May I keep this? Just for a day or two."

"Is there something you can determine from it?" What she did in her laboratory was as deep a mystery to him as the veiled woman who'd visited Callihan.

"I don't want to promise anything, but I can examine it more closely in my workshop and see what I can do."

She nibbled on her bottom lip.

Aidan swallowed hard. He wanted to kiss her again. Tonight. Now.

Before he could say more or thank her, the carriage stopped in front of the Merton town house. Diana slid the envelope into her reticule and placed her hand in his as he assisted her down from the carriage.

"Remember," she said, after he'd knocked on the front door. "Bess is clever. She's also rather bold and likes to ask questions."

Aidan wondered if she realized she'd described herself. "Were you close?"

"Good friends, yes. Bess and I both share a love of science, though she is more interested in chemistry. We spent a great deal of time together in school. Some said we were so alike we could have been sisters." She glanced up at him, and her eyes sparkled in the glow of the lanterns on either side of the Mertons' front door. "But we are truly very different."

"How so?"

"Unlike me, Bess has always wished to marry."

A SERVANT ANSWERED the door and saved Diana from the confusion in Aidan's gaze.

She was a fool. When he was near, he made her feel too much. Her mind quieted and her heart took over. It was terrifying. Every moment that they shared, every detail they revealed, made her want more.

Now he'd entrusted her with a piece of his mystery. A link to his past that he so desperately wanted to uncover.

The gesture felt as intimate as the kiss they'd shared in his study.

"Diana, I'm so glad you've come." Bess emerged from the drawing room once the servant had taken their coats. She wrapped Diana in a welcoming embrace. "Remind me to show you some of the decorations we've purchased for the reunion."

When she turned to Aidan, one blond brow arched high. "You must be Mr. Iverson. Diana sent me a note to say you'd be accompanying her."

"Thank you for allowing me to join the event, Lady Elizabeth." He bowed like a perfect gentleman over Bess's hand. "I've never attended a séance before."

Bess smiled, and it was an expression Diana knew well. The smile of challenge. Which usually meant her friend was about to mount an assault.

"I sense skepticism, Mr. Iverson," Bess said as she led them to the drawing room. "Come and meet the other guests. I'm afraid my father is at his club and my mother is indisposed this evening." She gestured as they entered the room. "But may I present Mr. Harker; Miss Gwendoline Ives; and her betrothed, Lord Egerton. Diana, I believe you two have met."

Diana stared in horror. Egerton was the last man in London she wanted to see.

"Miss Ashby and I are very briefly acquainted. My friendship is with her brother, Dominick." Though he didn't sneer, Diana doubted anyone in the room missed the disdain in Egerton's tone.

Aidan stepped closer. She felt the heat of him at her back, and his nearness gave her an odd sense of comfort that even Egerton's presence couldn't dispel.

"Are you all right?" he whispered low enough that only she could hear.

"The last time I saw him, we didn't part on pleasant terms," she told him quietly.

"Is he the one?" he whispered. "The unwanted proposal you spoke of?"

"Yes."

"Well, then I think I'm beholden to dislike him."

Diana inhaled sharply and fought the tickle of laughter that bubbled up. When Aidan placed a hand on her lower back and guided her to an empty settee, she let the frustration of encountering Egerton go. He was no longer any concern of hers.

"The room is ready, my lady." A servant waited on the threshold and directed them to a larger room across the hall.

Aidan followed close behind, almost protectively, and they took chairs side by side at the long, polished table that had been set out for the event.

"Oh, there are table cards," Bess told the guests. "Please sit in the spot you were assigned."

Diana's stomach churned at the sight of Egerton's card next to hers. Aidan's, it seemed, was on the opposite side of the table next to Bess. That made sense. Diana had been clear in her note to her friend about the intentions for their visit.

Once everyone was seated, the lights were dimmed and every candle snuffed. Faces were cast in shadows, and Diana kept her gaze on Aidan's.

In the darkness, someone moved toward the table with a light source. It was a glass bowl glowing with a greenish light that had a distinctive garlicky smell. Diana knew immediately how they'd created the illumination.

"Phosphorous?" Aidan mouthed at her from across the table.

She offered him a flash of a smile in return, and he grinned in triumph as if pleased to impress her with a bit of scientific knowledge. Someday she'd tell him about her experiments with phosphorescent illumination.

Her heartbeat ratcheted up. Someday. She was already planning a future with a man she was attempting to match to one of her friends. A friend who leaned over, whispered to him, and made him chuckle at whatever humorous quip she'd shared.

Bess had always been like that. Intellectually, they were fairly matched, but when it came to charm and socializing, Lady Elizabeth had always excelled.

"There are many spirits here tonight." The lady who'd deposited the glowing bowl had taken a seat at the head of the table. She was petite, dark-haired, and garbed in black from head to toe.

"Prepare yourself for the fakery," Egerton whispered too close to her cheek.

Diana eased away from him, and across from her, Aidan's hand balled into a fist. He looked ready to climb across the table if Egerton gave her trouble.

"I am prepared for anything, Lord Egerton," Diana quipped in reply.

She liked Aidan's protectiveness far too much. Oddly, it gave her confidence to deal with Egerton without his interference.

"Samuel," Miss Ives said softly, "the medium has directed us all to clasp hands."

Diana hadn't heard the woman's directive, and the last thing she wanted was to hold on to Egerton, but when he extended his hand palm up, she took it gingerly. Thank goodness she was wearing gloves.

Across the table, Bess had Aidan's hand clasped tightly too.

"Lady Elizabeth has asked to speak to her brother," the medium intoned in an odd singsong voice. "We will ask the spirits to speak to us."

The conjurer bowed her head, allowing the phosphorescent glow to cast her delicate-boned face in eerie shadows. "The brother says he misses you, Lady Elizabeth."

Bess let out a whimper. "What else does he say?"

"That you should follow your heart, my lady."

Bess turned her gaze shyly toward Aidan.

For a long while, the room filled with a strange tension. No one spoke. Diana wondered if anyone even breathed. They were all waiting, but she wasn't certain what they were waiting for.

"Another spirit comes," the medium said, her pitch rising.

Diana rolled her eyes in the semidarkness. She guessed that the medium would fabricate a dead family member for all of them. Nothing in her believed that the petite woman at the head of the table was truly speaking to spirits, but it didn't matter.

The séance wasn't truly the point of this evening. Matchmaking was why they'd come.

"Speak to us," the medium droned.

Diana drew in a long breath and chastised herself. She had no right to loathe the notion of Aidan marrying her closest schoolmate, but she did. Sitting across from them, staring at their clasped hands, a sickening mix of emotions built inside her. Jealousy was easy. That green biting envy welled up quickly.

But fear came too, and a gnawing uncertainty.

She hadn't quite worked out all that she felt for Aidan. She only knew that he made her feel. Not calculate or plan or engineer. Just feel. And, unexpectedly, she wanted more.

"A man. A father. He wishes to speak to the young lordling."

Egerton's fingers tightened on her hand and Diana winced.

"He says you must not squander the family's fortune."

"How dare you?" Egerton shot up from his chair.

Diana reclaimed her hand and rubbed at the spot where he'd pinched her.

"Lord Egerton, please sit down." Bess was using the no-nonsense tone she'd employed as a volunteer matron in their dormitory at Bexley. "You did know the evening could be provoking. I warned everyone."

Egerton scowled and remained standing. "I do not wish to be provoked by a charlatan."

All eyes shifted to the medium.

"What the lady said was a very impertinent thing to say," Miss Ives put in, her voice soft and youthful. "She should apologize."

Diana knew from long acquaintance that Bess Thorndyke could be a stubborn young woman.

"You are interrupting the spirits, Lord Egerton," Bess said in a cool, clear voice. "If you no longer wish to participate, feel free to depart."

"Elizabeth," Miss Ives squeaked. "Samuel is to be my husband and part of our family."

"I cannot work in such discord," the medium said tightly. "The spirits will not come."

Bess pushed her chair back and stood. "Would you

excuse us, Diana and Mr. Iverson? I would like to speak to my cousin and Lord Egerton a moment."

They stood and shuffled from the darkened room. Diana stepped into the drawing room where they'd gathered before the séance and Aidan followed close behind. He pulled the pocket doors almost shut behind them.

Diana sensed unspoken words from him. A strange energy buzzed in the air. She glanced at the carpet, the wallpaper, a gilded painting glowing in the light of a candlelit sconce.

"Bess likes you," finally made it through her lips. It wasn't what she wished to say. Only the words she knew she should say.

"How can you tell?" he asked, stepping toward the wall to examine a vivid painting of a battlefield.

"The way she looks at you is telling."

"How does she look at me, Diana?" He turned back to face her, those searching green eyes of his scanning her face.

"As if she's pleased with what she sees."

He grinned. A tantalizing flash of white. A cool shiver chased down Diana's spine, but other parts of her warmed. Her neck, her chest, and lower all the way to her thighs. To her very center.

"And you?" He had the audacity to quirk one auburn brow.

The scoundrel knew the answer.

"Sometimes I like you a great deal, Mr. Iverson."

Aidan came forward with such a look of determination that Diana almost stumbled back.

He cupped her face in his hands and swept his thumbs across her cheeks. He studied her lips, traced the edge with his fingertip. He was stoking her like a fire, and just when she thought she might burst into flames, his mouth came down on hers.

Not a gentle kiss. A hungry, searching joining. He dipped his tongue inside to taste her, stroked his fingers along her cheek, down her neck.

She wrapped one hand around his lapel to pull him closer and slid the other over his chest, all the way up to the taut muscles of his neck.

When he lifted his head, they were both breathless.

"First of all, stop calling me Mr. Iverson." He dipped his head to kiss her again. "And secondly, sometimes isn't good enough. I'd prefer you like me all the time."

"That seems a great deal to ask." Diana placed a hand on his chest, felt the firm swell of his muscles beneath. Relished the wild thrash of his heart, beating every bit as fast as her own. "And do you truly think a kiss is the way to convince me?"

His hand came up and settled over hers, as if he wished to keep her touching him for as long as he could.

"I'm willing to consider other suggestions."

Footsteps sounded in the hallway and Diana's heart skipped a beat. She jolted back out of Aidan's arms.

"We're ready to resume," Miss Ives said from the threshold before retreating back across the hall.

Aidan made no move to leave.

Diana stayed too. Not because she was uncertain of what to do. She knew what she should do. She had an instinct for practicality and knew exactly what a sensible young lady would do.

But not with him. He brought out some other part of herself that she rarely set free. A side driven by feelings and impulse, and emotions that frightened and thrilled her.

"We should join the others." Getting the words out was the first step, but she still hadn't taken the next and moved toward the doors. "Bess will wonder why we've lingered here."

"I have no more desire to return to that room than you do," he said from over her shoulder.

"But this is the deal we made." Clinging to their agreement seemed a shield she could hold up to protect herself from risking everything. Her heart. Her future. Her work.

And his future too. A noble wife was what he wanted.

She frowned as she turned back to him. "Why do you wish to marry?"

"Diana—"

"Why were you so eager to do so that you made a deal to fund a device you don't even believe in?"

"I believe in you. And now that I know what you're capable of, I believe in your device too."

His words were like a balm she didn't realize she desperately needed. It felt good to simply hear someone say he believed in her. It felt extraordinary to hear Aidan give her that assurance.

But she still wanted an answer. "I assume that as an untitled gentleman, you want the connections that marriage to a noble bride will bring."

His jaw tightened as he held her gaze. "Yes. That's what I wanted."

"I'm not a noblewoman, and I don't want the things that ladies like Sophie and Grace do. I can't bring you what you want."

"I remember our deal, Diana." There was such disappointment in his gaze that her breath tangled in her throat. Moving past her, he strode toward the room across the hall, but midway he stopped and glanced at her over his shoulder. "Perhaps I'm just not content with the terms anymore."

Chapter Twenty

$\mathcal{F}$or a week after the séance at Lady Elizabeth Thorndyke's home, Aidan did what he did best: he buried himself in work and did his damnedest not to think about Diana Ashby and the deal they'd made.

He was a fool for wanting what he could not have, especially when the opportunity to have what he'd longed for—connections, status, access to places of power that would always be closed to a commoner— was in his grasp.

Unfortunately, none of the noblewomen to whom he'd been introduced was the one lady who persisted in his thoughts day and night.

Diana was right. She had fulfilled her part of their bargain.

Yet here he sat, scribbling notes for an upcoming meeting and thinking chiefly of one dark-haired lady inventor.

A pile of papers sat at the edge of his desk, beckoning him. Diana's notes on all her friends. They'd spent most of the week in a drawer, but this morning he'd pulled them out. He'd told himself to attempt to find something among the lists and notes regarding her friends that appealed to him half as much as Diana herself.

It had proved a futile effort. Now something caused him to reach for the pages once more.

The notes on Miss Grinstead, he crumpled and set aside. The lady seemed utterly smitten with her young man. Though Aidan doubted her family would ever allow the match, she seemed steel-willed enough to find a way to marry the lad.

Lady Sophie was too fond of frivolity and giggling. He couldn't imagine a lifetime of the lady's high-pitched titter filling his ears.

In truth, the only real possibility was Lady Elizabeth. She had been kind the evening of her séance. He tapped his finger on Lady Elizabeth's list. Only one detail interested him. She had been matron of Diana's dormitory at their finishing school, and Diana said they'd been good friends. Though he had no desire to marry the lady, that didn't mean there wasn't merit in speaking to her about Diana.

"Coggins," he shouted through his half-open door.

The young man appeared a moment later.

"I'm afraid I won't be able to keep my next appointment this afternoon. Have a message sent to him, will you? We can reschedule for next week."

"Very good, sir." Coggins began to back out.

"Actually, do the same for the later appointment too."

The boy stuck his head in again. "Yes, Mr. Iverson."

Aidan donned his suit jacket and overcoat and made his way down to the street. He hailed a cab and directed him to the Merton town house. Calling unexpectedly might be considered bad form, but he couldn't resist the opportunity to learn more about Diana.

He was admitted by a friendly housemaid and waited in the same drawing room he'd visited a week prior. Strange how the room seemed cool and lifeless now. He'd remembered it as a more vibrant color, but the only thing he could truly recall was the rich purple of Diana's dress. The bright enticing blue of her eyes.

"Mr. Iverson." Lady Elizabeth entered the room and offered her hand in greeting. "You weren't frightened away by talk of spirits the other evening. How refreshing."

"I thought we were talking *to* spirits." He took the seat she indicated and crossed one leg over the other while she sat on the opposite settee and arranged her skirts. "Are the séances meant as a test to put off feckless potential suitors?"

"No. But perhaps they should be. Thank you for the idea."

After Lady Elizabeth had poured them both a cup of tea, she settled back against the cushions and assessed him over the gilded rim of porcelain as she took a sip.

"You didn't come here today as a potential suitor, did you, Mr. Iverson?"

"No." Aidan offered her a tight smile. He had no wish to insult the noblewoman, but he had no intention of feigning interest either.

"You haven't offended me, sir. I promise. Tell me why you've come to call."

"I wish to know whatever you're willing to tell me about Miss Ashby."

Lady Elizabeth's eyes widened in surprise. "I thought you two were well acquainted. Perhaps I assumed too much when she asked you to accompany her last week."

"Miss Ashby and I are . . . quite recently acquainted." He could hardly confess the truth. On the face of it, their agreement was inappropriate. He was beginning to wonder why it had made so much sense that day in Diana's laboratory.

But of course Diana was the reason he'd agreed. He'd been half smitten with her then. He was afraid to name what he was now.

"What would you like to know?"

Aidan worked his jaw and considered all his questions. Finally, he pulled one of Diana's lists from his coat pocket and handed it to Lady Elizabeth.

"Miss Ashby agreed to introduce me to eligible marriage-minded noblewomen."

"Like me?"

"Yes. For each lady she introduced me to, she produced a list like that one." He waited until she'd finished reading and chuckling under her breath at the effusive way her friend had described her. "I would like a similar list about Miss Ashby. You needn't write anything down, of course, but I'd like to know what you can tell me about her interests, her motivations."

Lady Elizabeth cast him a sympathetic grin. "Diana is not terribly mysterious. One of the things I like best about her is that she is utterly bereft of pretense. She truly loves her science and engineering and inventions. Occasionally, I've seen her play the piano or ride a horse for pleasure, but for the most part I remember her as a young woman who was driven to create and make sure others understood the usefulness of her designs."

"Do you know why she doesn't wish to marry?"

"Most of us at Bexley had moments of rejecting the notion of marriage. Surprising, perhaps, to hear about a group of young ladies sent away to a finishing school. I recall one classmate who was the most vehement disbeliever. She insisted marriage was an institution designed to subjugate women."

"Is that what Diana believed?" he asked Lady Elizabeth.

"I don't think so. Diana wants exactly what she says: she wants her inventions to succeed."

"The device she's created can succeed." Aidan admitted to himself that he hadn't been a believer when she'd presented her idea to the Duke's Den. But now, he understood how the device could be useful. "I believe in Diana, and I should have seen the potential in her invention."

"That's wonderful news." Lady Elizabeth beamed.

"So once Diana has the success she craves, what will she think of marriage?"

The noblewoman's mouth curved. "Unfortunately, the medium took her crystal ball with her when she departed the other evening, Mr. Iverson."

"Your best guess, Lady Elizabeth."

"I'm not a woman who offers guesses freely." She took another sip of her tea. "I prefer facts. A bit like Diana."

All his life, Aidan had been willing to take risks. He'd run away from the workhouse with nothing but the clothes on his back. He'd learned the ins and outs of gaming and risked pence and pounds in back alley betting for years before building his fortune. He owned a gambling club, for bloody sake.

But this was a different sort of gamble. One with consequences that he feared might break him in ways that the loss of money never could. While he sat stewing, Lady Elizabeth continued sipping her tea and casting him a skin-prickling look of assessment.

"You can tell me nothing to ensure I might win her?" That was it. The heart of why he'd come. The most open appeal he could make.

She tipped her head and her expression softened. Aidan had the sense she was considering whether to take pity on him. Finally, she drew in a long breath and let it out on a sigh.

Leaning forward slightly on the settee, she cast him a sympathetic grin. "Without risk, Mr. Iverson, is there any real value in the reward?"

DIANA LIFTED THE hammer again and again, working the strip of copper into the proper shape to fit into her third device. The metal gave way and formed itself against the wooden structure underneath beautifully. She was getting better at this part. Nothing like repeating the same processes over and over to become proficient.

"We're going, Di," Dominick called from the conservatory threshold.

Her next strike went wide and nearly caught her hand where she held the edge of metal in place.

"When will you return?" Diana hadn't paid close attention to the details of her brother and mother's outing. She only knew that they were answering a long put-off dinner invitation from a family friend.

"Late mostly likely." Dom applied his gloves and sounded as unenthusiastic as Diana had been at the prospect.

They'd all been invited, but Diana insisted she could not spare the time. That had turned into an argument and then another, until her mother finally capitulated and allowed her to beg off. It wasn't so much that Mama understood her need to spend every moment she could working on the devices for Mr. Repton, only that she'd tired of trying to change Diana's mind.

But this had nothing to do with stubbornness. Mr. Repton's deadline was fast approaching and she needed five devices in perfect working order by the end of the next week.

"There's apparently to be a musical performance, then dinner, then parlor games," Dom said in a miserable drone. "Wish me luck. Or simply knock me over the head with that hammer now. You choose."

Diana laughed and stood to stretch out the knots in her back and shoulders before approaching her brother.

"You'll survive, I promise."

"Not if someone plays the harpsichord. I have an almost preternatural loathing of that sound. Either I will destroy the instrument or it will destroy me."

Diana reached up to straighten his askew tie. "I'm glad you're taking this all in good stride." She winked at him.

"Be amused. You, in your metal-filled tower. I'll do the honorable thing and endure an evening of hellish entertainment for the both of us."

"You're very like a knight in shining armor."

"Tell Lady Sophie that." The moment the quip was out, his eyes widened and he attempted to cover the admission with a choked guffaw.

"Perhaps I will, brother dear. Perhaps I will."

"Don't," he said softly.

"Dominick." Their mother's call was muffled and barely audible.

"Go and enjoy yourself as much as you can."

Dom glanced around her crowded workshop, more cluttered now with the addition of materials for the five devices and three completed models. "Don't hammer or nail yourself to anything, and don't let anything combust."

"I haven't burned the house down yet."

He finally lightened as he departed, casting one of his charming grins over his shoulder at her.

Diana resumed her seat at the workbench and gripped her hammer. She ran her fingers over the copper, feeling for the spots that still needed shaping. When she'd determined where, she attacked the metal again.

A series of knocks rattled through the house and she turned her head a fraction just as the hammer struck the spot where she was holding the copper in place. Her thumb took the brunt of the strike. Shooting pain lanced up her arm, and she let her hammer clatter to the floor. Lifting her hand to examine her thumb, she realized her whole arm was shaking from the pain.

Tears streaked down her face, as if her body was determined to let the discomfort out somehow.

Still the banging continued. A visitor was at the front door and, for some reason, none of the servants seemed capable of answering.

She stood up from her chair and fought a wave of dizziness. The sharp sting had turned into a torturous throb and the edge of her thumb had begun to redden and bruise. She hadn't broken the nail and she could move the digit enough to convince herself she hadn't done any permanent damage. But it hurt like hell.

As she headed down the hall, she encountered the housekeeper.

"Sorry for the delay, miss. I can fetch the door."

"It's all right. I'll greet the visitor, but would you bring some ice and rags to my workshop, Mrs. Rudd?"

The older woman's face furrowed with concern when she noticed how Diana was sheltering one hand with the other.

"You've hurt yourself, miss. I knew it would come to that eventually."

Diana tamped down the flare of irritation. "I'll be fine. Just see to the ice."

Whoever was at the front door knocked again and it took her last vestiges of restraint not to shout at them to stop. After a quick swipe of her cheeks, she turned the knob with her undamaged hand and held the other close against her chest.

"Diana." Aidan cast her a look that was equal parts surprise and pleasure to find her answering the door. His mouth began to lift in a smile until he noticed her swollen thumb. "My God, what's happened?"

He began to reach for her and she instinctively pulled back, tucking her hand closer to her chest.

"An accident. Nothing serious. It won't slow me down. I can still get the five devices completed by the end of the week."

"To hell with the devices. Let me take a look at your wound." He stepped inside, shrugged out of his coat, and deposited it in an unceremonious heap on the entry table.

"The housekeeper is bringing some ice back to the workshop." Diana hated the tremulous quality of her voice. She realized it wasn't just her hand that was shaking. Her whole body had turned clammy and she couldn't stem a case of shivers.

"Lead the way," Aidan told her and then gathered his coat in one hand before following her.

Once she was seated in her workshop chair, he settled the garment around her shoulders. She didn't protest. The chills persisted, even though the pain in her thumb had begun to wane.

"How did it happen?" Aidan retrieved one of her wooden stools and sat in front of her. He offered his open palm, not touching her but indicating that she should place her hand in his.

"The hammer. I was shaping that bit of copper." Diana laid her injured hand gingerly in Aidan's palm and indicated the tool and project she'd abandoned. "I missed."

"Just as you requested, miss." The housekeeper entered the conservatory with a bowl of ice and a handful of rags, but she jerked to a stop when she noticed Aidan cupping Diana's hand.

"Shall I call for a doctor?" she asked pointedly.

"Perhaps you should," Aidan told her.

"No, you should not, Mrs. Rudd. The ice will take down the swelling and I'll have a fearsome bruise. No doctor required. Thank you," she told the older woman to stop her from gaping.

When the housekeeper retreated, Aidan leaned closer and ran his fingers gently along the edge of her hand. "Does it feel as bad as it looks?" Her nail had begun to discolor to a bluish plum shade and the skin of her entire thumb was still flushed a bright, angry reddish pink.

"It does hurt a bit."

Aidan seemed to admire her attempt at stoicism, but he didn't look as if he believed a word. "So what you're saying is it's agony?" he asked lightly.

"Yes." Diana pressed her lips together to keep from smiling.

"I have a flask in my carriage if you'd like me to retrieve it." When she simply offered a quizzical look in reply he added, "Whiskey. To help with the pain."

"I'll be fine. The pain is beginning to wane." The throb had grown duller, but Aidan's presence was a welcome distraction too. Focusing on him allowed her to fixate less on the pain. The gentle back and forth stroke of his thumb against the base of hers was soothing. She was grateful for his arrival, but it begged the question. "What are you doing here?"

He looked taken aback by the question, as if he hadn't expected it or hadn't prepared an answer. "I wished to see . . . how you're progressing with production. If you needed help, I intended to offer my services."

A strangled chuckle burst from her lips and he looked momentarily affronted.

"What services do you have to offer, Mr. Iverson?"

He narrowed one green eye at her. "A great deal fewer for a lady who addresses me so formally."

"And if I call you Aidan?"

He slid his gaze over her face and leaned an inch closer.

Diana forgot the pain, forgot to breathe. He was going to kiss her again and she wanted him to. Desperately.

One inch closer and his knees bumped hers.

She lifted her uninjured hand to touch his cheek, to feel the rough brush of stubble, the hard edge of his jaw. He waited, seeming not to breathe, until she lowered her head and pressed her lips to his.

Aidan responded instantly but gently, allowing her to take the lead, to taste and slide her tongue along his lush bottom lip. When she broke the kiss, his eyes were glazed with the same hunger she felt thrumming inside.

She edged closer to him on her chair, spreading her legs to let one of his knees rest between hers. The movement caused her thumb to bump his and she let out a whimper of pain.

Immediately, he lifted his hand. "I'm sorry."

"It's my fault. I was too eager."

Keeping his gaze fixed on her hand, he smiled. "I like your eagerness."

With infinite care, he slid back and rose from the stool where he sat. He approached the worktable where Mrs. Rudd had left the bowl of now partially melted ice. After soaking a rag in the cold water, he wrapped the chips of ice inside.

"See if this helps at all." He offered her the ice-filled rag and then bent to retrieve the hammer she'd left on the floor. "Now tell me what to do with this to help you finish your work."

A painful lump rose in her throat. She never let her mother into her workshop, and Dom was only ever allowed if he vowed not to touch anything. No one had ever come with the intent of assisting her.

"You see the spots where the metal isn't quite flat and fully flush against the shape beneath? Those need to be worked on."

"I can do that." He scooted his stool over toward where she'd been working and began tentatively.

"You can hit it harder. The metal won't break."

He did as she bid him, and he continued the work with impressive persistence. There wasn't a moment's disagreement when she redirected him to another spot on the metal or advised him how best to hold the hammer.

He was the most handsome, competent, and agreeable assistant she could have ever imagined.

Though there was little she could do with a rag wrapped around one hand, Aidan made it feel as if they were working in tandem. He asked her questions about her design as he worked

"Anything else?" he finally asked when the copper piece was finished.

Diana hesitated, uncertain whether she should ask him to do more.

"I want to help. I'm here to help," he insisted.

She pointed to another sheet of unhammered copper. "The same needs to be done to that piece and the one below it."

Without hesitation, he retrieved a fresh plate of copper and began shaping it over the wooden block. His strikes with the hammer were already deft. After a few moments of working away at the metal, he paused and tipped a grin at her over his shoulder. "Banging away like this is strangely satisfying. I could get used to it."

Diana's heart leaped in her chest. He'd made the comment lightly, his voice full of amusement, but the feelings it evoked were deeper. So potent that they frightened her.

He looked so strangely right in her workshop, just as his lips felt perfect against her own. They always had. Even before she knew his name.

"Yes," she whispered, unsure if he heard her. "I could get used to this too."

When he continued working, she unwrapped her finger and approached, resting her hands gently on his shoulders. He stilled, but the muscles of his shoulders bunched and flexed under her touch. Then he laid down the hammer and pivoted on his seat to face her.

"Thank you," she told him.

His eyes were bright, his mouth softened into a half smile. "You know those are words I will always owe to you, since the night we met."

"You can consider that debt repaid."

He chuckled. "After an hour of work? I must teach you to drive a harder bargain."

"In that case, I ask for a bit more than your labor."

Standing, he moved an inch closer, until their chests brushed in a delicious friction. "What else can I do for you, Miss Ashby?"

Diana twined her arms around his neck and lifted off her heels. He caught her around the waist, and every heated inch of him warmed her.

"Just this," she whispered before pressing her mouth to his. She kissed him boldly, slipping her tongue inside to taste him, nipping at his lip before she kissed him again.

He let out a moan when she stroked her fingers against his neck and tightened his hold on her waist, but he let her take the lead when their mouths met again and again.

When she lowered onto her heels, he bent and pressed his forehead to hers. They were both hot, breathless, and there wasn't an inch of space between their bodies.

"Is that enough?" he asked in a teasing tone.

She couldn't answer. Her body was humming with need and her heart ached with tenderness that frightened her. She was afraid of the answer too, because the kiss wasn't enough.

She wanted much more.

Chapter Twenty-One

Diana blew a stray hair from her brow and tightened the bolt into place. A strange sensation rushed through her, a wave of relief mixed with a heady thrill of victory.

She was finished. Five machines crowded her workshop, the metal polished and gleaming, every piece fixed in place, and all had been tested successfully.

Air whooshed from her lungs on a sigh, but the moment she relaxed onto her stool, exhaustion threatened to sweep in. She noticed the aches in her shoulders and back. Too many hours had passed since she'd stood and moved or had anything to eat.

"I've done it," she said to the empty workshop and five machines that had once been only an idea in her mind. "We've done it," she added more quietly.

Aidan had helped make this moment possible. She

wanted to tell him. He needed to know that she'd fulfilled their promise to Repton, and a day early.

Glancing at the hammer on her workbench, she recalled his hands curved around it, how diligently he'd worked to help her. And their kiss, and all the kisses before that one.

Her machines were done. Success was close enough to taste. But the joy of victory felt incomplete.

Somewhere along the way, what she wanted had shifted. She still craved success with her inventions, to see them put to good use. To be taken seriously as an inventor.

But now she wanted more. She couldn't deny her feelings, however they might complicate everything she and Aidan had agreed to.

She wanted him, and the need to tell him, to show him what she felt, was as strong as any desire she'd ever known. Whatever else might happen, whatever the future might hold, tonight she wanted to tell him the truth and hold nothing back.

She grabbed a rag and rubbed bits of grease from her fingers, then she untied her smock and headed for her room to wash and change.

"Diana? Is that you?" her mother called out from the drawing room.

"Mama, I was just going out." She hovered on the threshold, trying to avoid getting drawn into a long conversation.

"Of course you are, my dear. We all are. Have you forgotten that we're to dine with your uncle this evening?" Her mother flicked a hand toward her. "Go and prepare, Diana, so that we aren't late. And wear one of your ball gowns. I think he plans for a bit of dancing."

"Mama, I can't go tonight." There was virtually no part of her plan that she could explain to her mother. "I have an appointment that I must keep."

"Yes, you do. With your family." Her mother took on the stern look she wore when pleading and arguments would no longer have any effect on her resolve. "You're out unchaperoned far too often or hidden away in your workshop. Tonight you will accompany your family."

Diana nodded. She'd been working so feverishly to finish her devices, she'd barely spoken to her mother or Dominick in days. Accompanying them seemed unavoidable.

But as she made her way upstairs, her thoughts were on Aidan. She was determined that the night wouldn't end without seeing him.

AIDAN COULD NEVER decide whether it was worse attending someone else's party or hosting one's own. Two days after his visit to Diana's workshop, he sat on an overstuffed chair at the edge of his drawing room and decided that, at least on this night, playing host was most definitely worse.

Of course, it wasn't truly a party. Just a gathering of minds. He usually enjoyed gathering thinkers together to discuss myriad topics. He'd hosted dinner parties with conversation that focused on everything from industrial inventions to Peel's governmental reforms to the state of banking in the City.

Tonight he couldn't concentrate as the conversation ebbed and flowed around the topic of transportation. Present were a railroad engineer, the designer of a steamship, and two young men who vowed their steam-powered horseless carriage would soon be as popular on London's streets as an omnibus.

On any other night, the debates and discussion would have intrigued Aidan, and he would have hoped, if nothing else, a fresh investment opportunity might arise from the evening. But tonight, he just wanted everyone gone. A report from one of his investigators lay unopened on his study desk. In the busyness of preparing for the evening, he hadn't yet found time to read the report.

He swigged back the last drops of whiskey in his tumbler and was ridiculously pleased when the clock chimed the ten o'clock hour. It was early by the standards of many London parties, but Aidan had long ago designated it as the time when his gatherings drew to an end.

A couple of guests recognized the cue and began taking their leave.

Within half an hour, his drawing room was messy but blessedly empty and quiet. He rang for a maid and made his way back to his study, tugging at the knot of his tie and sliding it off as he entered the room. As soon as he settled in his desk chair, he heard someone rapping at the front door. Ignoring the sound, he slid a penknife across the letter from his Bow Street Runner. A guest often left some discarded personal item. He assumed one of the staff would retrieve it and send them on their way.

After meeting with Callihan, he'd asked his investigators to scour court records, but there was no record of a Mary Iverson ever being charged with any crime in Greater London for the years prior to his mother's death. There were also some notations regarding the Earl of Wyndham. If the investigators' information was to be believed, Wyndham had been abroad for months prior to Aidan's birth, though the investigator could not determine exact dates. The estimate made it improbable, though not impossible, that the man was his sire.

Of course, with no leads to offer, his investigator hadn't discovered a hint about Aidan's sister either.

"Bloody hell." Aidan pinched the bridge of his nose with his thumb and forefinger and fought the urge to tear the written report into shreds.

"Bad evening?"

Aidan snapped his head up and wondered if he was

dreaming. Diana stood in the doorway of his study, looking beautiful and nervous. She bit her lip as she watched him, and he realized that rather than greet her like a gentleman, he was staring at her like a starving man.

"Diana, come in." He stood and ushered her into the room.

She wore a pretty blue evening gown with a bodice that dipped low to display her neck and shoulders to mouthwatering advantage. The fabric was a paler blue than the sapphire richness of her eyes. He wondered what event she'd come from in such formal garb.

"My mother dragged Dom and me to dinner at my uncle's house." She nibbled at her lip again. "My father's brother, Sir William Ashby. I like him well enough but he's vehemently against any lady in the family doing anything like work. Obviously, he doesn't approve of me."

When she finally took a breath, a flush of pink colored her cheeks. She seemed to realize she'd been rambling and ducked her head.

"How did you get away?" Aidan never dreamed it was so easy for unmarried young gentlewomen to escape any kind of chaperone, yet Diana had done it repeatedly since they'd met.

"Oh, I simply left the house and hired a cab. Mama is abed and Dominick ventured out to one of his usual haunts."

"And you came here." Aidan approached and indicated the settee. "Would you like to sit?"

"No, I didn't come to sit."

He couldn't hide his smile. "Well, I'm glad you came, whatever the reason. Shall I ring for tea or would you prefer to join me while I partake of something stronger?"

When she didn't answer, he made his way to a cart near the far bookcase and poured himself two fingers of whiskey. He glanced back at Diana and caught her perusing his body, her gaze finally trailing up to his face.

"I came to tell you that I'm finished with the order for Mr. Repton."

"That's wonderful." A surge of pride bubbled in his chest. "You're ahead of schedule." He glanced down at the thumb she'd injured a few days before and marveled at her endless determination and tenacity.

"I still need to do some testing. I have ensured that every model works, but I want to test again and probably once more for good measure before we hand them over to Repton."

"You know I'm happy to assist you if needed."

"I know." She took a step closer to him and then another. "May I?" she asked, staring down at the tumbler in his hands.

"Of course." Aidan let her take the glass and watched as she sipped.

Her eyes widened and she coughed. "Strong," she managed on a hoarse whisper.

"Deliciously so," he said before retrieving the glass and placing his lips precisely where hers had lain against the cut crystal. He swigged down a dram and was tempted to swallow the rest when she reached up for the glass once more.

"Easy," he told her on a chuckle.

She tipped the tumbler back and swallowed every last drop.

"As soon as I finished the last device, I knew I needed to come tell you. Any success I find with this invention, it wouldn't have happened without your help."

"Someone would have invested. Your idea is sound and practical." He was glad that he'd been the one to help her and proud of what she'd achieved.

"As I told you, I never wanted any other investor. Just you."

Yes. He was definitely dreaming. That raw desire in Diana's eyes. He'd seen that in his dreams before. The lady had been coming to him in his dreams since the night he'd met her in Belgravia.

But when she reached for him, one hand braced against the center of his chest, he knew it was real and he didn't want it to end. Immediately, he clasped his hand over hers. His body hardened even as he marveled at the softness of her skin.

"On the carriage ride here, I told myself I simply wanted to give you the good news. But that was a lie." She swallowed and stared up at him. "I want more."

"Tell me what you want, Diana."

"You."

She breathed the single syllable once, but it echoed in his ears, sweeter with each reverberation. He was tempted to ask her to say it again.

"I want this night with you," she said on a husky murmur.

"I—"

Before he could agree, she pressed two fingers to his lips. "I know you'll tell me about propriety and warn me against ruination."

Aidan kissed the pads of her fingertips and smiled. When she removed her fingers, he told her, "I fear you give me too much credit. I was only going to agree." He wrapped a hand around her waist and pulled her closer, praying she could feel through the fabric of her skirt and petticoat just how much he wanted to agree to her request.

"I need you to do something that won't be easy." Her gaze turned earnest and intense.

He knew precisely what he wanted to do with her. All the ways he wanted to touch and tempt and worship her. All of it would be easy. Every moment with her was easy. It was part of why she intoxicated him.

"Tell me," he urged. "Whatever you need, I'll give you."

She drew in a deep breath. "I need you to refrain from thinking about the future."

His breath tangled in his throat. He understood what she was asking and he knew precisely how difficult it would be, if not impossible. But rather than deter her, he nodded. He couldn't deny her anything. Ever.

"We'll only have tonight," she said as she fitted her body against him, then lifted her hands to his shoulders. "Just promise me that for tonight we'll only think of these hours. Not tomorrow. Not any other moment than here and now."

He bent his head to kiss her.

She tasted of his whiskey and everything he'd ever wanted. When she moaned against his lips, he felt the echo of it reverberating through his body.

For some reason, she was offering him everything, and God how he wanted it. But a tiny voice in his head warned him to take care.

He knew with utter certainty that he didn't deserve her, but he desired her with everything he was made of, and he was nothing if not a man who chased after what he wanted with relentless drive.

Still, he had to be sure. Not of his own desires, but of hers. Lifting his head, he asked, "Are you certain?"

"I only had two sips of whiskey. I promise I know what I'm about." She reached up and slid her fingers through the hair above his forehead, trailing her fingers toward his neck and sending shivers all the way down the backs of his thighs. "I've wanted this for a while. Tonight I have no doubts."

"Good," he said, and couldn't manage another breath before taking her mouth. He wasn't gentlemanly or tender. His body had lit on fire. His mind was a spinning top. She wanted him and she'd come to him, and he refused to waste a single moment.

He kissed her again and again, hungrily, eagerly. She reached up to hold on to his shoulders. He lowered his hands to her backside, and pulled her tighter against where he was aching for her.

"Will you take me upstairs?" she managed on a breathless whisper between kisses.

Good grief, he was a brute. And her innocent and very practical question was precisely why he was dizzy with wanting her.

He had a primal urge to sweep her up into his arms and carry her up to his bedroom, but she'd probably tell him that sprinting side by side was far quicker.

He reached for her hand, and she threaded her fingers between his. The gesture was simple, instinctive, and yet it felt like a gift.

As they started up the stairs, side by side, hips and legs brushing each other's, fingers entwined, Aidan found he could easily imagine doing this with her every night. He turned and smiled at her.

Her skin was flushed with color, her eyes glassy and eager. "Just this one night," she whispered.

He nodded. He'd promised not to think of the future, but he couldn't imagine not wanting more.

Chapter Twenty-Two

The bed was the most elegant, opulent piece of furniture Diana had ever seen.

Slipping out of her family's house hadn't given her a moment's hesitation. Lifting her hand to grip the lion's-head door knocker on Aidan's front door had caused her only a moment's hesitation. Saying she wanted to spend the evening with him was the easiest part of all. It was what she'd wanted for perhaps as long ago as the moment she'd first met him.

But the bed. The bed was the first part of her plan to give her pause.

Not because of its size and opulence, but because it was the intimate spot where he laid his head every night. She'd bid him not to think of the future and yet now it was the only thing she could imagine. Would he sleep here every coming evening and think of this single night they'd shared together?

When he married his noblewoman, would they sleep in this same bed? Would one of her friends marry him and lay her head on these pillows?

"You're fretting." Aidan approached her from behind and pressed a warm kiss to the nape of her neck. "Tell me what you're thinking."

Diana leaned back against him. It felt good to let him take her weight. "How long do you have? There's never just one thought in my head. It's like a kaleidoscope."

"You offered tonight. We have until dawn. So tell me all of it."

He couldn't see her, but she smiled. How had she found the one man in England who truly wanted to know about the whirring thoughts in her head?

Maybe some other night. At that moment, the last thing she wanted was to talk. Only when Aidan's mouth was on hers, when his hands were on her body, did some of the constant noise in her mind stop. Feeling and sensation fought for their place and her loud thoughts quieted.

She needed that. She needed him.

Turning her head to look at him, she asked, "Help me undress?"

He didn't answer in words but in action. Expert fingers worked the buttons at the back of her gown and he slid the garment gently from her shoulders. Next came her corset.

Diana had no experience of other men, but Aidan worked the laces far faster than her corset unlacer ever could have. It seemed only seconds before she was standing before him in her chemise and stockings.

He cupped her breast through the thin fabric, his long, elegant fingers finding the taut peak of her nipple and rolling it gently beneath his fingertips.

She gasped at the intensity of the sensation.

"Now your clothes," she told him when he bent to kiss her.

She began with buttons and found there were far too many between his waistcoat, which went quickly, and his shirt, which she stopped and started to unbutton between kisses.

When she finally worked the last button free, she eagerly slid the fabric over his shoulders and gasped.

Feeling his muscles through layers of clothing was nothing like seeing them in the glow of lamplight. She slid her hand along the ridges of his shoulders and arms and chest, tracing every slope and swelling line.

Goodness, he was warm. Though she stood in little more than a thin layer of cotton, the heat radiating off his body like a furnace kept her warm.

He was patient as she explored, only tracing a finger across her cheek or stroking his hand down her back. He watched and waited, and when she'd finished he laced his fingers with hers and led her to the bed.

Diana settled on the edge and he knelt before her. He applied himself to removing her stockings, but turned the task into an opportunity to stroke and kiss every inch of her leg. When she let out a moan, he chuckled, his breath hot against her skin.

"Do you like that?"

"No," she told him honestly, "I love it."

He smiled and kissed her again, the spot above her knee, the inner edge of her thigh. When her stockings were off, she expected him to stop, but he didn't. His fingers found the lace of her drawers, and he slid them off as tenderly as he'd removed her stockings, adding kisses on every inch of skin he uncovered.

Then he sat back on his heels, his fingers skimming the tender skin of her thighs, slipping higher as he looked into her eyes. "Do you trust me, Diana?"

"Yes. I wouldn't be here if I didn't."

He smiled at that, then he shocked her by sliding his fingers along her sex, stroking at the part of her that was slick and aching. Then he bent and replaced his fingers with his mouth, flicking his tongue out to taste. Her body tensed with the keen pleasure of it, almost too much. But a moment later she bucked against him, desperate for more.

He lapped and suckled, and then she felt his finger slipping inside her heat, ratcheting up the pleasure. Her muscles tautened as he stroked her. The sensation was too intense, and yet she wanted more. She grappled for his shoulder and dug her fingers into his flexing muscles as her release shuddered through her. She held on to him as she gasped and cried out, and he kissed her through it, his mouth leaving a hot, damp trail along her thigh.

"You're incredible," he whispered against her skin.

Only when she sighed with a deep, languorous contentment did he stand, work the buttons of his trousers, and begin slipping them over his hips.

"Let me," she said, pausing him midslide.

She'd read books, seen sculptures. She had a fair notion of what he was about to reveal, but she wanted to uncover him herself. Hooking fingers on each side of his hips, she inched the fabric lower.

When the hard, smooth length of him sprang free, Diana inhaled sharply and licked her lips. Empirical knowledge was indeed far superior to crosshatch illustrations and the work of artists' hands.

She reached for him, shaping the length of him in her palm. His jaw tightened as his breathing turned shallow.

Every touch, every stroke seemed to make him harder and his breath seemed to sync with the rhythm of her movements.

"Diana," he whispered. A plea but also a warning. "If you don't stop—"

"I know." She released him reluctantly and reached down to lift her chemise over her head. She was completely bare before him, and there was no place else she wished to be. "Show me," she demanded softly. "Show me everything."

"Diana." Her name rasped out on a low, primal growl and he bent to draw her in for a kiss. He started slowly, tasting, and teasing, and all the while he urged her farther back onto the bed.

He followed her, his hard, warm body sheltering hers as they settled onto the mattress. He braced his hands on either side of her, held his body above hers so that he wasn't crushing her beneath him.

It was far too polite. Far too practiced. Diana needed him closer. She wanted to make him lose every bit of control.

"Closer," she told him. "You're too far away." Reaching up, she laced her hands behind his neck and tugged.

Aidan smiled down at her. "I do love your eagerness." He placed a knee between her legs, nudged her thighs wider, and settled between them. "But we needn't rush this."

The thick, hard length of him slid against her belly. Then he shifted and fitted himself against her, rubbing along her sex until she moaned for more.

He watched her with the tenderest expression. The way he'd always looked at her had filled a space inside her. Made her feel warm and wanted. No one had ever looked at her the way that Aidan looked at her.

"Aidan." Even the merest whisper of his name seemed to affect him. He captured her mouth in a searing kiss.

But when he retreated again, she gripped his shoulders to keep him close. "Wait," she told him. "Stay close."

"I'm not going anywhere. I'm right here, Diana." He rested his body against hers and finally let her take his weight. She spread her thighs, wanting him closer. He tangled one hand in her hair and then reached down with his other hand to slide a finger along her slit. Every nerve in her body drew to that single point where she was wet and desperate to feel him.

He seemed to know that she couldn't wait, but he still hesitated, sliding his length against her until she thought she'd go mad.

"Please," she whispered. Her mind might be pleasure-addled now, but she'd made this decision with a clear head, knowing the consequences.

As he often did, Aidan seemed to read her thoughts.

"You're certain, Diana?" As soon as the question was out, he bent his head and took a nipple between his lips.

It made it harder for her to speak, but it changed nothing about her answer.

"Yes," she hissed, and before she could take her next breath, he slid into her. Diana gasped at the sensation. She'd imagined how this night would go, everything that might happen between them. But not this, not how it felt to be so close to him. How right it felt when their bodies were joined.

He began to move, building a slow, steady rhythm. But Diana didn't want that; she lifted her hips, bucking against him, then lifted her head to pepper kisses along his jaw and take his lips.

"Diana." His thrusts quickened, deepened.

"I want all of you," she told him.

Aidan kissed her then, hungrily, possessively, and when his release came, he spoke her name again on a ragged whisper against her lips.

He lifted his body from hers and rested on his side, pulling her close. Diana laid her head against his chest and thought she'd never heard anything lovelier than the wild thump of his heartbeat.

"You're well?" he asked when his breathing had steadied.

Diana laughed and ran her finger down his chest. "That is an insufficient description."

"Tell me then."

"Wonderful," she told him quietly, though it was the kind of superlative she rarely ever used. But it was true as it had never been before. "And what are you?" She lifted her head to look into his eyes.

He smiled at her and stroked a hand through her hair. Then he frowned and his eyes widened, as if he'd come to some realization. "I'm content."

"You sound far too surprised." She pushed at his chest playfully.

"I am," he said earnestly. "I'm not sure I've ever felt it before."

"Why?" She thought perhaps she understood. She too felt a sense of rightness in his arms that she'd never imagined feeling with anyone. But she sensed there was more, and she knew instinctively that it led back to his family.

So she waited and laid her head against his chest. He took a breath as if to speak, but no words emerged for a long while.

Finally, he said, "I've never known where I belong." The words came out rough, as if his throat had gone dry. "To be honest, I'm not even sure of my name. The workhouse may have given it to my sister and me for all I know."

"You don't remember?"

"I try not to." He shifted, his hand tensing against her back. "I made a mistake that I can never fix." On a whisper, he said, "My sister Sarah. I left her behind. She was quite young when I ran away. I didn't want her to sleep on the streets, but I promised I'd come back when I found a place for us."

Diana swallowed back the sting of tears. The pain in his voice was raw, and part of her wanted him to stop, if only to keep him from the pain. But she had to know, and she suspected he needed to tell someone too.

He drew in a long breath and said on an exhale, "The workhouse burned. I lost my sister, or so I'd thought until a few days ago. A man at the lodging house where I was born says she's alive."

"Do you believe him? Has he told you where to find her?"

"I don't know what to believe, and he has no information. The envelope I gave you is the only lead I have."

Diana lifted her head again. "I'll help you if I can."

"You already have." He kissed her, a slow, tender caress of his lips against hers. Then he cupped her cheek against his palm. "I love you, Diana."

Her heart swelled, nearly burst inside her chest. They were the words she longed to hear. And yet her tongue felt thick and she offered him nothing in reply.

His gentle smile faltered, and she hated the disappointment that flickered in his eyes. But he stroked her back and pulled her closer, tucking her against him again. He kissed the top of her head but said nothing more.

Diana closed her eyes and fought the sting of tears. Something inside wouldn't allow her to give the words back to him. She'd told him they wouldn't think of the future.

Just this one night. That's all they could have.

Chapter Twenty-Three

*W*alking into Lyon's often required Aidan to re-acquaint himself with its sounds and scents. He'd never spent as much time at the club as Tremayne, who oversaw it with all the worry of a mother hen, or Huntley, who spent as much time there drinking and gaming as its most devoted members.

He smelled roasted ham and the distinct aroma of kippers and guessed that breakfast hours had been extended, as they sometimes were on Saturdays. The gaming tables were less crowded this early in the morning, but there were some inveterate risk takers still leaning over the green baize, hoping to make fortune their friend.

The club was just as impressive in daylight as lit by lamplight in the evenings. The gilded walls and crystal fixtures sparkled in the sunlight pouring in from the enormous multicolored glass dome overhead.

A few members recognized Aidan and lifted glasses in salute or offered nods of acknowledgment. Most didn't give him a moment's notice.

He scanned the upstairs balcony, where he knew Tremayne liked to hide, but he could see no one beyond the polished balustrade.

Aidan made his way down to the office and noticed a difference he never had before. A few paintings, mostly watercolors, had been added to the walls. He suspected Tremayne's wife was to blame. Or to thank. The art enlivened the grim space, and he was grateful his friend had found a woman who continually challenged him, both in business and in life.

Now that Aidan was contemplating marriage for himself, it was precisely what he wanted too.

Nick stood donning his overcoat when Aidan stepped into his office.

"You caught me," he said with a less than guilty smile curving his mouth.

"Are you on your way to an appointment?"

"No." Nick shrugged. "Not if you need to speak to me. I was simply going to go for a walk, if you must know. The air in the club begins to feel stale after a while. I thought a walk might improve my mood."

Slipping his coat off again, he indicated one of the chairs in front of his desk.

"Sit. Tell me what's brought you here so early."

"What brought you?" Aidan asked in all seriousness.

Nick spent more time at the club than he and Huntley combined, but he was often the last to depart in the evening, which meant he rarely managed to be the first in for early morning hours.

"If you must know, I was going to attempt a meeting with Lockwood on your behalf."

"Nick—"

He held up a hand. "Before you thank or chastise me, just know that the meeting never took place. I indicated the time and place, but I've received no reply to my correspondence."

"I do appreciate your effort," Aidan told him sincerely. "But I haven't come regarding the exhibition or my desire to win Lockwood's favor."

Nick nodded. "Good. It's better not to be too focused on one singular goal that might turn to disappointment." As soon as the words left his mouth, Nick drew his head back in surprise. "I can't believe I just advised you not to be single-minded."

Aidan chuckled, and the lightness of it eased a bit of the tightness that had been riding his chest all morning. "You are quite the most bullheaded and single-minded man I've ever known."

"Agreed." Nick stared at the carpet as if trying to sort out his fresh change of perspective. "But I also know that there are some pursuits that are futile. If Lockwood can't be bothered to answer a duke's letter for a simple morning meeting, then I'm not sure he's the sort of man you should wish to plan any event with."

Aidan smiled. "My main interest is in the industrial equipment and inventors who'll present at the exhibition rather than hobnobbing with Lockwood."

"Of course," Nick agreed. "But sit. Tell me why you've come today if not about Lockwood."

Aidan lowered himself into the chair and wiped a hand across his mouth. He still found it difficult to think of anything other than Diana, the night they'd spent together, and the fact that she'd been gone when he awoke in the morning. No note. No early morning good-bye. Just a cold, empty space in his bed.

The rightness of being with her. That was what he held on to. She had chosen him and that moment, and he didn't regret any of it. All he truly wanted was to find a way to have her in his life every day and his bed every night. His ambition, his hunger for success— that was a shadow of how much he wanted Diana.

"I need your advice." The four words were nearly impossible to get out and he felt a weight in the pit of his stomach the moment they were.

Aidan was comfortable with Nick. He trusted Nick. But coming to Nick, to anyone, for personal advice was something he'd never dreamed he'd find himself doing. Aidan had once advised Nick on how to survive. Perhaps, in some way, Aidan was now asking for the same in return.

"How can I help?" Nick asked, and then steepled his fingers to rest his chin on top as he assessed Aidan. "This is about a woman?"

"Is it so obvious?"

"To me. I doubt others would see it." Nick picked up and tested the heft of a paperweight in his hand. He kept his gaze focused on the polished stone, almost as if he sensed how difficult this was for Aidan and was giving him space to find the words. "Go on. Tell me everything and I'll help you in any way I am able."

"When did you know?" Aidan asked him. "When did you know you'd fallen and would give up anything to be with your wife?"

Nick lifted his head and stared at the back wall of his office; a smile tipped the edge of his mouth as if he was seeing the moment clearly in his mind's eye. "I met her the day I arrived at the estate. We clashed instantly, but I knew then that she would change everything."

"Yes," was all Aidan could manage. He too knew what it was to meet a woman in unexpected circumstances and know almost immediately that she would remain on his mind.

"So you've found your noblewoman, but you're not certain if she's the right one?" Nick prompted when Aidan fell silent.

"No." Aidan stood and began pacing Nick's office, struggling to gather his thoughts. "She's not a noblewoman."

"I don't understand." Leather creaked and the springs underneath his chair groaned as Nick settled back and crossed his arms. "Your intent was to woo a blue-blooded bride, was it not? Who is this woman who has you virtually speechless?"

For the first time, Aidan realized Nick might find some impropriety in his relationship with Diana. Not that either of them had ever worried much about propriety before. But nor had either of them had much to lose for most of their lives. Since Diana was one of the inventors to present before the Den, and the first woman, Aidan hesitated to explain more to his friend.

"She's an extraordinary woman, unlike any I've ever met before."

"But she cares for you and you for her? Which is enough to make you overlook your goals?" Nick sounded dubious as he drew out the words, as if he was attempting to piece together a puzzle and none of it quite made sense.

"She doesn't wish to marry." Aidan turned back to face him, hands braced on his hips. "Any advice on how to woo a woman who disdains the very notion of wedlock?"

Nick's furrowed brow and confused frown indicated he did not. "Iverson, what the hell have you gotten yourself into?"

Aidan closed his eyes and drew in a deep breath. Diana was there in his mind, and deeper, in his cold, walled-off heart. She'd proved all of his planning and strategies to be absolute nonsense. She'd proved that all the walls he'd thought he'd built were nothing but paper thin.

When he opened his eyes, he found Nick had stood. He wore an expression of such concern, Aidan let out a chuckle.

"I'm not sure because I've damned well never felt it before, but I think what I've gotten myself into is love."

The smile that broke over Nick's face came slowly, but finally spread into a beaming grin. "I'm trying so hard not to say I told you so."

"Not that hard, apparently."

"Don't lose her," Nick told him in a serious tone. "Don't apply your rules and strategies to this and attempt to turn it into some kind of fair exchange."

Aidan was on the verge of confessing that he had done precisely that.

"If this is right, you'll know and she'll know. Nothing will need to be forced or arranged."

"I know it's right. I'm not certain she agrees."

Nick crossed the room until they were face-to-face. "Then that, my friend, is where you begin."

DIANA PRESSED GENTLY as she rubbed the graphite over the envelope Aidan had given her. She'd vowed to help him, and she meant to keep her word.

A chemical test had revealed a nearly unnoticeable depression in the paper, and she prayed this simple technique would cause whatever might be imprinted to emerge. She used a brush to sweep away some of the dark flakes and gasped when a few faint letters became visible.

A *J* and an *S* with a space between them that she soon realized was an *O*. A man's name. *Joseph*. No, there was more. An *I* was almost indistinguishable but made an undeniable mark at the end. *Josephi* might be part of a surname or *Josephine*, a lady's name, which meant nothing to her. She hoped it might mean something to Aidan.

She could send a note with the information, but what she truly wished was to see him again.

Her nerves were frayed, her body ached in places it had never ached before, and her heart was full to the point of bursting. Inside her heart, she held an impossible mix of joy and anxious uncertainty.

Being with Aidan had been beyond what she ever imagined it could be. Leaving him in the early hours of the morning was the most difficult choice she'd ever made in her life.

She'd stroked a strand of hair from his forehead, traced her fingers along the line of his cheek, his jaw, his nose. She'd kissed him as softly as she was able, then dressed and tiptoed away when every step made her wish to turn back.

In the space of a few hours, she'd come to understand why people were willing to risk anything, do anything, for what she'd long imagined was poetic nonsense.

Love. Was that what was filling her heart this morning? Was that why she couldn't manage to focus on her work and thought instead of Aidan? One night with him and everything had shifted. She'd made him promise not to think of the future, and yet this morning she could think of little else.

She could no longer imagine a future that didn't include Aidan. The man had been on her heart and mind since the day they'd met, and now she felt he was a part of her.

But how could it work? She could conceive an idea and build and tweak and struggle until it worked just as she imagined, but she couldn't fathom how she and Aidan Iverson might make a life together.

What they felt for each other would only get in the way of his goals. She wasn't the noblewoman he needed to achieve the belonging he'd been seeking for so long.

And none of her own ambition had waned either. Glancing around the room, she took in her five completed devices and felt a surge of pride that she had achieved exactly what she'd set out to do. But the prospect of success didn't fill her up as she'd expected it to.

No matter how many devices she sold to Mr. Repton, no matter how many people used her machine, she knew she wouldn't be satisfied with the work alone.

Now there was more than toiling in a workshop and seeing one of her devices in a shop window; there was the simple bliss of being held and wanted, the joy of being in Aidan's arms. She wanted that too.

Gripping the lever, she applied her weight and moved the metal bar back and forth until she felt resistance. Lifting the tube of her machine, she drew up the collection of dust she'd deposited on her workshop floor. The mechanism worked just as expected and she turned to make a note regarding this final test.

Her wrist bumped against a small pile of post she'd left unopened. The name atop one envelope caught her notice. It was from Mr. Repton. She tore inelegantly to get to the letter and her jaw dropped as she read.

She'd sent him a note to let him know she'd completed the five models he'd asked for. She and Aidan had been waiting for confirmation that he wished to purchase and ship them to his shop in America. But he'd done more.

She read the lines again and again to make herself believe the words. The joy of it rushed through her, and more than anything she wanted to tell Aidan.

I have sold all five of Miss Ashby's cleaning devices to eager customers and only await the matter of delivery and payment. I am certain we can come to fair terms when we meet again next week.

Out of the corner of her eye, Diana noticed movement and a shift of light in the hallway beyond. The clip of heels on marble grew louder as they approached, telling her she'd soon have a visitor.

"Miss Grinstead to see you, Miss Ashby," the house-maid said from the conservatory threshold. "Shall I send her in?"

"Yes, do send her in." Diana didn't imagine even a visit from her dearest friend could alter the course of her wayward thoughts and the spectrum of emotions she'd passed through this morning, but she was eager to see Grace nonetheless. If nothing else, she understood her better now. Diana no longer questioned why her friend would risk scandal to follow her heart.

Grace wore a stunning green frock of shimmering satin and one of her elaborate hats with a veil pulled over her face. That struck Diana as odd, but as she rose to greet her fashionable friend with a welcoming hug, she understood why.

"Oh, Diana." Grace pulled out a hat pin and tugged off the large satin flower-covered hat. Beneath the veil, her face was splotched pink, her eyes swollen from crying, her lips quivering as if she was on the verge of tearing up again.

"Come in, Grace." Diana clasped her friend's hand and drew her to a corner of the workshop where she'd placed one of the family's old threadbare settees. "Tell me what's happened."

"Papa has refused us, of course. He's threatened Mr. Hambly and he's vowed to send me away if I pursue this course." Her chin wobbled and tears welled in her eyes, but she swiped at them and seemed determined not to cry.

"The worst part," she said on a broken whisper, "is that it's worked. Mr. Hambly has been frightened off, despite vowing he would persist."

Grace's shoulders slumped and she closed her eyes. A line of tears slid down her cheeks, but she said nothing more.

Diana didn't know what to say to lessen the pain. "I'm sorry, Grace," were the words that emerged, but she knew they weren't enough.

"He's withdrawn his proposal." She hiccuped and pressed a hand to her chest. "But even that hasn't satisfied my father. Mama says he plans to send me to the countryside for the Season so that I 'bring no more shame upon our family.'" After a ragged indrawn breath, she added, "I've lost everything."

Diana reached an arm around Grace's shoulders. She searched for anything to say that might soothe her. "Perhaps a few months in the country will be restorative."

Grace frowned at her. "Isolation? Banishment? I'm tired of my father dictating my life, Diana. Why do you think I was so keen to marry?"

"I thought you loved Mr. Hambly."

Grace pulled a lace-edged handkerchief from her pocket and pressed it to her nose. "Love is a fancy. You told me that yourself just a few days ago."

Diana opened her mouth but everything she considered saying caught on her tongue. She had been dismissive of Grace's romanticism, but she couldn't deny the potency of love anymore. Still, she hesitated to confess as much to Grace, not because she had any doubts about her feelings or Aidan's, but because the emotions were too raw for her to sift with a few words.

"I know you like solving problems, Diana, but I think I may have found a solution to this dilemma myself." Grace stripped off her gloves and turned to face her on the settee, a blush creeping up her cheeks.

"Good," Diana said, shocked by her friend's change in demeanor.

"I'll need your help," Grace told her with an eager glint in her gray eyes.

"You know I'll assist you however I can."

"Can you arrange another meeting with Mr. Iverson?" Grace reached for Diana's hand when she didn't reply. "I know he must think me a ninny after what happened at the Zoological Society, but we could make a fair match, I think. He has enough wealth to please my family, and I have something to offer him too."

Diana tried swallowing against the painful knot at the back of her throat, but she couldn't even manage that. She wasn't sure she could manage breathing. Every exhale got trapped in her chest.

"Remember how he mentioned the industrial exhibition?" Grace continued. "My father knows several of the men on the planning committee. Apparently, they rejected Mr. Iverson's proposal to join, but I think my father could convince at least one of the men to reconsider."

Diana nodded. Some rational part of her understood what Grace was saying. She could help Aidan, and Diana loved him enough to want that. If he wished to be part of this exhibition, then he must be. She understood how much he wanted to belong, and he'd helped her achieve her goals. Could she truly claim to care for him if she didn't do the same?

"Perhaps your family could host a dinner and invite us both." Grace rapped her nails against the table. "We could invite him to our reunion ball at Lord and Lady Merton's. Or perhaps I could simply go to him. It's not proper etiquette, but he doesn't seem bothered by such matters, and I'm too desperate now to mind a bit of a scandal."

"I'll speak to him and arrange a meeting." Diana heard her own voice and the words she spoke, but they reverberated painfully in her chest.

This morning, her heart had been full of joy and her mind raced with delicious memories. Now she felt

hollow, empty, and could only force out words she
knew she should say.

"Do you think he'll still consider marrying me after
that business with Hambly?"

Diana looked at her friend—blond, beautiful, clever,
and fashionable. A viscount's daughter. A noble lady
who wished for nothing so much as to marry and
manage a household of her own. She was precisely
what Aidan had wanted.

But the previous night, all their whispered words,
the way they'd loved each other. That was true too.

"Diana?" Grace prompted. "Is there still a chance?"

"I don't know." They were the most honest words
Diana could offer.

She was a woman who spent her days puzzling over
design conundrums and wanted nothing so much as
to solve every mystery she encountered. But Diana
couldn't calculate this. She couldn't be objective about
Grace's dilemma or her own. All she could do was
what she'd never done before. She could follow her
heart.

Her heart led her to Aidan, but she loved him enough
to want his happiness first. She couldn't be the cause
of his missing out on what he craved most.

"We shall see," she told Grace. "We'll soon see."

Chapter Twenty-Four

$\mathcal{A}$idan stared at the Ashbys' red front door and felt an odd wave of déjà vu rush over him. Less than a fortnight past, he'd paced the same pavement and pondered whether he should go inside and face Diana.

No debate plagued his mind now. He was aching to see her again, touch her, hold her. He knew what he wished to say. He'd practiced every word. Reaching up, he patted his upper jacket pocket and felt the square outline underneath.

Only one uncertainty lingered. He knew his intentions and desires, but he needed to discover hers.

And there was only one way to find out.

He approached the door to knock, but before he could lift his hand, Diana's twin brother emerged. He stopped in his tracks when he spotted Aidan.

"Iverson." Dominick Ashby looked shocked to find a visitor on their doorstep, but then he stepped aside and ushered Aidan in. "I take it you're looking for my sister. She's in her workshop, of course. Rarely out of it these days."

Rather than depart as he'd intended, Ashby shut the front door, crossed his arms, and quirked a brow as he stared at Aidan.

"This is the part where I ask what your intentions are toward my sister." Ashby's eyes were the same color as Diana's, his hair the same dark brown. There was a similarity in the lines of their faces, but her gaze was full of life and energy. Ashby's was awash in cynicism, even a hint of anger bubbling beneath the surface.

"They're honorable. In fact, I'd like to speak to your mother before I see Diana."

Ashby blinked and his lips parted slightly. "By God, you're a brave man."

"I suppose that's better than you telling me I'm a fool." Aidan slipped a finger behind the knot of his tie and gave a gentle tug. Ashby's words sparked a fresh ripple of nerves.

"How could I call you a fool? Any man who sees fit to admire my sister possesses good taste, at the very least. But you've taken it a step further." Ashby zeroed in on the bulge in Aidan's upper coat pocket. "In fact, it seems you're willing to take this all the way to the altar. I can only wish you luck."

"I am, and thank you."

The young man stuck out a hand and clapped Aidan on the shoulder. "A word of advice?"

"I'll take as many as you have." Somewhere along the way Aidan's disdain for taking the advice of others had been cast away.

"She's stubborn."

"So I've gathered."

"I don't know that she's ever truly followed her own heart." Ashby waved. "With her inventions, of course, she has, but sometimes I think it's all as much of a trap as her passion. She works like a woman possessed at times, as if she must do all the things our father did not."

Aidan sensed that drive in her, a kind of compulsion that fueled her. He'd once felt the same about achieving wealth and finding the truth about his past. Now he only wanted Diana and whatever future they could build together. All the rest would fall into place.

"Don't let her fob you off with excuses," Ashby went on. "She may refuse you and you must accept that—"

Aidan opened his mouth to protest but Ashby stopped him, a finger raised between them.

"I'm not saying she will. I only like to think of the worst so that I might occasionally be surprised when life is a bit less awful than I expect. If you love her, truly, I hope she says yes." Ashby's eyes turned sad and intensely serious. "She deserves no less."

"I agree, Mr. Ashby."

The young man smiled at Aidan and then turned his head toward the stairwell. "Mother, I'm off, but there's a visitor to see you." Without waiting for a reply, Ashby offered Aidan a final nod, opened the front door, and departed.

Aidan cast a glance down the hall toward Diana's workshop. His eagerness to see her was nearly unbearable.

"Hello, sir," a dark-haired woman called from the top of the stairs. "You've come to call on me?"

Aidan noticed she leaned on a cane and he climbed the stairs to offer his arm to help her descend.

"Chivalry is always appreciated, sir," she said when they reached the bottom step. "Thank you. But perhaps you should tell me your name."

"Iverson, Mrs. Ashby. My name is Aidan Iverson." *And I'm here to marry your daughter.*

"The man who is in league with Diana." She gestured toward the drawing room. "You'd better come sit down, sir."

For long silent minutes after they'd both taken a seat, she simply stared at him, studying and assessing.

Aidan decided that it was best to jump straight in. "Mrs. Ashby, I regret that we have not had the chance to meet until now, but I've come to know your daughter well and I . . ."

When his voice trailed off because he wasn't certain how to phrase the rest, Mrs. Ashby filled the quiet.

"What is it that you do, Mr. Iverson?"

"I own several commercial enterprises, Mrs. Ashby. I also invest and help others do the same."

She chewed on this information, clasping her hands in her lap and holding a slight noncommittal smile on her face. "And who are your people, sir?"

Aidan's hands tensed into fists against his thighs. He'd loathed the question when the matchmaker had asked him weeks before, and he hated the question now. There was still so much he didn't know, but he owed Diana's mother whatever he did know.

"My mother was in domestic service for much of her life."

He braced himself for her revulsion and judgment. Waited for her to scoff at the very notion that he could deserve her clever, beautiful, stubborn daughter.

"Well," she said after an endless stretch of nerve-racking quiet, "then you've come quite a long way, haven't you, sir?"

A jolt of shock rippled through him. He'd expected scorn or haughty disdain, not the respect he saw in the older woman's eyes.

"Yes, Mrs. Ashby, I suppose I have." She had no idea. Anyone who had not spent years inside the grimy walls of a Lambeth workhouse could have no idea.

"And now you've come about my daughter."

"I have."

"You've spent a great deal of time with her recently."

Diana's mother glanced toward the hallway, toward her daughter's workshop. "She's very committed to her work."

"I admire her commitment."

"You must convince her there's more."

"More?" Aidan didn't know whether he could convince Diana Ashby of much she wasn't willing to consider on her own. If anything, she'd been the one to change him. But to show her what kind of life they could build together, to shower her with the affection she deserved—that he could do.

"In some ways, she takes after her late father." She gestured toward the framed technical drawings Aidan had noticed when he'd visited the Ashby a fortnight past. "In the end, he did nothing but work. He'd disappear into his laboratory not just for hours but days. Something drove him relentlessly."

Aidan's pulse thudded loudly in his ears. She spoke of her late husband, but she might have been speaking of him. Or of Diana.

"Ambition is well and good," Mrs. Ashby said softly, "but there must be more. The joy of spending time with others. Contentedness in quiet moments."

"Yes, I'm learning that lesson, Mrs. Ashby." He would give half his bank account for another night like the one he'd spent with Diana. That was joy. That was contentedness.

"I hope she will too." Mrs. Ashby leaned forward

and tapped her cane on the rug. Quietly, she told him, "You have my blessing, sir. Though I suspect what you'll be most in need of is perseverance."

DIANA SAT IN the low lamplight of her workshop and listened to the echoes of voices in the drawing room down the hall. She couldn't make out their words, but her mother's voice and Aidan's deep, warm timbre were unmistakable.

She'd heard someone arrive nearly half an hour earlier, and she'd known instinctively that it was Aidan.

He'd vowed before that night they'd spent together that he would not think of the future, but he was an honorable man. No matter how often he told himself he wasn't a gentleman, Diana knew that he would behave like one in this matter.

Aidan had come to offer for her, and she could barely breathe through the pain of knowing that she would have to refuse him. What a change a couple of weeks had wrought. She'd bargained with her mother to prevent the very possibility that she would need to enter the marriage mart. Now she choked back tears at the prospect of turning away a proposal.

"Diana?" Aidan called to her softly from the threshold of the conservatory.

She stared ahead a moment, keeping her back to him, but unwanted relief washed over her at the sound of his voice. They'd been apart for only hours, but she'd missed him for every minute of those hours.

When she finally turned, his face lit in a devastating smile.

He strode forward and took her into his arms. She couldn't resist placing her palms against his chest, letting him tug her close.

His scent made her mouth water, and the heat in his gaze made her body respond as if they were bare and entwined and in his bed again.

"It's good to see you," he said with an open smile. Not even a hint of anger that she had left him without a word the previous night. The guilt of it still gnawed at her.

"I'm sorry I left without saying good-bye." She needed him to know that much at least. "It wasn't easy."

"Having you in my arms now is what matters."

She tried for a smile and felt her mouth trembling. Curling her hands around the lapels of his suit, she felt the outline of a box inside his upper suit pocket. He noticed her frown and reached a hand up to pull the box free.

"You're too clever for me to pretend this is anything other than what it is."

"Aidan—"

"I know I'm expected to get down on one knee, but that would require me to let go of you and I haven't even kissed you yet." He lowered his head and brushed his mouth against hers.

Diana had vowed to speak to him before the evening went this far, yet the moment he touched her, she forgot everything but the rightness of being in his arms. She opened to his kiss, slid a hand around his neck to pull him closer. She responded eagerly, letting him sense how much she wanted him and needed this moment.

When they were both breathless, he pressed his forehead to hers.

"This is what I hoped," he whispered. "That you'd kiss me exactly that way. That you'd want this as much as I do. When we're together like this, nothing else matters quite as much."

He kissed her forehead, then released her and took a step back.

Diana wanted him to return to her arms the minute he retreated, but she wouldn't be able to say the things she needed to say if he continued touching and kissing her.

"I am determined to do this properly," he said with a wink before lowering himself to one knee.

"Wait." Diana grabbed his arm to pull him back up. "Please don't."

He stood, his muscles tensing underneath her fingers. "You don't want me to propose." There was no question in his tone, just a miserable declaration.

"There's a matter I must discuss with you before you consider proposing to anyone."

"I will never propose to anyone but you, Diana." Uncertainty darkened his gaze.

She held up her free hand, urging him to listen. A man didn't rise to the level of wealth he had without his own brand of stubbornness and determination, but she knew he was a logical man too. A discerning investor, used to weighing various options and considering all the facts before making his decisions.

"There are things you don't yet know."

His bark of laughter shocked her. "I'm afraid that's been a theme in my life."

The comment reminded her that she had something that belonged to him. She opened a drawer in her workbench and retrieved the envelope he'd offered her the evening of Bess's séance.

"I'd almost forgotten to return this to you and tell you what I found."

His expression turned hopeful, intrigued, both auburn brows winging high on his forehead. "What did you find?"

"There's a technique I used to bring out depressions in paper." She pointed to the envelope. "I'm afraid it required me to discolor the envelope."

He stepped closer and reached for her arm. "I don't care about that. Tell me if you discovered anything."

"Part of a name, possibly." She turned the square of paper and shifted it in the light so he could see the ghost remnants of handwriting too. "*J-O-S-E-P-H-I* is what I can make out clearly. Perhaps a surname or a lady's name. Does Josephine mean anything to you?"

Aidan shook his head. "No, but it's something. I can hand it over to my investigators. Perhaps someone in Wyndham's household will know that name."

Diana offered him the envelope and he placed it inside the same coat pocket he'd retrieved the ring box from.

"Thank you," he said with genuine warmth. Then he squared his shoulders and released his hold on her. "Now what else did you wish to tell me?"

The breath Diana drew in to try to steady her nerves only agitated the ache deep in the center of her chest. Her exhale turned ragged and she struggled to look into Aidan's eyes.

"Grace Grinstead," she began.

"No," he said emphatically before casting her a bemused look. "I didn't come here to discuss anyone else, Diana. Only you and me."

"Please listen to what I promised her I would say."

His eyes fluttered closed and he reached up to pinch the bridge of his nose. Turning, he paced the small path she'd created between her worktables covered with pneumatic cleaning devices.

"Mr. Hambly withdrew his offer of marriage."

He glanced up at her and shrugged as he continued to pace. "Not unexpected. Presumably Viscount Holcomb objected to the match and the young man balked."

"Quite so."

"And?" he prompted her gently, but his every movement indicated that impatience was getting the better of him.

"Grace thinks you would be a better prospect."

He stopped in his tracks. "You're still trying to play matchmaker?"

"I'm fulfilling a promise I made to her."

He came forward and didn't stop until they were toe to toe. "What of what we said to each other last night?"

"What of the reasons you agreed to a deal with me in the first place?"

He flinched but said nothing, though she could see the pain in his expression. His eyes shuttered as they had before when he sought to hide his past from her. She hated the distance she felt opening up between them.

Diana bit her lip, afraid she'd angered him or pushed him too far. Then his hand came up and he cupped her cheek in his palm.

"Much has changed since we made our deal." His gaze turned open and tender again. "I have changed. You have that effect on me."

Diana nuzzled her cheek against his skin and told herself not to look into his eyes. "Grace asked me to arrange another meeting."

"So we can tell her about our engagement?" he teased. "I'd love to."

Diana stepped away from him and approached her worktable, gripping the edge between her fingers. She needed to ground herself, remind herself how this had all begun. He wanted a noble bride. She wanted his investment.

"She possesses everything you want in a wife."

"I've changed my mind."

He approached and stood behind her. She prayed he wouldn't touch her. If he reached for her, she didn't know if she could cling to her resolve.

"She knows Lord Lockwood, or her father does. If Grace could help you find favor with him—"

"Diana, listen to me."

Turning around to face him was a mistake. He was so close, she could taste his scent on the air, and his gaze was so hungry that her body began to pulse with need.

"I don't want what we agreed to a fortnight ago in this room."

"But—"

He bent and kissed her before she could get a word out. One quick claiming and then he straightened. "I'm going to kiss you every time you interrupt. Let me say the rest."

Diana offered him the slightest of nods.

"I love you, Diana Ashby. The only part of our agreement I ever truly wanted was you. I should have never let you offer yourself as guarantee. I don't want you to accept my proposal because we made a deal. I want you to accept because you know, as I do, that nothing feels as right as when we're together."

Diana wanted desperately to believe him, to simply let herself feel and give in to the temptation to say yes. But thoughts rushed in, as they always did. Not only doubts and fears, but memories.

She knew what it was to yearn for belonging and acceptance. She understood the desperation, the willingness to do anything, promise anything, for the chance to succeed in a world where many would say she didn't belong.

If they married, he would gain none of what he'd wished to achieve. What if she agreed to be his bride and he came to resent her for what their marriage cost him?

"What about the exhibition?" she asked him weakly, desperate for him to think as she was struggling to do, not only with his heart but with his head.

"Diana." He took her hand in his and swept his thumb along the backs of her fingers. "I feared you'd resist this, but I hope you'd at least hear me. I have changed. The exhibition doesn't matter to me as much as you do."

"Because you're infatuated." It was a fear she'd wrestled with all day. She remembered their conversation at the Zoological Society. Infatuation, he'd said, was something one couldn't prepare for. Perhaps that was what he felt for her.

"This is more than infatuation. How shall I convince you?" He slid a hand around her neck and tipped her head toward his. "Will this convince you?"

Diana lifted onto her toes for the kiss. She wanted it as much as he did. He plundered, stroking his tongue into her mouth again and again until her knees began to quiver. She lifted a hand to steady herself, and he smiled against her lips. The rogue knew the effect he had on her, and he loved it.

"Convinced?" he asked on a breathy whisper.

"Aidan."

He wrapped an arm around her back and lifted her off her toes, settling her bottom onto the worktable at her back. As he kissed her again, he reached down and dragged his fingers along her stockinged legs, rucking her skirt up so he could press in between her spread thighs.

"I want you like this," he said against her lips. "Shall I take you right here in your workshop, Diana?"

"Yes," she hissed between kisses.

He raised his head and looked down at her, eyes blazing with need. "Then would you believe me?" He kissed her cheek, her nose, nipped at her lower lip. "Then would you marry me?"

"Aidan, I can't."

The three words froze him in place. Even as his body tensed and he seemed to hold his breath, his expression crumbled. All the joy, all the desire of a moment before, were swept away by disappointment.

Stepping back, he reached out and settled her skirts around her legs, then lowered her onto her feet.

"I'm sorry." Diana's whispered words brought no relief. Not to her and, from the devastation in Aidan's gaze, not to him either.

He stunned her by stepping forward and pressing one quick kiss to her forehead.

"I'll meet with Grace Grinstead," he told her in an emotionless tone. "I'll let you keep your promise to your friend. Send me the details once the arrangement has been made."

Without another word, he started out of the conservatory. Diana pressed her lips together and willed herself not to cry out and call him back. But then his footsteps slowed. She turned to find him watching from the threshold.

"I'm not giving up, Diana. You may be stubborn, but I'm as tenacious as hell."

Chapter Twenty-Five

*I*f anyone had observed Aidan for the next several days, they would have assumed he was simply a hard-working London man of business who rose early to go to the office and didn't leave until the wee hours at night.

Closer inspection would have revealed hours of pacing, an excessive consumption of whiskey, and rants shouted at the walls of his office that none heard but his trustworthy secretary.

This morning he was attempting to make sense of investment notes that he'd scribbled during a meeting the day before. Usually he took care with his hand-writing, since it was a skill he'd struggled to learn at the workhouse. Yesterday, apparently, he hadn't given a damn.

Something else he didn't give a damn about was the invitation perched on the edge of his desk. For days he'd been waiting for word from Diana. He'd expected an invitation to meet with Grace Grinstead. He'd hoped for a letter declaring her love. In the end, he'd received neither. Instead, a note had come from Lady Elizabeth Thorndyke inviting him to a ball that the Ashbys and Miss Grinstead would attend.

Aidan couldn't imagine anything worse than attending a ball with the woman he desperately wanted to wed and two of her friends to whom he'd been introduced for the purpose of matchmaking. No, actually, he could imagine something worse. Another sleepless night spent without Diana in bed beside him. Or under him. Or on top of him.

Damn it all to hell.

He stared around his office and loathed every inch. He stood and his chair groaned as loudly as his muscles. He'd almost become welded to the damned thing over the past handful of days. One night he'd slept in the chair, his head resting on his desk. For half a day, he'd considered installing a day bed in the corner and living in his office.

What was the point of going back to an empty tomb of a town house with more rooms than he'd ever have use for? Work was what he understood. Work was the only thing he'd ever done well.

But he'd spent so many hours in these four walls of his office that he was beginning to detest them too.

Approaching his curio cabinet, he stared at the figurines he'd purchased, the books he'd chosen mostly because the cover and title intrigued him rather than any pursuit of scholarly knowledge. He was an amateur at collecting just as he was an amateur at being a true gentleman. He possessed only the polish that money could buy, but he'd always be a mudlark deep down.

The fiddle reminded him of those days. He'd bought it from a street seller shortly after escaping the workhouse. Learning to play had occupied hours, and when he'd gotten good enough, he'd sometimes claimed a corner and earned a few bob for a ditty.

Now he could only look at the violin and think of Diana and the song he'd played for her. God, he'd behaved like a smitten fool. He was, in fact, a smitten fool. And of course he'd chosen to fall in love with the one woman in London who was as stubborn as he was.

Lord, he'd made a muck of it.

"Mr. Iverson." Coggins's voice came before his usual three short raps. "Visitor to see you, sir."

"I have no appointments. Send them away."

Aidan opened the curio cabinet and retrieved the violin. The wood had taken on a dark patina over the years and he could almost feel its history when he held the instrument. Even when he'd been chased from a doss house for not paying or had to change lodgings sharpishly, he'd made sure to retrieve the instrument.

In a sense, it represented a sentimentality he hated acknowledging in himself. Perhaps it was time to put such nonsense aside. As far as he could determine, the dividends of sentimentality were wild expectations, hellish disappointment, and misery.

He let the violin fall through his fingers and drop to the carpet below. Then he lifted his foot and considered crushing the thing to pieces.

"Mr. Iverson," Coggins called. "May I enter, sir?"

Aidan sighed wearily. The young man was as tenacious as cold in winter. "Come."

Coggins stuck his neatly greased head inside the room. "She says she insists on seeing you, sir. I've spent the last few moments trying to put her off, but she won't be dissuaded."

"She?" Aidan swallowed against the ridiculous surge of hope that welled up. "Who is it?"

"She says her name is Brook, sir. Lady Josephine Brook."

"Josephine?" Aidan's mouth went dry, and his heart crashed painfully against his ribs. He peered past Coggins at the woman in the outer office. Tall, darkly garbed, veiled. She fit Callihan's description.

He wanted to run out and confront her, but part of him was also terrified to hope.

"Send her in," he told Coggins.

After the young man closed the door, Aidan swept a hand through his disheveled hair and worked to tighten the necktie he'd gradually loosened over the course of the morning.

His sister. For so many years he'd believed he'd lost her. Failed her. But a tiny seed of hope had remained, and now it had bloomed into desperation to see her again, to know that she was well and safe.

His hands shook as he retrieved his suit coat from the back of his chair, shrugged into it, and waited.

"Lady Josephine Brook," Coggins announced as he led her into the room.

"Have a seat?" Aidan gestured toward the chairs at the front of his desk.

"Thank you, Mr. Iverson." She sat stiffly on the chair and anxiously clutched the reticule in her gloved hands. "I don't wish to take up too much of your time." Her voice was rich and her accent polished, just as Mr. Callihan had described. After a moment, she lifted her veil.

Aidan's heart stopped. He scanned her features, desperate to find something he recognized.

Nothing. Her hair was brown, her eyes a pale blue. He had few memories of his sister, but he knew that her eyes were the same green as his and her hair had been a brighter red.

"You're not my sister." The words came out flat, emotionless, as empty as he felt.

The lady's eyes widened in shock. "I beg your pardon?"

Aidan had remained standing after she took a seat, but now he sank into his desk chair. The fatigue he felt went bone deep. Soul deep. The foolish hope he'd let blossom inside him withered. It felt like a weight now, as heavy as the guilt he'd carried for decades.

"Lady Josephine," he said with as much civility and patience as he could muster. "Please tell me why you've come here today."

The woman started to speak and then pressed her lips together. She tipped her head and studied him, then proceeded to pull off her gloves and fuss with arranging them neatly on her lap.

"I'm sorry to come into your life this way." There was a tremulous quiver in her voice that didn't match her ramrod posture and steady gaze. "I know much that you do not, so allow me to clarify, Mr. Iverson."

When she fell silent again, Aidan sat forward and urged her, "Go on."

"I am your half-sister. Your mother was not my mother, though I knew her well." A little smile lifted the corner of her mouth. "I grew up with Mary in our household." She looked up and cast him a sympathetic look. "I'm sorry that you weren't able to know her.

"We do share the same father, Mr. Iverson." She assessed him, as if looking for a resemblance. "That makes you my brother, sir," she added almost wistfully.

Realization dawned in fragments. "You're Wyndham's daughter."

"I am."

The earl was his father. And he had a sister. Perhaps other half-siblings. Aidan gripped the arms of his chair, squeezing until his hands ached. All these years of searching, and now the truth was coming too fast. Grief welled up, anger, but he needed to know the details. "My mother was a servant in your household?" Good God, the irony of his search for a noble bride when all along he had blue blood in his veins.

"For many years. She was kind and tenderhearted. I'm afraid our father could never claim the same traits. He can be a cruel man."

Aidan didn't doubt that, but he couldn't believe what she said about his mother. "A tenderhearted woman who deposited her children in a workhouse?" Aidan struggled to reconcile that description with the hell he and his sister had endured. "My sister . . ." The next word wedged in this throat. The grief of losing Sarah had always been there, tangled up in shame and regret. After Callihan's story, he'd allowed himself a fanciful hope. Now there was no hope left to cling to. Sarah was gone. "She died in that workhouse, Lady Josephine."

The elegant woman's ladylike demeanor faltered and Aidan was shocked to see tears well in her eyes. "I'm so sorry, Mr. Iverson."

Aidan wouldn't let himself crumble. Not yet. He still needed answers.

"What did my mother tell you about us?"

"Nothing at all. She shared few details about her history, but I do know there was always a melancholy air about her. I found a letter from Mary in my father's papers that indicated she had children—his children—and had once resided in Lambeth. That prompted me to visit Mr. Callihan's boarding house to learn more."

"Is Wyndham aware of who I am?" Aidan wasn't sure he wished to meet his father. Ever. He now knew who the man was. That was answer enough.

"He is, Mr. Iverson. He's been on his sickbed for many months. After learning a bit of the story from Mr. Callihan, Father relented and told me the rest."

"And you wished to meet your bastard brother?"

"You're the only sibling I have." She lowered her chin as if abashed, and then lifted it high again. "Father is dying, and I thought that I, at least, should come to make amends. He won't ever acknowledge you as his son, but he is capable of guilt, and I suspect he'd want to bequeath you something to ease his conscience."

Aidan chuckled. "I don't need his money."

"No, of course not." She glanced at the ledgers lining a shelf behind him. "And I know that no sum can atone for his actions, but I could arrange for the funds to be donated to one of your charitable endeavors."

When Aidan snapped his gaze to hers, she smiled.

"As soon as I learned your name, I found out as much as I could. You're a benevolent man and the success you've achieved is most impressive." She took in more of his office, noted the violin on the carpet, and then squared her gaze on his again. "You owe him nothing, but I could arrange a meeting with our father if you wish."

"That's not a good idea."

"No. I understand." She lowered her veil over her face, as if preparing to depart. "I'll take my leave of you for now. If questions arise, I've left a calling card with your clerk." She stood and Aidan did the same. But rather than starting for the door, she hesitated. "You may reach me in the future at any time. I would welcome a visit, even if you don't wish to see Father."

"Thank you." Aidan wanted to say more. He knew he should say more. But the two words were all he could manage.

Lady Josephine simply nodded in reply. She started for the door, but then pivoted on her heel to face him again. "If there is ever anything I might do for you, Mr. Iverson, please know that I would assist you if you're in need. We never knew each other, but we are family by blood."

Aidan had the mad impulse to embrace Lady Josephine. Not because there was any true familial tenderness between them, but because she was his sister and she had come to tell him as much when she might have kept the secret of her father's bastard children forever. He knew that the earl's illness and imminent death was what freed her, and he felt a swell of sympathy for her, despite their difference in history and circumstances.

"You may call on me too, my lady. I have only money to offer, but if you're ever in need, you know where to find me."

Beyond the dark lace of her veil, her mouth curved in a momentary smile. "Good day to you."

Aidan dropped into his office chair the minute the door shut behind her. He had answers now, but they brought no real peace.

The guilt he'd felt for years sharpened into a pain that pierced him through. He should have known that mad flare of hope he'd felt in Callihan's lodging house was folly. Every newspaper account had made clear that none had survived the workhouse fire.

He slid a hand across his desk and rested his palm on the carved box that held the only memento he would ever have of Sarah. Lifting the delicate scrap from its resting place, he thought back on his few precious memories of her. He smiled remembering her dimpled grin.

He'd never been able to see her grow up, to see her become the kind and clever woman she would have been. Aidan swallowed hard to hold back the sting of tears. He bit into his lower lip and struggled to draw breath past the searing ache behind his ribs.

"I'm sorry, Sarah," he whispered to the drawing she'd once made for him. "I would have come back for you."

Returning the drawing back to its resting place, he let out a shaky breath. He needed to lay Sarah to rest too. He'd never provided her the memorial he should have. Now he had answers. He knew who their father was and what had become of their mother. It was time to remember Sarah as she deserved.

He stood and retrieved the old fiddle from the carpet. Smashing the damned thing would have brought momentary relief, but it wouldn't erase his history. Those days of struggling and regret were his forever, a part of who he was and why he'd climbed as high as he had.

He could answer the question now. *Who are your people?* But it changed nothing about who he'd become and what he wanted.

Why in the hell had he ever cared about being accepted by noblemen like his father? Men who would use a woman and discard her. Men who used their privilege to hide their sins.

His goals seemed frivolous now. Belonging to an exclusive club. Currying the favor of men involved with the prince's exhibition.

None of it mattered as much as Diana. Just the thought of her made his heart beat faster, and everything became clear.

She was what he needed. Loving her and spending the rest of his days by her side were the only goals worth pursuing.

After replacing the violin in the cabinet, he collected the invitation from Elizabeth Thorndyke that lay at the corner of his desk.

He'd told Diana he would meet with her friend, but there was no question of a match with the lady, with any other woman but Diana. He could no longer imagine marriage as a simple transaction or practical exchange.

But he was still a practical man. And he'd always been fond of conquering two problems with a single tool. If he attended the ball, he could keep to his word to Diana and she could fulfill her promise to her friend.

But most importantly, he'd have a chance to see her again.

Chapter Twenty-Six

$\mathcal{D}$iana escaped to the back garden as soon as she arrived at Bess's town house. She knew she should go back inside and assist with whatever preparations might be needed for the ball, but the cool air was preferable to an overheated drawing room. And being alone with her thoughts was far easier than pretending she was excited about the prospect of a successful match between Grace and Aidan.

Diana wanted to wish Grace well. She wanted Aidan to have all that he'd desired.

She also wanted to return to her workshop and keep herself busy so she didn't have to think about any of it.

"I know people say I'm a terrible gambler . . ." Dominick said as he stepped into the garden to join her.

"That's because you *are* a terrible gambler."

He sniffed haughtily as he came to stand beside her. "I did acknowledge that people say so. But if I admit to being bad at games of chance, you'll have to admit you're a dreadful liar."

"I'm not a liar at all."

"What would you call this then?" He nudged his chin to indicate the gathering inside.

"A reunion and ball with my closest friends from finishing school."

"Who all think that you're here to support Grace in her efforts to win the heart of the man you're enamored with."

Diana swallowed and shot her twin a glare. "That's neither here nor there."

"You never get angrier than when you know you're wrong."

"You don't understand." Diana wheeled on him. "Even if I go and tell them, it will change nothing."

Dom yawned as if her anger didn't affect him in the least. "Telling the truth is good for the soul, or so they tell me. Also, you can't truly play a game fairly when someone is withholding cards."

"Now you're saying I'm a cardsharp."

"Essentially." He shrugged. "You're holding back relevant information. Grace can be ambitious, but do you think she would truly pursue this course if she knew of your feelings? Or his?"

The scoff she gave him felt so good, she did it twice. "You're lecturing me on feelings? The man who claims his heart is black as night and can never be won by any lady because it's shriveled to the size of a chestnut."

"I was twelve when I said that."

"You've done nothing to disprove the claim since."

He laughed, and she wanted to punch him because his merriment sparked a tickle of laughter in her belly too.

"Do you want my advice, sister?"

"No."

"Well, too bad. It's yours for free." He stepped closer and placed a hand on her shoulder. "Stop pretending. Turn around and go tell your dearest friend that her plan has a snag. Namely, you are in love with her marital prospect and he is utterly smitten with you." He tipped his head and screwed his mouth into a thoughtful moue. "You might also add that Mr. Iverson proposed to you just a few days ago."

"That won't go over well, and there's more to it."

"Then tell me."

"I'm not what he wants." Speaking that truth aloud was far harder than letting it chase around in her head.

"You're wrong, Di. I spoke to Iverson before he proposed. He looked as hell-bent as any man I've ever seen."

That news didn't surprise her. "*Want* is the wrong word." Attraction had always been there with Aidan, mutual and irrepressible, from the moment they'd met. "I'm not what he needs."

"I'm flummoxed." Dom looked utterly confused. His brow crumpled and he ran two fingers along his dark brow. "It's as if you're telling me one of your hideous mathematical equations and expecting me to solve it."

"He helped me, don't you see? And in return I was to help him."

Dom nodded and rolled his hand in the air. "Yes, that much I follow. And then he fell in love with you."

He had. She knew Aidan loved her, not just because he'd spoken the words, but because of the way he looked at her and treated her, because of his willingness to give up his goals to choose her.

But she couldn't let him do that.

"Aidan wants belonging more than anything. To make connections and be accepted at the highest levels of society. He needs to marry a noblewoman." Diana sighed when it was all out.

Her reasoning was logical. It made sense.

And it was breaking her heart.

Dom's frown had only deepened. "He proposed to you, Di."

"I remember." She recalled the pain of refusing him and the agony of seeing that pain reflected in his eyes.

"Then all of what you just said, all the reasons and rationales, must not matter to him. He's a clever man, one who would consider all factors before something as momentous as a proposal." Dom leaned in, placed a hand on her arm. "You must be more important to him than impressing a few titled prigs."

"There's more you don't know. Details from his past that aren't mine to share." Diana's head was throbbing. Her heart was aching. Perhaps she couldn't make Dom understand, but she still knew what she had to do.

Dom shocked her by wrapping an arm around her shoulders. He wasn't one for physical displays and she half expected him to offer some quip or to retreat. Instead, he held her and finally said, "This may be the only time you'll ever hear me admit this, so listen carefully."

"You have me trapped. I have no choice but to listen."

"Love is rare, in my experience. Precious. Something to be cherished."

Diana arched her brow and glanced at her brother's profile.

"All the things poets say," he added with a dismissive flick of his hand. "If you've found it, don't let it go." He puffed out his chest, gave her a squeeze, and released her. Reaching up, he fussed with his neck cloth and added, "There endeth my advice."

"Thank you." She did appreciate his sincerity and she couldn't disagree with a word of what he'd said, but he didn't understand the circumstances and Aidan's goals as she did. "So when are you taking your own advice?"

"Beg pardon?"

"Don't be coy, Dom. Part of the reason you're a terrible gambler is that you're as dreadful a liar as I am and every inch as impractical."

"This feels like when you used to make up riddles and insist I solve them."

Diana had once been good at riddles. "This one isn't too difficult. I'm talking about Sophie, of course."

He tented his eyebrows in a dramatically bemused expression. "And why, pray tell, are we talking about Lady Sophronia?"

"You're smitten with her. You always have been and you pretend you're not by picking frivolous fights with her."

Diana was sure he'd deny her claim. She'd hinted as much before and he'd always fobbed her off with a joke or sarcasm. Now his mouth tilted in a mischievous grin and she expected the same again.

Instead he squared his shoulders, looked directly into her eyes, and said, "You first. Show me how it's done."

"I can't. But we should go inside. The ball will begin soon." Diana started back and then paused, waiting for him to join her on the threshold.

"How will you get through it?"

"Wish me luck?"

"You've never needed luck, and you know mine is terrible." He shocked her by bending to brush a kiss on her cheek. "I wish you happiness, Di. I hope you'll allow yourself to have it."

INSIDE, DIANA FOUND Grace and Bess chatting in the drawing room.

"Come and join us," Bess called. "The musicians are in the ballroom. All the candles are lit. Everything is in place and we only await the arrival of Mr. Iverson and a few other guests."

Dom took a chair near the ladies and Diana opted for the edge of the settee nearest the fireplace. She felt hollow and couldn't get warm.

"So you're looking for a mercenary marriage, Miss Grinstead."

"Dom." Diana matched the sharpness of her tone with a quelling glare that had sometimes worked on him when they were children.

"Forgive me," he said too flippantly for anyone to believe he felt a bit of remorse. "I have been reading too much poetry of late and have developed the foolish notion that marriage should be based on love."

"Love can grow in time," Grace said, though there was a distinctly uncertain wobble in her tone. "Admiration is a fine start, and I certainly admire Mr. Iverson."

"Even if he's smitten with my sister?"

"Dom!" Diana shot out of her chair at the same moment Grace gasped and a tall, auburn-haired investor stepped into the room.

"He is, actually." Aidan's voice often sent a burst of warmth through Diana's body. The sound of it now set her nerves aflame.

She wasn't ready to face him. Grace, on the other hand, was.

"Mr. Iverson." She rose and swept forward to greet him, offering him her fingers in a brief handshake. "How good it is for you to play along with Mr. Ashby's nonsense and to agree to attend this dance."

Diana's mouth went dry as dust. Her thoughts scattered like leaves in a stiff breeze. He was here and this was truly happening. She was going to have to watch her friend attempt to win him.

"Shall we go into the ballroom? We have some refreshments assembled there," Grace said brightly.

"Yes," Bess said instantly. "I'm famished." She rose from the settee and Dom stood and followed too, but Aidan hadn't moved.

He stood, blocking the threshold, his eyes locked on Diana's.

"No," he said with unexpected firmness.

"Is something amiss, Mr. Iverson?" Grace blinked in confusion.

"I need to speak with Miss Ashby." He glanced around, his gaze skimming each of them. "Privately."

Bess and Dominick moved past him into the hall, so that only Grace remained, standing between the two of them. She looked from Aidan to Diana, and then let out a weary sigh.

"This is most unusual," she said with more understanding than Diana expected. "But I will ensure that you have some privacy and tell the others we'll hold off dancing for a quarter of an hour. Will that do?"

When neither of them answered, Grace exited the sitting room and pulled the door closed behind her.

"I met a Lady Josephine Brook today." His voice was strained, raw. "She is my half-sister."

They were the last words Diana expected to hear, and she approached immediately to lay a hand on his arm. "The name on the envelope? How did you find her?"

"She found me." He stared down at his boots a moment before meeting her gaze again. "My father is an earl and my mother was his servant."

"You've found your family," Diana said quietly. She was glad he had answers, and yet heartbroken that he'd endured so much and grown up without a family.

"What I've found is that I'm no longer as concerned with where I came from as with what the future holds." His gaze was lit with warmth, and though he spoke with his usual confidence, there was a raw intensity in his tone. He reached for her, stepping closer until they were bodice to waistcoat. "You know that I can't marry Grace Grinstead."

"Can't you?" Diana found that the nervous anticipation of seeing him again was nothing compared to the rush of pleasure that poured through her veins like warm treacle when he was this close. "She will be disappointed."

"I don't want to talk about Grace," he said firmly. "I want to talk about us."

Diana moved a bit closer and wondered why she'd ever thought she could resist him and the feelings he stoked in her. "I thought I explained everything."

"Do you trust me?" When they were so close his trouser legs brushed the bell of her skirt, he reached for her. Sliding a hand around her waist, he held her very much as he had the night they'd met.

"You know that I do."

"Then believe me when I tell you that I've realized what's important. Those goals you think I was clinging to don't matter to me at all." He bent closer and said quietly, intently, "Diana, a future with you is what I want. You matter to me."

"But I'm not what you n—"

He lifted a finger and pressed it to her lips. "You *are* what I need."

Diana scooted an inch closer, savoring the heat of him. "You're certain?"

One ruddy brow lifted and his mouth tipped up in a

smile. "I intend to show you how certain every single day." The smile ebbed and his mouth turned down. "That is, if you'll allow me to."

She lifted a hand between them and wrapped her fingers around one of the buttons of his waistcoat. Her mind had quieted, and she knew only one thing for certain.

"I've confessed all," he said softly. "But you must tell me what you want."

The words were there on the tip of her tongue, bursting to break free, but some last threads of resistance held her back. "I spoke to Dominick about all of this," she told him with a smile.

"What did you tell him?" He leaned down and nuzzled her cheek.

"I told him I was fond of you."

"Fond?" He pulled back and chuckled. "That's it? You describe your pneumatic device with more enthusiasm. And what did you tell him of my feelings for you?"

"I said you admired me."

"Too tame, Miss Ashby."

"He's my brother. I didn't want to be too explicit."

"But here, now, it's just you and me." He wrapped his other arm around her, pulled her an inch closer, and stepped one leg forward so that his thigh pressed between hers. "You can be very explicit."

"You did say you love me. I am recalling accurately, am I not?"

"I could repeat it again, if you like."

"Could you?"

"Mmm. We could make it a daily ritual." He slid a hand up her back and stroked a delicious trail back down again. "I love you, Diana."

He bent his head. Diana licked her lips, starving for the taste of him. But after just brushing her lips with his, he pulled away.

"What will you say when I repeat the words every day?" He tipped his head and cast her a mischievous smile. "It seems to beg some kind of response. I'm curious what yours would be."

Diana held the words on the tip of her tongue a moment longer. Then she couldn't hold them back anymore.

"I love you, Aidan Iverson." She sealed the words by bouncing onto her toes, slipping a hand around his neck, and pulling him down for a kiss. She was so relieved to have him in her arms that she sighed against his mouth and kissed him again. And once more.

"Do you think it will get repetitive?" he teased, as he trailed hot, openmouthed kisses down her neck. "Me telling you. You telling me."

"Perhaps," Diana told him on a gasp when he ran his tongue along the dip at the base of her throat. "There are times when actions speak louder than words."

She felt him smile against her skin.

"You're such a clever woman." He lifted his head

and stared down at her, a question in his eyes. "Shall we start now?"

"A quarter of an hour isn't much time at all."

He reached a hand down to cup her bottom and sighed. "And a practical woman too."

"Then we should join the others?"

"We should," he agreed, and then pressed a quick kiss to the tip of her nose. He lowered his arms, but immediately clasped her hand. "I'm not sure I'll be able to stop touching you even once we're in the ballroom. Will it scandalize everyone terribly?"

"Probably." Diana chuckled, and her heart felt lighter than it had in days. Years. Perhaps ever.

She let Aidan lead her to the sitting room door, but he stopped short and turned back.

"We're forgetting something very important," he told her with a frown.

"Are we?"

Aidan released her hand and dug in his pocket. Then he got down before her on one knee. "We never quite did this last time, did we?"

"You know my answer, Aidan."

"Do I? You know I'm a man of business. I like the details." He reached for her hand. "And you deserve this to be done properly."

Diana grinned.

"Will you be mine, Diana Ashby?" He offered her a small band of gold, inset with a string of tiny diamonds.

The words were so raw. No negotiating terms or thoughts of what they might exchange in this bargain. Just an offer of belonging, and a promise of love.

"Yes, I will be yours."

His smile said she'd given him the moon and stars and everything in between. He got to his feet. His hands shook as his slipped the ring on her finger, and his mouth trembled when he kissed her.

"Did you expect this when I saved you in the Belgravia mews?" Diana whispered when he lifted his head.

"I knew you were beautiful, fierce, and utterly unforgettable."

"I feared I'd never see you again," she confessed. "Now I know I don't want to be without you."

He looked at her as he always did, as if she was the most interesting woman he'd ever seen, as if he didn't want to take his eyes off her. But now there was something else. Contentedness. She felt it too.

Being in his arms felt right, but having him as her own felt like a gift.

"You never have to be without me, love. I'm right where I belong."

Chapter Twenty-Seven

May 1846
Mayfair

"Have you seen my wife?" Aidan quizzed the crew of workmen who were converting his billiard room into a workshop and laboratory for Diana. The space was large enough and had a sufficiently high ceiling to allow her to work on larger prototypes and stack raw materials several feet high, if she so desired.

When the three men grumbled and shook their heads, Aidan made his way down the hallway and was befuddled by the absence of servants. Usually there was a maid or butler about, especially this close to the dinner hour.

His day at the office had been long, tedious, and full of meetings with men who blustered too long and had very little of interest to say.

In short, he wanted to see his wife.

"Diana!" he shouted, not caring which of their neighbors heard him.

"Aidan." She approached from the opposite end of the hall, a smile on her face, and the evening post clutched in her hand. He scooped her into his arms and kissed her before she could tell him about the post. He didn't care who'd billed them for what service or which invitations they'd received from the Tremaynes or Huntley or one of his Lyon's Club cronies.

She kissed him eagerly, hungrily, and Aidan sidestepped with her into the study, kicking the door shut with the toe of his boot.

"I missed you," she told him, "and I—"

He kissed her again and she laughed against his lips.

"Is this one of those you'll-kiss-me-every-time-I-interrupt-you moments?"

"No," he said, dipping his head to kiss her cheek, her neck, the spot just below her ear. "I've simply missed you too and haven't had my fill of you yet."

"You'll want to hear this news," she said, waving one of the letters in her hand.

"Tell me." He didn't want to let her go, but he could hear the eagerness in her voice and didn't wish to stifle that either.

"I think you should read it for yourself."

With a long-suffering sigh, Aidan released his wife and took the letter she offered. He frowned as he read and then both brows winged up.

"He's invited us to dine at his home," she told him.

"So I see."

The letter was from Lord Archibald Lockwood, and Aidan didn't feel an ounce of the interest he expected to feel upon seeing the old man's name embossed on the missive's letterhead. Aidan had followed news of the burgeoning industrial exhibition with interest and even privately advised several inventors to submit their designs for inclusion in the exhibition. He'd encouraged Diana to do the same. A few of the men whose devices he'd invested in had been selected, and Aidan had contented himself with being involved in the project in that small way.

Now Lord Lockwood had invited the Iversons to dine at his Sussex country house. What a difference a few months had wrought.

"He says he wishes to speak to you about the exhibition and discuss my newest invention," Diana said as she came to stand beside him, her backside resting next to his against the desk. "Someone must have spoken to him about me. And you."

Lockwood's letter was almost opposite in tone from the one Aidan had received in response to his inquiry long ago. In that reply, Lockwood had been arrogant, insulting, dismissive. The letter Aidan held in his hand now was almost fawning. The question was, who'd taken it upon himself to turn the old man in their favor?

Aidan let his mind sift the possibilities, then cast the letter aside to move and stand in front of his wife.

"Shall we accept his invitation?"

"You'd consider refusing?" She sounded shocked.

He understood her confusion. This exhibition had once mattered to him so much that he was willing to marry a woman for the blood in her veins and how far back she could trace her family history in *Debrett's*. He winced to think of how mercenary he'd been, how he'd let ambition cloud everything else.

But his heart was full now. Love had changed him. Diana had changed him. And loving her made everything he'd sought, everything he'd achieved, worthwhile. He had a home. He had belonging. The hunger had abated.

Except when it came to his wife, and she was the reason he wished to accept. "I think we should go," he said decisively.

Lockwood's letter implied not just an opportunity for Aidan, but for Diana too. Perhaps one of her inventions would be featured in the exhibition. That would make him happier than sitting on a committee and enduring a series of mind-numbing meetings with pompous noblemen.

"This is a cause to celebrate," she told him, "so I've asked the servants to prepare a table for us in the conservatory."

He was hungry, but it wasn't for an elegantly arranged four-course meal in the conservatory.

"How long until dinner?" Aidan slipped a finger inside the square neckline of her day dress and pulled Diana closer. She laced her arms around his neck and smiled.

"Long enough, I think."

"Excellent." He stroked low inside her bodice, reaching his fingers down until he found the peak of her nipple.

She let out a delicious gasp and reached down to ruck up the skirt of her gown, spreading her legs so that he could step between. He'd lost count of the number of times he'd taken her on his study desk, but he was more than happy to add to the number this evening.

When she reached for the opening of his trousers, it was his turn to gasp. She stroked him eagerly through the fabric, and he bent to take her mouth.

Someone rapped on his study door and Aidan groaned miserably against Diana's lips.

"Ignore them," he begged her.

"It's probably one of the workmen. They promised to come and report on their progress before they finished up this evening." She pushed gently at his chest and then lowered herself from the desk, her body sliding enticingly against his.

Aidan sucked in a deep breath and tried to stifle his urges while he helped her settle her dress.

She fussed with a few strands of loose hair as she made her way to the door. Aidan took his eyes off her long enough to notice that some of the post had fallen onto the carpet. He bent to retrieve the letters and noticed one small, neatly constructed envelope with an address written in an elegant looping script.

The name Josephine stood out, and he grabbed at the envelope, tearing eagerly at the seams.

Aidan,

I hope you don't mind me addressing you as such. If we ever meet again, please do call me Josephine. We are family, after all.

I believe you will already have received a note from Lord Archibald Lockwood. I understand through various sources that you were quite keen on participating in the industrial exhibition being planned by Prince Albert in the coming year. Based on your experience and knowledge of industrial devices, you seem a perfect fit to advise in such a matter, but I understand that Lord Lockwood was not initially receptive to that proposition.

He is now. A few words were little enough to offer on your behalf, and I am glad if I have assisted you in any way.

Our father has passed on. If you would ever

wish to call at Wyndham House, you will be welcomed.

Your sister,
Josephine

Diana had urged Aidan to invite his sister to their wedding, but Josephine had not come. Now he understood why.

He'd once thought his tendency to refuse the help of others was smart. A means of protecting himself. Now he saw the selfishness in it and the folly.

"What is it?" Diana asked as she approached and noticed the note in his hands.

"My sister. She's the one who spoke to Lockwood."

"That was very kind of her." She stepped closer and rested her hand over his. "I'd like to meet her. It sounds like we owe her our gratitude. Do you think perhaps we should invite her to visit?"

"Yes, let's do that." All the old hurts had faded with time. He still mourned Sarah and wondered about his mother, but all the old resentments seemed anemic now. His happiness with Diana was the belonging he'd always sought. Still, he'd spent years searching for his family. Now that he knew he had a sister, he wanted to welcome her into his life.

Diana's love was as boundless as her imagination. He needed to follow her example.

He hooked her arm around his and began to lead her toward the door, but she pulled him back.

"I thought we had time before dinner to . . ."

Aidan chuckled and turned to pull her into his arms. "Do we still have time?"

"I want us to make the time."

"Mrs. Iverson," he said as he pressed the study door closed and nestled her back against it, "you're the cleverest woman I've ever known."

"So you married me for my mind?"

He bent and reached for the hem of her gown, tugging the fabric higher and pressing kisses against her hip, her waist, her breast as he slid the skirt up to her waist. "That was one consideration, certainly."

"What were the others?" Diana nipped at his bottom lip.

He groaned when she began to kiss him in earnest, stroking him with her tongue.

When he lifted his head, he told her, "You are kind, driven, and quite skilled at using an umbrella as a weapon whilst screeching like a banshee at brutish men in back alleys."

"That was a battle cry," she insisted as she worked the buttons of his shirt free and slipped her hand inside to feel the warm, muscled ridges of his chest. "Like an Amazon."

"I stand corrected, love. Forgive me." He nuzzled her cheek and then trailed openmouthed kisses down her neck.

"You're forgiven."

He stilled, lifted his head, and cupped her face between his hands. "Thank you, Diana."

"I told you that debt is forgiven."

"Not just for that night in Belgravia, but last night, and this one, and every bit of bliss you've given me since we met."

Diana bit her lip, and tears welled in her eyes. "Thank you for being as stubborn as I am."

He laughed. Then she chuckled too. They were pressed so closely together that he wasn't sure if the reverberation of joy in his chest was her laughter or his.

When her hands dipped low to the edge of his trousers, he let out a little hiss of pleasure.

"You know, love," he whispered, "I rather liked your Amazon cry." He cupped her breast and stroked his thumb against her through the fabric. "I wonder if I could draw one out of you again."

"I do hope you'll try," she said as she lifted off her heels to kiss him.

He smiled against her mouth. He would take any reason to be close to her, any chance to make love to her. Diana and her love were a gift that he was grateful for every day.

Nothing he'd achieved, nothing he'd ever earned, mattered as much as moments like this.

She was the one thing he could not do without.

**And don't miss the first romance
in Christy Carlyle's wickedly
delightful Duke's Den series,**

A Duke
Changes Everything

Nicholas Lyon gambled his way into a fortune and ownership of the most opulent, notorious gentlemen's club in England. But when Nick's cruel brother dies, he inherits a title he never wanted. The sooner Nick is rid of the estate that has always haunted him, the sooner he can return to the life he's built in London. But there's one obstacle—the exquisite Thomasina Thorne.

When the new heir to the Tremayne dukedom suddenly appears in Mina Thorne's life, she's flustered. Not only is he breathtakingly handsome, but he's also determined to take away her home and position as steward of the Enderley estate. If Mina learns what makes the enigmatic duke tick, perhaps she can change his mind—as long as she doesn't get too close to him.

With each day Nick spends with Mina, his resolve weakens as their colliding wills lead to explosive desire. Could she be the one woman who can help him finally bury the ghosts of his past?

Available Now from Avon Books!